ARROW'S EDGE MC

CW00819555

PRAISE FOR FREYA BARKER

Freya Barker writes a mean romance, I tell you! A REAL romance, with real characters and real conflict.

~Author M. Lynne Cunning

I've said it before and I'll say it again and again, Freya Barker is one of the BEST storytellers out there.

~Turning Pages At MidnightBook Blog

God, Freya Barker gets me every time I read one of her books. She's a master at creating a beautiful story that you lose yourself in the moment you start reading.

~Britt Red Hatter Book Blog

Freya Barker has woven a delicate balance of honest emotions and well-formed characters into a tale that is as unique as it is gripping.

~Ginger Scott, bestselling young and new adult author and Goodreads Choice Awards finalist

Such a truly beautiful story! The writing is gorgeous, the scenery is beautiful...

~Author Tia Louise

From Dust by Freya Barker is one of those special books. One of those whose plotline and characters remain with you for days after you finished it.

~Jeri's Book Attic

No amount of words could describe how this story made me feel, I think this is one I will remember forever, absolutely freaking awesome is not even close to how I felt about it.

~Lilian's Book Blog

Still Air was insightful, eye-opening, and I paused numerous times to think about my relationships with my own children. Anytime a book can evoke a myriad of emotions while teaching life lessons you'll continue to carry with you, it's a 5-star read.

~ Bestselling Author CP Smith

In my opinion, there is nothing better than a Freya Barker book. With her final installment in her Portland, ME series, Still Air, she does not disappoint. From start to finish I was completely captivated by Pam, Dino, and the entire Portland family.

~ Author RB Hilliard

The one thing you can always be sure of with Freya's writing is that it will pull on ALL of your emotions; it's expressive, meaningful, sarcastic, so very true to life, real, hard-hitting and heartbreaking at times and, as is the case with this series especially, the story is at points raw, painful and occasionally fugly BUT it is also sweet, hopeful, uplifting, humorous and heart-warming.

~ Book Loving Pixies

ALSO BY FREYA BARKER

ARROW'S EDGE MC SERIES:
EDGE OF REASON
EDGE OF DARKNESS
EDGE OF TOMORROW
EDGE OF FEAR
EDGE OF REALITY

ON CALL SERIES (Operation Alpha):
BURNING FOR AUTUMN
COVERING OLLIE
TRACKING TAHLULA
ABSOLVING BLUE
REVEALING ANNIE
DISSECTING MEREDITH
WATCHING TRIN

ROCK POINT SERIES:
KEEPING 6
CABIN 12
HWY 550
10-CODE

NORTHERN LIGHTS COLLECTION:
A CHANGE IN TIDE
A CHANGE OF VIEW
A CHANGE OF PACE

SNAPSHOT SERIES:
SHUTTER SPEED
FREEZE FRAME
IDEAL IMAGE

PORTLAND, ME, NOVELS:
FROM DUST
CRUEL WATER
THROUGH FIRE
STILL AIR
LULLAY: A CHRISTMAS NOVELLA

EDGE
OF
REALITY

ARROW'S EDGE MC

FREYA BARKER

ACKNOWLEDGMENTS

As always I need to thank you, the readers, for putting your faith in me. Whether this was your first time reading me, whether you've faithfully followed me since I published my very first words, or have discovered my books along the way. Your feedback—the notes, reviews, comments, recommendations—is always fuel for the next book.

I have such an amazing, small and intimate Barks & Bites reader group. An interactive place where all of us can feel free to share our love for books, have a few laughs, get into some serious (or not so serious) discussions, cheer each other on, and lift each other up.

My group is very welcoming, so if you enjoy my books and would like to join, we'd love to have you: https://www.facebook.com/groups/FreyasBarksandBites/

There's a group of individuals without whose support I wouldn't be able to function: Karen Hrdlicka, Joanne Thompson, Deb Blake, Pam Buchanan, Petra Gleason, Krystal Weiss, Debra Presley, Drue Hoffman, CP Smith, and my agent Stephanie Phillips of SBR Media,. Each of these women make me look so much more polished than I really am. They (at times quite literally) hold the mess that is me together.

Last but definitely not least I'm grateful for my family, my quiet cheer team. My kids who may not be intimately familiar with my stories (they'd prefer not to know their mom isn't as 'innocent' as they'd like to believe) but never fail to celebrate me with each book I release and every milestone I reach . My husband who has the patience of a saint and puts up with my crazy schedule, my mood swings, my insatiable writing drive, and my lack of communication for long stretches of time. He doesn't quite understand what it is I do, but that doesn't stop him from making sure everything is taken care of while I disappear into the writing cave.

He simply is the very best man. Sorry ladies, he's mine and I'm keeping him!

My love to you all.

EDGE OF FEAR

1

Mel

"I'M SORRY. YOU just missed her, she's on her way to meet with a client."

Lindsey rolls her eyes dramatically as I pass by her desk on my way out the door.

My daughter, my legal assistant, and my gatekeeper. She's the face of this office. Not only much friendlier, she's also much more diplomatic and politically correct than I ever was or will be.

I'm not making any apologies; my much bristlier personality has served me well in my profession. Especially in family law—my preferred field—where emotions always seem to run high, my lack of bedside matter and unwillingness to coddle tends to cut right through to the business at hand. I don't think I have many clients who actually like me, but they sure like the results I can get them.

I'm known as a ballbuster, which is mostly manspeak for a woman who won't put up with their bullshit. It's probably also the reason I'm single. I'm too much to handle. Even that badass biker I thought had potential seems to be keeping his distance.

I mentally shrug my shoulders. Oh, well, so be it. I guess if he can't take me the way I am, he's not worth my time anyway. Screw him.

I pull open the door when I notice Lindsey hanging up the phone.

"Who was it?"

"Mesina's lawyer. Howell Redfern. That's the third time he's called in the past day or two. He really wants to talk with you."

"I'm sure he does, but he'll have to wait until I've had a chance to talk with my client."

My client being thirty-three-year-old Shauna Mesina, wife of Carlos Mesina, the man whose lawyer is probably as dirty as he is.

Shauna came to me a week ago expressing a desire to leave her husband. He made it clear it wouldn't end well if she tried. He has good reason to be worried, it turns out Shauna knows far more about his shady business dealings than he probably suspects she does. That's why I convinced her to talk to the FBI. Some of the information she shared with me will be of great interest to them.

Fucking drugs and money, the downfall of society, and Carlos Mesina is apparently up to his eyeballs in both.

The one blessing for Shauna is that she doesn't share kids with the man. Not by his choice—he was eager for offspring—but by Shauna's. Despite staying with him for over ten years, she was never sure she wanted to bring kids into his world.

Turns out that was a smart choice or he would've had some serious leverage to keep her in check.

Anyway, Shauna is in federal protective care as we speak and I'm on my way to meet with her and SAC Damian Gomez at the Durango office. Which is also why I've avoided speaking with Howell Redfern. I don't want to run the chance Carlos finds out his wife is about to have his ass handed to him. He'd probably disappear before the FBI can get their case together.

In the meantime, I'm going to proceed with the filings for their divorce as if that's all we're interested in.

"Are you gonna be home for dinner?" Lindsey wants to know.

"Plan to."

"Do you want to stop at The Backyard Edge and pick us up some brisket? I have a dental cleaning this afternoon and I was hoping to squeeze in a yoga class."

"Sure. Sounds good to me"

Lindsay and I have been alternating weeks for kitchen duties since she moved back in with me two years ago. This is technically her week, but we regularly opt for takeout because we both have pretty busy schedules.

Our place isn't big, a modest two-story house with a nanny-suite in the basement in a decent neighborhood, not far from the college. I didn't want big when I bought it. It would only mean more clutter and more cleaning, neither of which I'm a fan. But I did like the option of Lindsey having her own space for her visits.

Then when she came back to Durango permanently, having her move in made more sense than having to pay rent somewhere else. It gave her a chance to get back on her feet, and although we share the kitchen and the rest of the main floor, we each have our own self-contained space as well. It works for us.

When I start my ancient Subaru, it makes a noise like a frickin' race car. I really need to get that exhaust checked out; it's starting to sound like the cars Lindsey's father used to drive when he was still racing NASCAR.

I met David Zimmerman when he was at an event at my alma mater. I was just twenty-one and was drawn to his almost reckless sense of adventure. Everything he did, he did to the extreme. Including me, which is how I ended up pregnant after a whirlwind two months of dating. My parents hated him on sight, which was all the more reason for me to say yes when he surprisingly asked me to marry him.

I can't say being with him was a mistake, because I got Lindsey out of it, but I should've thought twice before marrying him. Needless to say, the impromptu marriage lasted about as long as it took to give birth to Lindsey and for the reality of parenthood to scare the absolute shit out of David. He was gone before the ink on the birth certificate was dry.

You'd think I would've been heartbroken, but instead I felt liberated and oddly empowered, managing new parenthood by myself while still in college. It wasn't easy but I made it through both, earning my law degree just before she turned eight.

Lindsey grounded me, forced me to shed any remaining wild hairs I may have sported. I grew up alongside my daughter, and I don't mind admitting she taught me as much as I taught her.

Of course Lindsey had her own bout of rebellion right around when she left for college. No pregnancies—thank God—but it took every last ounce of patience I had, cost me many sleepless nights, and added many a gray hair before she managed to get herself together.

David was only peripherally present in her life, but his monthly child support payments were as regular as clockwork. It's only in the past few years since he quit racing that he's started showing his face a little more often. Lindsey isn't that gung-ho but I try to stay out of it. She's an adult and more than capable of making decisions of her own.

Heck, sometimes I think she's become the adult in *our* relationship. If I'd listened to her, I wouldn't be driving through downtown Durango with a muffler hanging on by a thread. She tried to get me to buy new wheels when she went to pick up her Toyota RAV4 from the dealer, but I was being stubborn.

As promised, my client is at the FBI office on Rock Point Drive waiting for me. SAC Gomez doesn't want me to know where they're keeping her—totally fine by me—which is why he arranged this meeting.

"Has he been asking about me?" is the first thing out

of my client's mouth.

I have to curb my annoyance at her question, or I might say something to set her off which could jeopardize the investigation.

"I'm not his lawyer, Shauna. I have no reason to talk with Carlos and any communication is through his attorney."

I don't bother telling her I've been ducking his calls for days.

"So no messages?"

I glance over at Agent Gomez, who seems as unimpressed as I am.

"No messages, and don't forget that's a good thing. Now," I firmly steer us toward the real reason for this meeting.

I pull the documents we need to go over from my briefcase, which is really more of a knapsack. It fits my personality better. At least I wore black pants and my Chucks today, instead of my cargo pants and flip-flops, which made Lindsey happy. She's responsible for the sleek-looking offices we occupy, I was fine with the old furnishings I had before. It was all still serviceable and I don't put a lot of stock in looks. The only luxuries I tend to spend money on are my laptop, which is always the latest model, and my shampoo, which costs a whack but makes my hair look and feel fabulous.

Oops. Guess I have a hint of vanity after all.

It's already after five when Gomez finally walks me out of the office.

"Tell me she's not this difficult for you to deal with?"

I ask him.

"Me? Half an hour was enough for me to want to put my fist through the wall. No, I handed the interviews over to Luna, who's doing a good job of handling her. Better than I could."

Luna is one of Gomez's agents but also happens to be married to the president of the Arrow's Edge, a motorcycle club I regularly work for. They foster troubled boys—mostly runaways—get them to school, give them direction, and teach them the value of family. I may have been apprehensive at first, but I've seen them in action and completely stand behind their mandate.

"As long as you're getting somewhere with her." I hold up the documents I got her to sign. "I'll get these filed, which should buy us at least another month. I'm guessing that's how long it'll be before we'll even get on the family court docket."

"Fingers crossed we'll have enough evidence to nail him before then."

"I hope so too."

The parking lot behind The Backyard Edge isn't too crowded. Hopefully, it won't take them too long to get my takeout order ready. Don't get me wrong, I love this restaurant, and I adore Sophia who manages it. The place is owned by the Arrow's Edge MC and the food is phenomenal. Sophia is actually married to Tse, one of the club members. Nothing wrong with the club, this restaurant, or Tse, I just prefer to avoid one of his brothers.

The first person I see walking in is him, his ass parked

at the bar.

Murphy's fucking law.

Paco

WELL, DAMN...MY day is looking up.

She tries to avoid my eyes but I know her well enough, she won't be able to resist the challenge I'm putting out there.

Mel Morgan.

As I've seen her do before, she straightens her shoulders, lifts her chin, and then looks at me, her eyes cool.

"Mel."

"Paco."

I indicate the barstool beside me and I see the brief hesitation before she takes a seat.

"Hey, Mel," Emme, one of the bartenders, greets her. "What can I get you?"

"I'm just here to order takeout."

"Have a drink while you wait."

I don't even have to say a word, Emme is doing all the work. Means I won't risk shoving my size twelves in my mouth again, which is what I seem to do every time I open my mouth around her.

At first, I could've sworn there was something there, the way she looked at me with blatant interest when we were first introduced last year. I looked too but figured I'd pace myself, get familiar. Then I tried giving her a compliment at Brick and Lisa's wedding and I got my first taste of that ice-queen look she's mastered.

As soon as the words left my mouth, I wished them back. I'm good with my hands, my mind works fine, but I've never been good with words. Shit, I never needed them. Back when we'd still have club chicks showing up at the clubhouse, a look and a raised eyebrow was all it took.

Mel is definitely not a club chick. She may have a mouth on her and balls of steel, but underneath that woman is all class and I told her with some hair dye and makeup she'd be a looker. *Fuck*. Don't know what the hell I was thinking. Her hair is awesome and she doesn't need anything to enhance her beauty.

"Yo, earth to Paco. Refill?"

Emme waves my empty under my nose.

"Yeah, sure."

I sip my beer, as Mel chats up Emme, and wait for an opportunity to get a word in. Ten minutes later, when her order comes out and she gets up from her stool, I can't do much more than watch her leave.

My opportunity comes five minutes later when I've settled up with Emme and make my way to the parking lot.

Mel's car is still there and she's standing beside it, giving the fender a swift kick.

"Need a hand?"

Her head snaps around as I approach.

"Stupid car," she mumbles, looking annoyed. "I thought it was just the muffler."

"Let me have a look."

I hold out my hand for the keys and after a hard glare, she drops her keys in my palm with a deep sigh. I'm not a mechanic, but I'm pretty handy with engines. I can handle the basics.

Having about six inches or so on Mel, I have to move the seat back to be able to get behind the wheel. The engine coughs to life when I start it, then makes a god-awful racket before sputtering out again.

Mel sticks her head in the door opening. "Can you fix it?"

It's on my lips to tell her no amount of fixing this piece of shit is worth it, but I've learned my lesson so keep it to myself.

"Don't know."

I ease out of the car and pull my phone from my pocket and dial Brick.

"Talk to me."

Brick is one of my brothers and runs an auto shop for the club. Mel helped him get custody of his grandson last year.

"Yo, brother, Mel's car crapped out. Parking lot at the Backyard."

"Finally," Brick deadpans. "Was waiting for that piece of crap to die."

I chuckle and catch a sharp look from Mel.

"Can you swing by?"

"Does she need a ride?"

"I'll take care of that."

Been wanting to get that woman on the back of my bike and now is my chance.

"Good. Leave the keys behind the sun visor, I'll pick it up when I'm done here."

I end the call and lean back into the car, leaving her keys where Brick instructed.

"You can't leave the keys in the car. Someone'll steal it."

I straighten up and turn to her, pulling an eyebrow up.

"No one's going anywhere with this car unless they have a tow truck, Darlin'," I point out. Then I put a hand on her elbow. "Come on. I'll drive you home."

She pulls her arm free and says stubbornly, "I'll wait for Brick."

"You'd be waiting a while and your dinner's gettin' cold."

She looks down at the bag in her hand and mutters what sounded like a curse under her breath.

"Fine. Where are you parked?"

I don't bother hiding the grin as I point at my bike parked next to the restaurant's back door.

"You've got to be shitting me."

2

MEL

"IS THAT ALL?"

Lindsey indicates the stack of documents on the kitchen island, sarcasm dripping from her tone and her expression.

She's ticked I spent my weekend catching up on work instead of taking her up on her offer to go shop for a new vehicle, but I don't want to jump the gun. I briefly talked to Brick Saturday morning, who said he'd look at it over the weekend. Before I invest in new wheels, I want to be sure my Outback is not salvageable.

"Yup."

Lindsey offered to stop by the courthouse to file some documents before heading in and I have to be at the office early for a conference call on the Mesina case. I picked up a rental car on Saturday so we won't have to carpool. It would've been a pain in the ass to coordinate.

We leave the house at the same time and I choose to ignore the disgusted look my daughter aims at the small compact rental parked beside her shiny new SUV.

I wave at her as I get behind the wheel and let her back out of the driveway first.

We have a top-of-the-line coffee maker in the small kitchen at the office my daughter knows how to operate. I tried but my coffee sucks. Since I'll be on the phone for a while, I stop at the drive-through across from the office to pick up some necessary fuel.

The law office is just north of downtown Durango. I picked that location because none of the downtown has proper parking and I don't have the patience to have to hunt for a spot every day. The office has four spots in front and two at the rear, where Lindsey and I park.

My phone rings as I get out of the car. It's Brick.

"You're early."

He chuckles. "We've got kids in the house, there's no sleeping in here."

"Wait until they hit their teens, you won't be able to get them out of bed," I note from experience. "Not sure which is worse."

"Guess we'll find out soon enough. Anyway, was calling about your car."

I groan as I lean in to grab my knapsack. I can already hear in his voice the news isn't going to be what I want to hear.

"Lay it on me."

"The good news is, I can fix it. The bad news is, even if I used refurbished parts it's going to cost more than the vehicle is worth. If you want my honest opinion…"

At first, I don't see anything wrong. Then I fish my keys out of my pocket to open the rear door and notice it's not quite latched. Looks like someone cracked the doorpost with a crowbar to break it open. I promptly drop my untouched coffee and the hot liquid splashes my feet.

"…Mel?"

"Sonofabitch!"

"Mel?"

"Looks like some asshole broke into my office. That piece of shit alarm didn't go off."

Cursing under my breath I reach for the door.

"Don't go in," Brick barks in my ear, somehow guessing that's exactly my plan. Then I hear him say to someone else, "Break-in at Mel's office," before he gets back on the line. "Hang up. Call 911 and wait in your car. We're on our way."

Great. Just what I need, the cavalry rolling in.

I call it in, but as soon as I hang up, my phone rings again. This time it's my conference call. I explain my situation quickly and apologize for having to reschedule. Redfern, Carlos Mesina's lawyer, is clearly annoyed at the inconvenience, voicing how imperative it is he speak with me, and I struggle to stay professional as I end the call.

Now I'm really pissed, both at that pompous ass and at the miscreant who broke into my office. Fueled by anger, I ignore Brick's warning and pull open the door. Good luck to anyone still hiding in there, I'm so fired up I'm pretty sure I could do serious damage.

Yet no one is hiding, but whoever was in here certainly left a mark.

The door to my private office is wide open, papers strewn all over the floor spilling into the hallway. The four-drawer filing cabinet behind my desk is tilting away from the wall, weighed down by the drawers someone forced open.

That crowbar got quite the workout, since my filing cabinet is always locked, as are the drawers in my desk.

I slip from my office and peek into the kitchen, which looks untouched. Same with the conference room which only holds a table and six chairs, no additional furniture. The front is another disaster, with Lindsey's desk upturned and her filing cabinet, where the general office files are kept, received a similar treatment.

Clearly someone is looking for something in my files and one name immediately comes to mind.

"Hands up, please."

I swing around to find a young police officer standing at the end of the hallway, his weapon drawn. On *me*.

"Put that damn gun down! This is her office, you moron."

I hear his furious bark before I see him.

Paco.

How the hell he got here at the same time the cops did, I don't know.

After the ride home on the back of his bike a few nights

ago, I promised myself I'd be making an increased effort to stay out of his way. Despite being a jerk, the man is a magnet and I enjoyed the short ride home plastered against his back, the engine of his Harley humming between my legs, a little too much.

Ignoring the heated discussion developing between Paco and the officer, I sink down on a chair in the small waiting area and drop my head in my hands. I don't want to deal with this without some caffeine enforcement and I left my drive-through coffee all over the back step.

I get the feeling I've caught one of those slippery patches I seem to hit every so often, where every step you take seems to keep you off-balance until you finally find yourself laid out on your ass.

That's just awesome.

"You okay, Darlin'?"

I look up to find him crouched in front of me, his hand resting on my knee and his eyes intense.

"No. I'm ticked off, and I haven't even had a sip of the coffee I dropped by the back door," I complain.

The stern face in front of me morphs into stunningly handsome when he cracks a smile.

"I can fix that."

As much as I don't want to, I believe him. He's talking about coffee, but looking into those eyes I believe he can fix anything.

PACO

As LUCK WOULD have it, I was just up the street at the

gym meeting up with Wapi, one of my brothers, to burn off some frustration when Ouray got hold of me.

He happened to be in the shop when Brick was on the phone with Mel and immediately called me.

Got here in record time, only to walk in on some dumb rookie aiming a fucking gun at Mel.

"I'm gonna have to ask you to wait outside until the detective gets here," the dumb kid says, looking at me cautiously like he expects me to flatten him. I'm tempted, but I'm pretty sure that wouldn't get a warm reception from Mel.

"Come on, Darlin'," I tell her, ignoring the cop. "Let's go grab you another one of those coffees across the street."

"I'm sorry, but I need you to stay on the premises."

I slowly get to my feet and fix my eyes on the rookie.

"That's too bad. You can try to stop us but I'd strongly advise against it. She's known to wipe the floor with guys like you, and I'm already tempted to rearrange your face. It won't take much."

I reach for Mel's hand and pull her to her feet. She has her head low and I wonder if she's crying and trying to hide it. Shit, I can handle Mel when she's busting balls, but I'm at a loss on how to handle her crying.

"We're going across the street and if you need us you know where to find us."

I send the cop a last glare as we pass him. The moment we step out the back door, Mel lifts her head and I'm surprised to see she's not exactly crying.

"I can't believe you're laughing."

She snorts but I don't get an explanation because at that moment a Durango PD SUV pulls up and Ramirez steps out with that new detective.

"Hey, Mel, are you okay?" Detective Ramirez asks as he approaches.

"Will everyone stop asking me that?" she suddenly snaps. "He somehow managed to disable my alarm and used a crowbar to break open the back door. This wasn't a robbery; he was looking for information. Tossed my office and the front office. I'll give you a statement *after* I get some goddamn coffee inside me."

Tony Ramirez presses his lips together

"Sounds good to me. We'll have a look around and talk to you after."

"That would be much appreciated." Unexpectedly she grabs my arm. "Let's go."

We haven't even left the parking lot yet when she tugs on my arm.

"Shit. I should wait for Lindsey." She glances up at me and explains, "She stopped by the courthouse on her way in. I don't want her to freak out."

Wapi is standing by our bikes talking on his phone, probably giving Ouray an update. I wave him over.

"Can you keep an eye out for Mel's daughter? We'll be across the road."

"Will do."

A bit later we're sitting by the window, watching cops go in and out of her office across the street, while she moans with every damn sip of coffee she takes. My head is still spinning, both with her apparent mood swings

19

and the fact she's sitting here having a coffee with me. Something I haven't been able to accomplish since I met her.

"Why were you laughing? Earlier," I add.

"Don't really know, I guess it was one of those moments where it's either that or cry, and I loathe crying."

Interesting, and I have to admit I'm relieved to hear it.

She takes another sip of coffee and looks at me over the rim of her cup.

"How did you guys show up so quickly?"

"We just got to the gym up the road when Ouray called."

She puts her cup down and leans her elbows on the table, propping her chin on her hands as she studies me.

"And you came straight here?"

Since that's evident, I don't bother answering.

"Better be careful it doesn't become a habit you can't shake; showing up to my rescue. Unless of course that's your plan."

It sounds like a tease but I can hear a question mark in the comment as well. She's curious and that's mildly encouraging. Maybe I should…

"Are you okay doing a walk-through with me?"

So focused on Mel, I completely missed Ramirez walking into the coffee shop.

"Absolutely."

While they do that, I stay outside to make a call to the clubhouse. Honon, another of my brothers, answers and takes down my list of supplies needed to secure Mel's office.

"Give me an hour," he says.

"Okay, and bring tools. Mine are in the back of my truck at home."

"Sure thing."

I end the call and tuck my phone back in my pocket when I notice Wapi walking up to a Toyota RAV4, trying to get into a parking spot occupied by a police cruiser. Mel's daughter jumps out of the vehicle, clearly concerned with the police presence, but Wapi blocks her. I can't hear the conversation, but from her reaction I can tell she has her mother's fire.

My brother may be young, but he has more patience than a saint and a softer touch than you'd expect from a biker.

"Mom!" she yells, almost shoving Wapi aside.

I swing around to see Mel walking out, the second detective—I think his name is Evans—right behind her. He stops beside me as the women meet in the middle of the parking lot, and we watch as Mel explains things to her daughter.

"Name's Bill Evans," the man beside me shares and holds out his hand.

I give it a firm press.

"Paco."

He raises his eyebrows.

"No last name?"

I've been Paco for almost as long as I can remember. The name I was given at birth is just a name I find on official documents or bills.

"Driver's license says Nathan Philips, but it's been

so long since someone actually called me that it's highly likely I won't answer."

The guy grins.

"Gotcha. I've had a chance to meet a few of your brothers and thought I'd come introduce myself." He motions in Mel's direction. "Ramirez tells me she's the club lawyer?"

I figured there was a reason he's chatting me up.

"Watch yourself. She won't take too kindly to that label if she hears you call her that."

He lifts his hands defensively.

"Didn't mean any offense."

I believe him.

"You know what the club does?" I ask him.

"Other than own a growing number of businesses in town? Yeah, I've heard about your work with displaced kids."

Good. It appears he's done his homework.

"Mel helps us with the legalities around the boys. Setting us up as legal guardians," I explain. "Making sure everything's aboveboard."

I'm making a point he seems to get as he nods in understanding.

"Officer Staab mentioned you had a bit of a confrontation?"

So the dumb rookie has a name. My temper instantly flares.

"Damn right we did. Idiot had Mel at fucking gunpoint when I walked in. At an unarmed woman standing in her own goddamn office. I made it clear I wasn't down with that."

Evans's face loses all expression. Only a slight flare of his nostrils tells me this is news to him. Now he knows the kid is a loose cannon. In any tense situation he's likely to shoot first and ask questions later.

"Understood. I'll look into it."

I have no doubt he will. Staab could be a liability that reflects on the entire department.

He nods and joins Mel and her daughter while Wapi comes to stand next to me.

"What's the plan?"

"Honon's picking up new locks and a better security system before coming here. You can go if you've got somewhere to be, but I've got shit to do here."

He shoots a quick glance in the direction of mother and daughter before his gaze settles on me.

"Nah, I'll stick around. I'm sure you could use a hand."

That's true, but I have a suspicion his true motivation is about five foot six, with honey blonde hair, and a sharp tongue much like her mother's.

3

MEL

APPEARANCES NOTWITHSTANDING, I like things organized. Everything in its place.

That can't be said for the current state of my office.

The police just left, after traipsing through the place most of the morning, but Paco and some guys from the club are still here. They're fixing the door and putting in some kind of new security system he insisted I need. Already out of sorts, I didn't have the gumption to argue.

Now I'm standing in the middle of my office, looking around, not sure where the hell to start.

"Mom!"

Jesus, what now?

"What?"

I stomp out of my office to find SAC Damian Gomez

standing beside Lindsey but my eyes are drawn beyond them. Paco is standing on a chair outside doing something above my door. A strip of stomach is visible between the hem of his shirt and the waistband of his low-slung jeans, and I'm momentarily distracted by the glimpse of his happy trail leading down.

"Mom!"

I jump at Lindsey's voice. Good Lord, what is wrong with me?

Giving my head a mental shake, I turn to the agent.

"Damian? What are you doing here?"

"Heard about the break-in." He looks around the front office, where Lindsey has already made a decent dent in the mess. "Your alarm didn't go off?"

It always surprises me how fast news travels.

"Actually," Lindsey volunteers, a blush on her cheeks. "That's my fault. I was late for a dentist appointment Friday afternoon and apparently forgot to set it."

She'd mentioned it was a distinct possibility to the detectives earlier. I've forgotten to set it at least a handful of times myself that I can remember. It's not like we're that interesting, just a family law office, hardly a place where you'd find a lot of valuable stuff. Both Lindsey and I work on laptops we always take home. The only thing that might be worth hocking is the damn coffee machine.

I watch my daughter fiddle self-consciously with the seam of her pencil skirt. As always, she's dressed in appropriate office attire, unlike me.

"Not the first time, Linds," I reassure, throwing her a

smile.

"It happens," Gomez states. "Anything missing?"

"Nothing valuable, but we haven't had a chance to make sure all the files are here," I volunteer. "They were obviously looking for something."

"Any specific files they focused on?"

I know where he's going with this, and to be honest, it's the first name that popped in my head.

"Are you asking whether they were after the Mesina file?"

He shrugs. "Ramirez said you mentioned his name. He's aware of our investigation into the man," he explains.

I guess local PD would at least be aware of a local FBI investigation. It makes sense the detective alerted Gomez.

"It's hard to tell. I took the file home to look over before the conference call I had scheduled for this morning with his lawyer."

"I can't imagine anyone else would go through the trouble," my daughter contributes. "This is a family law office, it's not like we represent criminals."

"Not willingly, anyway," I add dryly. "But Lindsey is right, most of my clients are simply trying to get out of a bad marriage."

Of course we deal with divorces where domestic violence is involved and my client is in hiding, but other than Shauna Mesina, we don't have any current cases like that. Besides, we never keep records of their secure locations.

"Which only confirms Mesina is likely the one behind this," Gomez concludes. "Probably getting antsy he isn't able to get a bead on Shauna. What was the call with Redfern about?"

"Just a courtesy call. Lindsey filed Shauna's affidavit in support of her application for divorce with the court this morning. Mesina will be served with a copy but Redfern's been hounding us. Instead of having him blow up our phone for the time it takes for the documents to be served, I thought I'd go over the highlights with him and avoid that annoyance."

"He's on a fishing expedition."

I grin at the agent.

"Of course he is, but we both know that affidavit won't tell him anything we don't want him to know."

He doesn't stay long after that, but as he exits the front door I notice him stop to talk to Paco, and I find myself wondering what they're talking about. Then I watch Gomez walk to his vehicle and feel Paco's eyes on me. I meet his gaze through the window and for a moment our eyes lock.

"I've moved your appointment with Janice Munk to Wednesday," Lindsay says behind me and I swing around to face her.

"Good," I mumble, convinced the sudden heat I feel shows on my face. "That's good."

I try to duck past her, but my daughter has sharp eyes.

"Are you okay, Mom? You seem out of sorts."

I attempt to rearrange my features into a picture of innocence as I turn around, but I already know she won't buy that either.

"Not every day we get broken into, Lindsey."

She narrows her eyes.

"I call bullshit since you have been out of sorts for a while now."

Her gaze slides out the front window where Paco had been just moments earlier.

"Is it him?"

I try for a derisive snort, but what escapes me sounds more like the bark of a seal.

"Who, Paco? Puleeze…"

"You could do worse, you know?"

"Don't be ridiculous," I sputter.

"Why not? I've seen him looking, I'm pretty sure he's interested. Even just a fling. How long has it been, Mom? It would be good for you. Especially now that you've hit the change."

I'm still processing the fact she thinks he's interested when the rest of her comments register.

Wait.

"I've hit the what?"

"The change, the big M, menopause, Mom."

It's like a punch in the stomach. The shock similar to when I discovered my first gray hair at twenty-two. I was totally gray by the time I turned thirty but religiously dyed my hair in an attempt to preserve my youth. Then one day I decided to embrace it—embrace the true me— and let it all hang out.

Menopause, though? That's for old women. Right?

"Bullshit," I snap. "I'm too young for that."

"The mood swings, you don't sleep well, and last week I found you with your head in the freezer."

"My doctor would've said something," I protest weakly.

Lindsey barks out a laugh.

"Mom, you haven't been to the doctor in years. When's the last time you had a period?"

She's got a point. She's also right that I haven't been sleeping well and get overheated all the time, but it's been a hot summer. And the last time I remember having a period was back in April when Sophia and Tse had the twins. I was never regular, but it's been almost six months.

"I don't wanna talk about it," I state firmly before swinging around to hide out in my office.

Except Paco is blocking my way.

Paco

"What pissed her off?"

Honon throws the tools back in the bed of the truck. We both just watched Mel speed off in her little rental car.

I have a pretty good idea after catching part of what her daughter said, but I'm not about to share that with my brother.

"Cut her some slack. She's had a shit day."

In her hurry to get out of the office, she shoved Honon—who was coming to look for me inside—out of the way.

I was tempted to go after her, but held myself back. Something tells me she wouldn't have appreciated that.

"Whatever. I'm heading back to the clubhouse, you coming?"

"I'll be there for dinner. I want to go over the new security system with her daughter and install the software."

Lindsey is inside sorting stacks of papers she collected from the floor.

"Sorry about that," she says when she spots me coming in. "I pushed Mom's buttons when she was already stressed out."

"No worries," I mumble. I really don't want to discuss the subject I walked in on earlier with Mel's daughter and quickly change the topic. "I'm going to need to install the software for the new security system on your computer so you can monitor the cameras, even when you're not here."

"Cameras?"

She looks surprised as she pulls her laptop from a briefcase.

"Yeah, covering your entrances. I can install a few in here as well but wasn't sure if you'd want that. I can always add those later."

"I'll check with Mom." She sets the laptop on the front desk, logs in, and turns it to me. "Have at it."

It takes me half an hour to get it set up and show Lindsey how to monitor the cameras and manipulate their angle. Then I ask for her phone and download the app that will allow her to set the alarm remotely, in case she forgets.

"At some point, I should probably do the same with your mother's computer and phone," I tell her. "I assume she'll need to access the system as well."

"She probably has her phone on her, but I don't think she had her knapsack with her laptop when she ran out of here earlier."

She disappears down the hall and reappears a few moments later with a worn leather backpack.

"Are you able to access it?"

"Uh huh, fingerprint. Just in case something ever happened, we made sure we could get into the other's computer."

"Probably smart."

While I work on Mel's laptop, Lindsey is able to refile the sorted paperwork and moves to her mother's office to tackle that. When I'm done, I find her in there.

"Laptop is done, I should get going."

"What about Mom's phone?"

"I can do that another time, or you can do it yourselves. You saw me do it, it's not complicated."

She puts down the stack of papers in her hands and puts them on her hips. She suddenly looks just like her mother with that challenging lift to her chin.

"You know, my mother may be a little rough around the edges but she has a good heart."

"I'm sure she does," I agree, unsure what that has to do with the price of eggs.

"I've seen how you look at her. I hope you're not the kind of guy who lets a little outburst like earlier scare you off."

I grin to myself. It's funny her daughter is concerned her mom's rough edges might put me off. Heck, I'm nothing but rough edges.

"Not gonna lie and tell you I'm not interested, but you're reading me wrong if you think your mother's strong personality is gonna scare me off. Been patient a long time and had my eyes open, but I've seen enough to know Mel is not a woman you rush or you get shut down quickly."

I don't tell her I'm able to monitor their cameras from my phone as well, and I'll be watching even more closely now. Reason I don't plan on telling either of them is so they can't say no. Monitoring remotely is the only way I can keep an eye on Mel without pissing her off too much.

Lindsey tilts her head slightly and a grin twitches at the corner of her mouth.

"Yeah," she drawls. "You'll do."

Amused at the vote of support, I shake my head and take my leave, but before I step outside, I call over my shoulder.

"Lindsey!"

"Yeah?"

"Don't forget to set the alarm!"

4

MEL

"READ THESE OVER and we'll talk at your follow-up appointment."

My doctor hands me a stack of pamphlets, detailing the different treatment options for menopause she explained to me.

Lindsey was right and I'm not looking forward to eating crow. She's likely to lord it over my head to infinity.

Menopause.

Fuck.

I needed another reminder I'm not getting any younger like I needed a hole in the head.

"Now, since I finally have you in my office," she continues when I'm about to get to my feet. "You haven't had a Pap smear in four years and you're well overdue for a mammogram. While we're at it, we may as well refer you for a colonos—"

"Don't," I snap, holding my hand up before she can finish that thought. "Don't even think about it."

She promptly burst out laughing. "Eventually," she threatens.

"Maybe, but…" I pause, squinting at her far-too-amused expression. "You bitch, you're yanking my chain."

That results in a renewed bout of laughter from my best friend since high school.

"Only a little bit," she snickers. "I was serious about the Pap and the boob squeeze." She gets up and walks over to the treatment table, flips up the stirrups, and pats the paper cover. "Hop up. We can get one thing over with today."

Half an hour later I get behind the wheel of my rental, toss the pamphlets and the mammogram reminder on the passenger seat, and tear out of the parking lot.

Instead of going back to the office, I pick up a burger and an ice tea at Sonic. Then I drive up to the college where I park at the West Hall, grab the pamphlets and Sonic bag, and walk to the lookout point. No one is there so I take a seat on the bench and eat my lunch while staring down on the town.

This is what I do when something is eating at me, when I feel my balance slipping; I sit here watching daily life in Durango go by below, people and cars reduced to ant-sized proportions. It helps me reclaim the illusion of control.

I need it today.

The truth is, this entire past week has thrown me, starting with the break-in at my office. Or maybe even before that with the breakdown of my car. A car I have yet to replace.

Change is not my thing. It makes me feel unsettled. I never used to be like this, at least not when I was young. I was adventurous, outgoing, and yes, a bit of a rebel as well. On the outside I may still look the part, but it hides a deep need for predictability.

A new car, the chaos at my office, and now this whole menopause thing all have me feeling rudderless. And to add to that, there's Paco.

He has the ability to throw me off completely and I don't know what to do with that. There's a reason I've successfully avoided relationships since the demise of my marriage. Alone I know what to expect and that was enough for a very long time. My don't-mess-with-me attitude helped to keep any hopefuls at bay. But meeting Paco made me wonder about what I was missing for the first time.

Then last year when he made that comment about my appearance it stung, but I hoped it would cure my attraction to him, give me a reason to vilify him, but that clearly hasn't worked. I'm still very much aware of him and even worse, I think that awareness may be mutual since he seems to keep showing up lately.

Although, I haven't seen hide nor hair of him since last Monday and I can't help wonder if what he overheard from Lindsey and my conversation that day had anything to do with it.

As if on cue, I hear the rumble of a motorcycle engine on the road behind me and swing my head around.

It's not him, the bike is a crotch rocket he wouldn't be found dead on. Judging by the backpack the biker is wearing, probably a student late for class.

I'm instantly pissed at myself for feeling disappointed.

Shoving the rest of my burger in my mouth, I gather my pamphlets, dump my trash in the receptacle, and head for my car.

That's enough self-doubt for today. Time to pull my big girl panties up and learn to embrace change.

"AT LEAST CONSIDER a Forrester or a Crosstrek," Lindsey suggests.

The young guy at the Subaru dealership nods eagerly. Whether because his eyes have been on stilts since catching sight of my gorgeous daughter or because the price tag—and therefore his commission—is higher on those vehicles versus the Outback I asked him to show us. It's a toss-up.

My look at Lindsey is annoyed. Mostly for trying to push me outside of my comfort zone. Still, I glance over at the pearly white SUV she indicates and picture myself behind the wheel. The mental image comes easily, and I have to admit, it *is* pretty.

"It's got heated seats, Mom."

Damn. That would be nice come winter.

"Yeah, but what's the gas mileage on that?" I ask stubbornly, determined not to give my headstrong daughter two victories in one day.

Or maybe it's me who's the headstrong one.

"Not much different from the Outback," the salesman assures me.

I throw him a doubting look; not so sure he wouldn't say just about anything to seal the deal.

"Here, look for yourself," Lindsey prompts, shoving her phone at me.

She's pulled up the *Consumer Reports* website comparing the two vehicles. Almost identical.

I'm running out of excuses.

Taking a deep breath, I hand her back her phone and turn to the young guy.

"I want to test drive it."

A big grin splits his face. "Of course. Let me grab the keys."

Forty-five minutes later, Lindsey is almost skipping along beside me as we make our way back to her RAV4.

"Don't look so smug," I grumble. Not that it makes a difference; she's smiling all the way home.

I'm cringing at the whack of money I just spent, but tomorrow I'll be picking up my brand-new SUV.

I'm embracing change.

PACO

"YOU USED TO be fun."

I don't even bother turning my head to watch her stomp off pouting. It's not the first time this week she's approached me.

Betty. One of the Mesa Riders' club girls.

It's been a while since we've been at the Mesa Riders' clubhouse. Not much has changed here; parties almost nightly and no shortage of booze or women. That's the way it used to be at Arrow's Edge as well, but things have changed over the past ten, fifteen years. The club changed direction, got out of the illegal trades, and things have quieted down significantly since then.

With quite a few of my brothers now hitched and having families, these wild parties are a thing of the past. I wasn't happy about that at first, but in the past few years discovered I wasn't really missing them or the effortless hookups they guaranteed.

Never thought I'd say this, but getting wasted and fucking random chicks is not nearly as much fun north of forty-five if you can't remember a damn thing the next day and your body hurts like a sonofabitch.

"You good, brother?" Red, the Mesa Riders' president, wants to know.

"Yeah. I'm good." I throw the rest of my beer back and set the bottle on the bar. "I should probably crash. We're heading out early tomorrow."

'We' being Honon, Ouray, and myself, as well as the young boy we finally found this morning.

Red called us last week about this kid spotted along the shores of the Colorado River, just north of Moab. Some of his guys reported seeing a small boy wearing a sky-blue T-shirt, ducking between the rocks and brush along the water. One person actually saw him in the Lions Park parking lot near the bridge, diving into a garbage bin.

Red figured he was a runaway and called us in. It took the three of us days to track the boy down and cornered him in a drainage pipe. He was fighting like crazy when we managed to pull him out.

Fucking heartbreaking. The kid can't be more than six, maybe seven years old, and hasn't spoken a word. If I had to guess, I'd say he was maybe out there for a week at most and other than a few scratches and bug bites, he looked to be in decent shape.

Still, we took him to the hospital to be checked out. We were met there by our local contact at Child Protective Services and she was able to inform us there were no reports of young boys with his description missing. The boy checked out and Ouray is back at the motel with him.

The social worker for CPS is getting the paperwork ready, placing the boy under the club's temporary guardianship, so we can take him back to Durango tomorrow. With the child still not talking and clearly afraid of something or someone, she agreed with us the best and safest place for him would be the Arrow's Edge clubhouse.

Under Ouray's guidance we've built up a good reputation and it's not uncommon we get calls from neighboring states. In part because of Trunk, one of my brothers, who also happens to be a certified child psychologist. If anyone can get the boy to talk, it would be him.

"Feel free to crash in one of the back rooms," Red offers.

"Nah. I've only had two beers. I'm heading back to the motel. Thanks anyway."

I clap a hand on his shoulder and scan the clubhouse for Honon. I spot him at the pool table and whistle between my teeth. He looks up, catches me gesturing to the door, slaps his cue on the pool table, and meets me there.

"You don't seem too heartbroken to leave," I note when we get on our bikes.

"Not my scene," Honon shares. "Not anymore."

"You and me both."

The motel is only a five-minute drive from the Mesa Riders' compound. When we drive up, I see Ouray leaning against the wall beside his door, smoking a cigarette.

"Thought you quit that," I point out when I get off my bike and approach him.

"Fuck off," he grumbles, his glare darting from me to Honon. "I've had a shit night. Poor kid just passed out ten minutes ago. He's been curled up with his knees to his chest in the corner beside the bed all night, watching my every move. Won't accept anything to eat or drink, and I'm pretty sure he pissed his pants because the kid is too scared to go to the bathroom."

"Jesus."

"Yeah. Something happened to that boy." He drops

his head between his shoulders and shakes it. "Fuck, he's so little. And I'm so goddamn sick and tired of seeing kids like him scared."

I nod but don't need to say anything. We all feel that way from time to time. The kind of work we do, you see and hear heartbreaking things. For a few of us brothers, it's a difficult reminder we were once just like these scared, traumatized kids.

Nudging Ouray I point at the smoke in his hand.

"Got any more'a those?"

Honon bums one as well and the three of us smoke them in silence. Ouray is the first one to announce he's turning in, and Honon follows suit, unlocking our shared room next door.

"Coming in?"

"I'll be a minute," I tell him. Then I take my phone from my pocket and dial.

"It's fucking late, Paco," Gomez says by way of hello.

"Whatever," I dismiss his complaint. "Any progress on the break-in?"

"You could've bugged Ramirez," he grumbles. "He's investigating the break-in."

"Wasn't Ramirez who wanted to make sure the club had Mel covered. That was you. I've been out of town, but she's had eyes on her every move this week and I've been monitoring the office. Now, is there any progress? Do you know if it was this Mesina guy she mentioned?"

I looked up that name. Wasn't really able to find anything that would explain the FBI's interest in him, but that only means he's hiding it well.

"You fucking know I shouldn't be discussing an active investigation with you. However, since you already know more than you should, I'll share we didn't find any evidence—no prints, no witnesses, and no video feed from neighboring businesses—to suggest it was him. He also has an alibi for most of the weekend."

"He could've hired someone," I suggest.

"It's a possibility, but the fact remains, we have no physical evidence."

Not what I want to hear. I'd rather know who to keep an eye out for.

"Too bad."

"I know." He pauses briefly and then continues, "Well, if that was it, I'd like to get back to bed, if you don't mind."

"Right. I'll be back in town tomorrow, I'll check in."

"Fine," he groans. "As long as you don't do it after midnight."

I chuckle at his disgruntled tone.

"I'll do my best," I offer, not leaving a chance to needle the man unused.

We may get along okay now but there was a time Gomez had me in his crosshairs for something I didn't do. That's not something you forget easily.

"Asshole," he mutters right before the line goes dead.

I quickly check the video feed from Mel's office, like I've done a few times a day.

Nothing. It's quiet.

Good.

Maybe by the time I get back tomorrow, Mel will be

over her snit and a little more pliable.

Maybe…but I'm not holding my breath.

It's Mel after all.

5

MEL

"WHAT THE HELL are you doing here?"

It slips out before I can bite my tongue.

Paco is on my doorstep, trying to hide a grin, and holding what looks to be a bag from Royal Cumin, a new Indian restaurant Lindsey and I discovered a few weeks ago.

How the hell did he know I...*Lindsey.* I swing around to see her ducking down the stairs to her apartment. Traitor. My own flesh and blood.

I turn back to find Paco still grinning on my front step.

"You may as well come in. You obviously already know I'm a sucker for chicken vindaloo, thanks to my loose-lipped offspring. I can smell it from here."

I reach out, grab the bag from his hand, and head for

the kitchen. His footsteps follow me.

"There may be a stray can of beer in the fridge."

Grabbing plates and cutlery, I hear the fridge open.

"What about you?"

I turn to the kitchen island where I left the food and set out the plates. I do my best not to ogle Paco standing in front of my fridge. Just having him in my house is already causing weird flutters in my stomach.

"I'll grab a water."

I hear the fridge door close and the hiss of the can opening. Then he walks into my view, his eyebrow raised, as he takes a seat on one of the stools on the opposite side of the island.

"You don't drink?" he asks.

"Not anymore," my daughter, who's just coming back up the stairs, answers for me. "She says it gives her hot—"

That little... She's been rubbing it in my face all weekend, which hasn't exactly improved my moods.

"I swear to God, Lindsey Amelia Zimmerman, I'm going to superglue your mouth shut when you sleep!"

Unimpressed, she sidles up to me and kisses my cheek.

"Don't be a grump and don't wait up for me, I'll be late."

"Where are you going?" I call after her, mildly panicked.

"Out!" is the last thing I hear before the front door slams shut.

"Your daughter's a card."

One side of his mouth is pulled up and his eyes are sporting laugh lines. The man is far too attractive.

"She's a pain in my ass," I grumble, taking the containers from the bag and pulling the lids off. I close my eyes and inhale the fragrant scent of spices. "Damn, that smells good."

"Yeah. I noticed that."

I glance up at him as I start loading the plates. "Have you had their food before?"

"No. Can't say I have a lot of experience with Indian food. Or any. This'll be my first time. Good thing your girl suggested what to order or I would've been at a loss."

He eyes the food I'm piling on his plate dubiously.

"Can't believe you've never tried it," I comment. "You're in for a treat. It's spicy though."

"I can handle a bit of heat."

Oh, I just bet he can.

The suggestive tone in that gravelly voice causes a full body flush. Before I break out in a sweat, I beeline it to the fridge to grab the jug of water I keep cold in there.

"Want a glass?" I ask over my shoulder.

"I'm good with my beer."

"Dig in," I tell him when I round the island with my glass and catch him watching.

I sit down, leaving one empty stool between us, and take a bite. My eyes close automatically when the intense flavors hit my taste buds. *So good.* The sudden clearing of a throat has me dart a quick glance at Paco, who is grabbing for his beer. Beads of sweat break out on his forehead and I stifle a grin.

"You weren't kidding," he says hoarsely, his eyes watering. "It's like eating fire."

He takes another gulp from the can.

"You're better off taking a bite of white rice," I recommend. "It cuts the heat."

We don't talk much while we eat, only a few comments here and there about the food. But when both our plates are empty, he turns his body so he's facing me.

"Is that a new ride I saw in the driveway?"

"Hmm. Lindsey arm-wrestled me into getting it. Picked it up today."

He smiles at the mention of my daughter and my stomach does a little flip. He really is quite handsome and having him in my house —without my daughter as a safety buffer—is a little bit unnerving.

"Good choice. Great safety record and it'll hold up well in winter weather."

"Glad you approve."

My words come out a bit snippy, but it doesn't seem to faze him. In fact, he appears annoyingly unflappable. Eager for something to do I slide off my stool, gather the dishes, and head for the sink.

"I was in Moab all week," he volunteers while I run water in the sink. "We got called in to look for a boy seen roaming around the riverbanks just west of town. Took us a couple of days to track him down. Kid's messed up."

I turn off the water and turn around.

"What do you mean?"

"Just a little guy—five, maybe six—and he's scared out of his mind. Won't talk, and—"

"Won't or can't?" I interrupt.

"Won't. Ouray had him in his motel room and said the boy was restless all night, crying in his sleep and calling for his mom. He has a voice, he's just too afraid to use it."

My heart squeezes in my chest.

"No clue who he is?"

Paco shakes his head. "No kids matching his description missing. We checked."

Of course they would've.

"It's tourist season, maybe he was accidentally left behind?" I try.

"The family would've backtracked and reported it."

Poor lamb, God only knows what he's been through.

"Where is he now?"

"Clubhouse. Lisa's lovin' on him and Trunk is there keeping a close eye."

"What can I do?"

I assume the reason he's here is because they need some kind of legal intervention.

His smile for me is appreciative. "Nothing at this point. Our contact at CPS was able to fast-track temporary guardianship, but depending on what we find out that might change."

I nod my understanding. If there was any sign the boy was mistreated or abused, the club would want to change that temporary document into a more permanent one. That's when I'll jump in to provide the legal backing.

"And the boy isn't the reason for me stopping by," he adds, catching me off guard.

"It isn't?"

"No. Just thought I'd explain why you haven't seen me this week."

"Oh."

I turn back to my sink of sudsy water. I'm not sure what to think about that statement, it's not like I saw him all that often before, but I refuse to let my mind make more of it than it is.

"Mel?"

"Hmm," I hum without turning.

My shoulders inadvertently straighten when I hear him getting up and closing in.

"Mel."

His tone is firmer now, and right behind me. He doesn't touch me, but I can feel his proximity with every cell of my body.

"Doesn't mean I haven't kept an eye on you." I make an unintelligible sound in the back of my throat. "Been monitoring your office feed on my phone," he continues. "And my brothers have been keeping watch."

Wait.

The plate I was holding hits the water with a splash as I spin around, the wet dishrag still in my hand spraying suds.

"You had me watched?"

PACO

I FIGURED SHE wouldn't be happy.

Heck, that's why I texted Lindsey to find out what

her mother likes to eat. Thought I'd butter her up with food before telling her we've had surveillance on her. I wanted to do that myself before she clued in on her own or one of my less discreet brothers let something slip.

Didn't think to bring a change of clothes, though.

The front of my shirt is soaked but she doesn't even seem to notice, she's too busy glaring at me.

"Hear me out," I plead calmly, but she's not done.

"Someone's been following me around?"

"For your safety, and Mel—"

"Without my knowledge? That's an invasion of privacy. What? You had them watch my every move and report back to you? That's…that's…that's stalking!"

Oh, she's pissed all right. She's starting to stammer and agitatedly blows at a strand of hair that came loose from the bun piled on her head.

Unfortunately for her, instead of intimidating me she turns me the hell on.

"Hardly," I return dryly. "Just some added security. From what I understand, the guy you mentioned, who might be responsible for the break-in, is bad news. Bad enough he's under investigation by the feds. Do you think if he wants something from you, he'll limit himself to tossing your office? Especially if he didn't find what he was looking for?"

An irritable grunt is her only response.

"Mel," I try, infusing a lot more patience than I feel. "Gomez has his hands full guarding your client, he doesn't have the manpower to put a guy on you, so he asked if I'd keep an eye out."

I thought that might calm her down but it only seems to upset her more.

"Oh, so you were watching me because Gomez asked you to?"

Fuck me. The woman is a challenge.

"No, but—"

"I'd like you to leave," she interrupts, putting her hands on her rounded hips and jutting out her chin defiantly.

What I'd like to do is kiss that stubborn mouth of hers, but I figure that'll probably get me a knee in the nuts. She'll need some time to cool off. Again.

Melanie Morgan is gonna be more than a handful but I'll bet she's worth it.

Having pissed her off enough for one day, I do as she asks and head for the door. I hear her footsteps behind me. With my hand on the doorknob I turn to face her.

"For what it's worth, I didn't need Gomez to ask me. I would've watched out for you anyway. You're important to the club…"

She nods, a derisive smile on her lips. "The club…" she echoes.

"But more than that, you're important to me," I finish what I intended to say.

I've apparently caught her off guard again, as her expression softens a bit.

For a moment we stare at each other, and I try to read the emotions swirling in those pale eyes.

"You should've told me," she finally says in a more subdued tone, her eyes lowering to a point in the middle of my chest.

Instead of accusatory, she almost sounds hurt.

Taking a risk, I touch her shoulder and slide my hand to the side of her neck. Then I duck my head so I can look her in the eye.

"I would've if we hadn't been called away, but I was on your doorstep not two hours after we got back. I'm telling you now."

As I straighten, her eyes travel up, hesitating briefly on my mouth. I may not be the savviest or smoothest guy around, but I'm pretty fluent in body language.

Taking a chance, I bend down and lightly brush her lips with mine. The small gasp when I break the light kiss has me do it again, this time allowing my tongue a little taste before I pull back.

I'm grateful to see the deepening flush on her cheeks. *Good*, I'm not the only one affected. That'll give her something to think about.

I turn away and open the door.

"Lock this behind me," I remind her as I walk down her steps.

It takes her a minute, but when I get to my bike parked in the driveway, I hear her call out behind me.

"I can take care of myself, you know!"

"YOU LOOK SMUG."

Honon moves closer on the other side of the bar.

With our club prospects busy—I just checked in with

Shilah, who is parked a few doors down from Mel's place, and Mika is probably in the boys' dorm with the younger kids—Honon is manning the bar tonight.

Instead of heading straight home as I intended, I ended up at the clubhouse instead. After kissing Mel I knew I'd be too wired to relax anyway. A beer and some distraction seemed a better option.

"Had a taste of the good life," I blurt out.

My brother's eyebrows shoot up to his hairline.

"I thought you said you were checking in on Mel," he points out.

"I did."

I couldn't keep the grin from my face if I tried but the truth is, I just don't give a damn. I watch as Honon clues in.

"Well, thank fuck." He grins back at me and reaches over the bar to give my shoulder a pat. "Been dragging your ass on that for so long, I thought you'd given up on it." He checks his watch before looking back at me. "What the hell are you doing back here so soon?"

I shrug, taking another sip of my draft.

"One step at a time," I tell him.

He nods his understanding. That's the thing about brothers, they often know you better than you know yourself.

"Probably smart. Not the kind of woman you'd rush anyway."

"You've got it," I agree.

Can't remember the last time I kissed a woman and didn't end up naked as a result, but then most of the time

I wasn't looking for more than a physical release. Not so with Mel, which is exactly why I only allowed myself a taste.

Trust my brother to recognize the significance of that.

"How's the boy?" I ask, changing the subject.

He grins. "Kiara performed her magic on him. She had him eating dinner beside her at the table. I'm sure she'll eventually have him talking too. Lisa took him back to the cottage with them."

Lisa is our club mother and married to Brick. Ouray may run the club, but Lisa runs the clubhouse. They live in a cottage at the back of the compound with her two grandchildren, Kiara and Ezrah, and Brick's grandson, Finn. Both Brick and Lisa tragically lost their daughters, and ended up raising their grandkids.

Kiara, unlike her quiet older brother, is a chatterbox and has been able to melt the hearts of more than a few hardened bikers. The little boy was no match for her.

Good. Whatever it is the kid's had to endure in his short life, he'll be well taken care of here.

I drain my glass and slide it across the bar to Honon.

"I'm outta here."

"Already?"

"Yeah. Gonna get an early start tomorrow. I've got some stuff to do around the house."

I flick a few fingers at a group of my brothers playing cards at a table nearby and scratch Jack—Ouray's dog—behind the ears on my way out the door.

The house is dark when I drive up, looking a little lonely.

The front looks good. I spent quite a bit of time this past spring putting in some shrubs and flowerbeds. The rear is still a work in progress, but I did manage to put in a garden. A lot of the vegetables I planted are done—most of them went to the clubhouse for Lisa to use—but I still have tomatoes, peppers, a few beans, and a shitload of carrots. Having been gone for a week, I'm sure I'll have a ton of picking to do tomorrow morning. Maybe I can drop some off at Mel's too.

I flick on the lights when I walk in the door. I built this house with the help of my brothers, and there are times I still can't believe it's mine. For all of my adult life, the clubhouse had been my home up until we finished building this place last year.

Most of the time I enjoy the quiet up here on the mountain, but I'm thinking maybe a dog like Jack, or Van—Sophia and Tse's rescue—would make the house feel less empty.

Maybe after I tackle the yard tomorrow, I'll go check out the animal shelter in town.

I wonder if Mel likes dogs.

6

Mel

"BUT WE'RE GETTING married in three weeks. I already gave my notice here."

I take in a deep breath in an effort to stay calm while my client, Jessica Huberfelt, dabs at her eyes with a tissue.

When I first took her on as a client eighteen months ago, my first impression of her had been one of innocence. I felt compelled to look out for her. She appeared naïve, but I've since discovered she uses her wide-eyed tears to manipulate if she doesn't get her way.

Her now-ex-husband—whom she accused of verbal abuse and cheating—turned out to be a very reasonable, nice guy. Nicer than I would've been under the circumstances for sure.

As it turned out, it was Jessica who had the affair, something she eventually admitted to me. She didn't have a choice since Philip—her ex, who wasn't stupid—hired a private investigator, who came up with the photographic evidence to confirm it.

I had a long talk with her back then, recommending we mediate an agreement to avoid dragging what should be a fairly straightforward divorce into court. A judge might not look kindly on the false accusations she made in her original divorce application. Her objective had been sole custody of their two children, but given Philip could show he had taken a very active role in raising them, she finally conceded to joint custody.

Their divorce was final two months ago, but now she's back, looking to move to Austin, Texas with the kids. Her fiancé—the man she previously had an affair with—lives and owns an ad agency there.

"Like I explained before, you cannot just move the kids to another state when you and Philip have joint custody. Not without a change in the custody arrangements or consent from Philip."

"He's just being stubborn. This is his way of getting back at me," she complains. "He doesn't want me to be happy."

I'd really like to bang my head against the table.

"He found out from the kids last week, Jessica. Are you really surprised he's not throwing you a goodbye party? He has the same rights you do. Of course he's not just going to roll over and give up without a fight."

"That man is ruining my life!" she explodes

dramatically before turning on the waterworks in earnest.

Christ, give me patience.

By the time I manage to coax her out of my office with a promise I'll connect with Philip's lawyer, my nerves are frayed.

"Drama much?" Lindsey comments dryly, holding out a few messages. "I could hear her all the way out here."

I grab them from her hand. "She's a pain in my ass. Can you get hold of Miles Davies' office? See if he has time tomorrow to talk to me about the Huberfelts?" I sift through the messages and startle when I see the name scribbled at the top. "Carlos Mesina? He called himself?"

"Yup. Said it was urgent he speak with you," she confirms.

"Did you tell him to get in touch with his own lawyer?"

Lindsey rolls her eyes. "Of course I did, but he said it was imperative he talk to you directly."

It's highly unusual, but curiosity has me sit down at my desk and dial the number he left with Lindsey. While it rings, I hit the record option on my office phone. You never know. It's an old thing that still records on micro cassettes, but those recordings are much harder to tamper with than their digital cousins and therefore hold more credibility in court, if they were ever needed.

"Ms. Morgan, it's a pleasure."

I've never even spoken to him so I couldn't tell you if the man who answers is in fact Carlos, but his smarmy tone fits the picture I conjured in my head.

"Mr. Mesina. I believe my assistant already explained

it would be more appropriate to have your attorney contact me."

"Ah, yes, your lovely daughter."

My back snaps straight. That is not common knowledge. At least not in this office. We agreed early on we'd keep our interactions professional around clients. She doesn't call me Mom in front of them, and I refer to her as my legal assistant unless we're alone.

The fact Mesina knows has a cold chill crawling up my spine. It feels like a threat.

"Mr. Mesina, I—"

"A beautiful young woman," he continues as if I hadn't spoken. "Seems very together but still you must worry. She drives the same Toyota I bought my wife. In fact, she reminds me a little of Shauna, who I'm very worried about."

"Mr. Mesina—" I try again.

"My wife is not well, Ms. Morgan. Beautiful, like your daughter, but not nearly as capable. I'm afraid she's unstable, suffers from paranoia and delusions—"

I almost laugh at the obvious ploy. The only thing this man worries about is what his wife might share with me. Little does he know it's not me he has to worry about but the FBI.

"Mr. Mesina!" I say loud enough I'm sure Lindsay heard in the front office. "Any communications with this office need to go through your attorney. I suggest you contact him."

With that I firmly hang up, only to immediately dial Damian Gomez's number.

"I think Carlos Mesina just threatened me," I blurt out the moment he answers the call.

"PLAY IT AGAIN."

We're in a storage room in the back of a secondhand bookstore I didn't know belongs to Gomez's wife.

When I mentioned on the phone earlier I'd be heading home soon anyway and could drop the tape off at the FBI office, he told me to stop at the bookstore instead. The friendly brunette waved me through to the back, indicating they were already waiting for me.

They ended up being Detectives Ramirez and Evans, as well as Gomez and one of his agents by the name of Jasper Greene. A bona fide welcoming committee. Except the moment I handed over the tape I was all but forgotten.

Agent Greene came armed with a laptop and a small dictation machine he connected to the computer. He plays the conversation again as requested.

"Definitely a threat," Evans concludes.

"I'm not arguing that," Gomez responds. "But I can tell you as evidence it's flimsy. It certainly isn't enough to bring Mesina in."

The next five minutes arguing is exactly what they do. The lines are drawn in the sand with the cops on one side and the feds on the other. The FBI doesn't want to blow their investigation by jumping the gun unless they have tangible evidence that'll stick, and the detectives are more concerned about the possible implications of Mesina's threat.

If anyone had bothered asking my opinion, I'd have told them I have a foot on both sides of the fence. From a legal perspective I agree with Gomez, but on a personal level you bet your sweet bippy I want that man nailed right now. He threatened Lindsey.

"As fascinating as it is to sit here and listen to you guys yammer, I'd like to get home where I can keep an eye on my daughter," I announce, getting to my feet.

"She's looked after," Gomez states.

"What does that mean?"

"I called Paco."

Jesus F. Christ, these guys. High on their own damned testosterone.

Throwing him a scathing look I move to the connecting door to the store.

"Give me a minute and I'll make sure you get home," he calls after me.

"I can find my own way home, Special Agent Gomez. Lived there for near twenty years and haven't gotten lost once."

I think it's Evans I hear laughing but I don't wait to find out, I march through the store and straight out to the parking lot.

Fifteen minutes of road rage dealing with downtown rush hour later, I pull into my driveway next to Lindsey's RAV4. A pickup truck I recognize as Paco's is parked at the curb.

Paco

"WHAT THE HELL is that?"

Mel, who just came storming in the door, aims a pointed finger at her daughter.

"Her name is Cookie," Lindsey says, unfazed by her mother's temper. "Isn't she adorable? I told Paco I'm going to keep her."

She did tell me that when I showed up with three bags of vegetables I was supposed to drop off at the club and the little mutt tucked under my arm.

What can I say? I stopped by the shelter and was checking out a mastiff named Bull when this little thing in the cage beside him kept barking for my attention. The moment I looked in her direction, the little tail started wagging like crazy and when the older woman working there opened the gate, the pooch almost tripped over her own feet to get to me.

Bull had pointedly ignored me the entire time I stood in front of his cage, but this tiny thing greeted me like a long-lost family member.

How could I resist?

I cringed when I was told her name, but since she's two years old and already used to it, I don't have the heart to call her something else.

I was signing the adoption papers when Gomez called.

"You got us a dog?" Mel looks at me with abject horror plastered on her face.

Well, shit. I guess she doesn't like dogs.

Before I have a chance to tell her the pooch is mine,

Lindsey pipes up.

"Here, Mom, say hi."

She shoves the dog at her mother, who has no choice but to grab hold. Excited to meet a new person and not at all intimidated by her bad mood, Cookie proceeds to lick every inch of Mel's face she can reach.

It takes her about ten seconds, give or take, to force a tentative smile on Mel's lips.

"Well, aren't you a cutie? Happy little thing, aren't you?" she coos.

I catch her daughter winking at me from behind her mother's back.

"Fine, she's cute. But how do you propose we look after her, Linds? We both work all day."

"Chill, Momma. I was just yanking your chain. She's Paco's."

"Yours?" Mel asks me, her eyes wide and her lips twitching. "I didn't know you had a dog."

"Picked her up at the shelter this afternoon," I grumble, noticing her barely contained laughter. I'm sure I'll be getting more of that when the guys find out.

"I've gotta say, not what I would've expected you to pick."

Then she doesn't bother containing it anymore and bursts out laughing, the dog happily barking along. I'm about ready to grab my dog *and* my vegetables to go sit outside in my truck until I can get one of the brothers to take my place, when she hands Cookie to me. The pooch curls up in the crook of my arm and promptly goes to sleep.

"I promise I'm not laughing at you," she says, putting a hand on my arm.

"Sure as fuck looked like it to me."

"No. It's just…unexpected."

"Oh, and Mom? Check out the vegetables he brought over," Lindsey points out, shooting what little is left of my street cred all the way to hell.

I expect renewed hilarity, but instead, Mel's mouth falls open when she rummages through the bags.

"You grew these?" She picks out a pepper and a tomato and admires them. "How the hell do you get them so big?"

"Mom tried to grow tomatoes once," Lindsey clarifies. "They ended up looking like raisins."

"They did not," her mother objects, which makes Lindsey laugh at her.

"Sure they did. Remember the birds wouldn't even touch them when I stuffed some in the feeder?"

Mel huffs and focuses on me.

"Anyway…I certainly couldn't get them to grow like these. These look amazing."

I have to say I'm a little surprised at her reaction—especially after the way she laughed at my choice of dog—but I'm more than a little pleased at the compliment. The gardening is something my brothers like to rib me about, but they'll use anything as an excuse to torment. I'm used to that, and since they don't complain about the food Lisa makes with my produce, I don't take the ribbing to heart. Besides, if the roles were reversed, I'd be giving them a hard time too.

It's different with Mel. For some reason her approval is important.

"The garden at my place faces south and the soil's good."

"That's right, your place is just down from Tse and Sophia. I've seen it in passing a few times, but at the time it was still under construction."

This conversation leaves me an opening I'm not going to miss.

"About time you see the finished product. I'll show you the garden, give you some pointers."

Lindsey gives me a thumbs-up over Mel's shoulder.

Cookie starts squirming, wanting to be let down. When I put her on the floor she immediately starts sniffing, turning in circles.

"You may wanna take your dog out before she pees on my floor."

"I'll do it."

Lindsey scoops Cookie up and rushes her outside, and I watch as she plops the dog on the grass to do her business.

"I learn new things about you all the time."

I swing around. Mel is rinsing the vegetables in the sink, her eyes focused on what she's doing. I wait for her to elaborate, but she doesn't.

"Hope only good things."

She darts a glance at me from the corner of her eye.

"Some," she qualifies, and her serious tone tells me I'm about to hear what had her storming in earlier. "But I don't appreciate being managed. Like you did when you had your boys watching me while you were gone, or how Gomez calls you to keep an eye on my daughter and nowhere in there am I consulted or notified by him, but most importantly, by you."

"Don't remember you calling to let me know that dirtbag threatened you."

"Not the same, Paco. This is *my* daughter we're talking about. And it's *me* who was threatened."

"And I'm the man who's gonna make sure nothing happens to you *or* your girl," I add resolutely.

There's a stubborn set to her mouth I'm fast becoming familiar with, and as much as I want to kiss those rigid lips soft, this is something which needs to get hashed out sooner than later.

"I like you, Mel. That can't be news to you. And I respect the hell outta you, but I ain't gonna hold back when it comes to your safety. I'm gonna do what I can, it's just who I am."

Any hope I have with her hangs in the balance, right here, right now. This is something that goes right to the core of me and if she can't accept it as part of me, we have a problem.

She takes her time drying her hands, but there's no anger in her eyes when she turns to face me.

"Fine, but next time could you at least keep me in the loop?"

My grin is instantaneous.

Sure she's negotiating, she's a lawyer, but I don't have a problem agreeing to that.

"I can do that. Now, wanna tell me about Mesina?"

1

MEL

"THIS IS RIDICULOUS."

I look up from the work I was hoping to finish today. Seeing Lindsey standing in my doorway—mutiny on her face—I'm pretty sure that's not going to happen.

Resigned, I close my laptop and lean back in my chair.

"You'll have to be more specific," I tell her.

"Dale just called, canceling dinner tonight," she huffs.

Dale is a process server she met at the Durango courthouse a few weeks ago while filing documents for me. By my count tonight's dinner would've been their third date.

My daughter doesn't date a lot—most guys don't meet her lofty standards—but Dale made it past two dates, which means she really likes the guy. Or maybe

I should say 'liked' because she doesn't appear too enamored today.

"I'm sure he had good reason," I suggest carefully, but judging by her derisive snort it wasn't good enough.

"He said something came up and he'd be busy for the foreseeable future." She accompanies her sarcastic tone with air quotes. "Said since it looked like I might have some issues I should probably deal with first and perhaps our timing was off."

"Where would he get that idea?"

"What do you think?" She throws up her hands dramatically. "Every step I take I have that stupid biker dogging me. The other day he sat in the row behind us at the movies. Of course he scared Dale off."

She slumps down in the club chair facing my desk.

I'd love to point out if Dale was so easily discouraged, he's obviously not the right guy for her, but I keep my mouth shut. Best she figure that out by herself. She's smart, she will.

The stupid biker she talks about is Wapi, who clearly takes his assignment to keep an eye on Lindsey very seriously. Since Paco and I came to an understanding after Mesina's call, I've tried to ignore the occasional glimpse of a biker following me around.

"I know it's annoying to have eyes on you at all times, but they're just looking out for us."

I can't quite believe that just came out of my mouth. Just a few days ago, I was spitting nails myself at the perceived invasion of privacy. Does that make me enlightened, or a hypocrite?

Paco stopped by again last night, without the adorable pooch this time. According to him, Cookie seemed to have a bit of separation anxiety and he was training her to be alone. He stayed for maybe ten minutes before announcing he had to go. If you ask me, it could well be Paco with the separation anxiety instead of the dog. On his way out the door, he asked if I'd like to come over to his place after work today, and since Lindsey had dinner plans and I'm really curious about his house, I said I would.

"Look, why don't you come with me? I was going to stop by Paco's after work. Get a look at his house, check out his garden."

"No, Mom. Just because my date fell through doesn't mean I want to ruin yours."

"There's nothing to ruin since it's not a date," I insist. "Besides, I'm sure five minutes with that dog of his will cheer you up."

That seems to grab her attention.

"I almost forgot about Cookie."

We end up taking my vehicle up the mountain, leaving Lindsey's parked behind the office for the night.

"This is *nice*," my daughter observes when I turn onto the driveway.

The house is set back and only partially visible from the road. A mix of stone and rough-hewn logs, it suits the rugged landscape. It also matches the man who lives here.

The front is nicely laid out, the lines of the beds following the natural curves in the landscape, and the plant material used effortlessly blends in. Even though it's late in the season there are still pops of color: some fountain grasses, a clump of snapdragons, sedum, and goldenrod. Still a little bare but I'm sure it'll fill in nicely in a couple of years.

Paco is already waiting in the open front door as we walk up to the house. He doesn't appear too surprised Lindsey came along, but I'm sure there isn't much going on these days he doesn't have an eye on.

Cookie immediately draws the attention of my daughter, who quickly mumbles, "Don't ask," before scooping up the little mutt and squeezing past Paco who looks at me quizzically.

"Apparently having a big bad biker breathing down their necks at the movies the other night was too much for her date. He blew her off."

As much as he tries to hide it, I can tell he's amused.

"She upset?"

I shrug. "Nah, her pride is stung more than anything, but it might be prudent for Wapi to keep his distance for a bit."

That makes him grin, those laugh lines fanning out from his eyes adding to his appeal.

Oh, who the fuck am I kidding? The guy is hot, and the fact he grows vegetables for fun and adopted a feisty purse-sized dog doesn't do anything to change that. Quite the contrary. These days he occupies far more of my thoughts than I care to admit. Of my fantasies too.

"Are you gonna come in?"

His question startles me and I realize he's been

waiting for me. Heat burns my cheeks and I hope to God my musings weren't plastered all over my face.

The inside of his house reminds me of him. It's simple, sparse, and straightforward, but high quality and geared toward comfort. Lindsey has already made herself at home on the sectional sofa, curled up with the dog, her feet tucked underneath her, looking like she belongs.

Paco walks right past her to the kitchen, as if he's used to having her around.

"Drinks?"

"Wine?" Lindsey looks over her shoulder.

"Sorry. Beer and…" He pulls open a cupboard over the fridge.

"Ooo, I see tequila. I'll have that. Straight up."

"Linds, it's five fifteen and you haven't eaten yet." I can't stop my inner mother from speaking up.

She turns to me with a saccharine smile.

"Then it's a good thing you're driving."

I bite my tongue. My daughter is twenty-seven years old and can make her own decisions. Even those that won't end up pretty. Good thing she's self-contained in the basement, any messes she makes she can also clean up. I just hope she doesn't end up puking all over my nice new car seats.

"Mel?"

"Just water for me, thanks."

He grabs a bottle from the fridge for me and gets my daughter her shot of tequila. Then he grabs my hand and leads me to the sliding doors in the back.

"Where are you taking me?"

"Garden," he says over his shoulder. "Linds? Wanna come?"

"Hell, no," my daughter calls back. "I'll keep Cookie company. You guys can go play in the dirt."

I groan at her comment but Paco seems to think it amusing.

"Now there's an idea."

PACO

I OBSERVE MEL as she walks between the rows of plants in front of me, bending down occasionally to check the crop or test the soil. She seems genuinely interested, which is a pleasant surprise.

"Why don't you pick us some?" I suggest when she turns up a row of pepper plants I haven't harvested yet. "I'll toss them on the grill with the elk steaks. You eat meat, right?"

"Yes, but you don't have to feed us." Her eyes dart back to the house. "I thought I was just dropping by to see the place. Otherwise, I wouldn't have been so rude to invite Lindsey along."

She looks a little flustered compared to the competent and confident attitude I'm used to. I like it.

"Dinner was my plan all along," I admit. "Figured it was less likely you'd turn me down if you were already here."

"I wouldn't have," she protests, but then concedes at my raised eyebrow. "Okay, fine. I probably would've."

"Why?"

She seems surprised at my question.

"I'm not really sure." She glances at a point somewhere over my shoulder as I take a step closer. "Maybe because I wouldn't know what to expect."

"A meal?" I tease her.

She rolls her eyes at me, but her mouth is smiling. Encouraged, I take another step, bridging the distance that remains. She doesn't object when I slip one arm around her and press my palm to the small of her back. My other hand I lift to her face, running a silky soft strand of her hair between my fingers.

"Your hair is amazing," I mumble.

"So now you're saying I shouldn't go out and spend a whack on coloring it?"

Her comment isn't harsh—the smile still lingers on her lips—but the message is clear. I fucked up and I did it in a way that left a mark. She's warning me it's gonna take more than an easy compliment to fix it. That's fine. I don't mind working hard, especially when she's leaving it open for me to try.

"Please don't. This suits you."

I slide my fingers in her hair and curl them around the nape of her neck. This time when I kiss her it's not a tentative brush of lips. This time I kiss her deeply, loving the way her mouth opens under mine. Instead of using words I show her how gorgeous, how desirable she is to me.

"I don't date," she says, a bit short of breath when I end the kiss.

"Works for me. I don't date either."

She pins me with an annoyed look, but her hands are still fisted in my shirt. I call that a win.

"So…what do you call this then?"

"You think it needs to fit in a box?" I challenge her.

"Well…no, but—"

"It is whatever we make of it. Doesn't have to be predictable."

"Hey!" Lindsey calls out the back door. "Do you have anything to eat? I'm starving."

Mel drops her forehead to the middle of my chest as I start to chuckle.

"Wanna bet she's already tossed back half your bottle?"

I give her hip a squeeze.

"Let's get some food in her to help soak up the tequila."

Mel wasn't far off.

Luckily there was only a third left in the bottle to begin with, but Lindsey had made quite a dent in that. She offered to help cut vegetables for the foil packets but Mel wisely waved her off. She was bound to cut herself.

"Why do men have to be such wimps?" she complains, hanging over the deck railing beside the grill while I flip the steaks.

Not sure if she really wants me to answer, I figure it's safer to keep my mouth shut. Sure enough, she picks up her tirade without any need for prompts.

"I thought I was done with losers but they always find me. Why is that? Why can't I find a good man? A decent one who is willing to fight for me?"

Her voice gets more and more slurred and if I'm not mistaken, her eyes are starting to water. She looks like she could burst out crying any minute. A little panicked, I glance over my shoulder where I can see Mel putzing around in the kitchen. She offered to make a tossed salad and set the table, but I'm regretting I took her up on it.

"Like you. You're fighting for Mom, right? You're not scared off," she sniffs, "not even when she's being hormonal."

I'd love to get off this fucking topic and for a moment I consider throwing Wapi under the bus. One mention of him would have her fuming again, which I much prefer over this.

"Is there something wrong with me?" She lifts up her arm and sniffs her pit. "Do I give off funky phero... whatever those things are called?"

"Lindsey!" Mel's stern voice sounds from the door. "Why the hell are you sniffing your armpit?"

I let out a sigh of relief when Mel firmly takes her daughter by the arm and pivots her inside.

I'll say one thing though; these women are not boring.

By the time I head inside with the meat and roasted veggies, Lindsey is smiling again, sitting on the floor against the back of the couch, playing tug-of-war with Cookie.

Mel is by the coffee maker, cursing under her breath.

"Doesn't anyone have an ordinary machine anymore?" she grumbles when she catches sight of me. "I'm trying to get some coffee in her but I can't figure out how this thing works."

I slide the food on the counter and bump her hip. "Move over."

Five minutes later we're sitting at the table, Lindsey with a coffee beside her plate, and I realize this is the first time I've ever eaten here. Most of the time I sit at the kitchen island or eat over the sink when I'm home, and I still take a lot of my meals at the clubhouse, although not this week.

Feels good, having some life in this house.

I glance over at the dog, who is sleeping in front of the fireplace in the little hammock bed I got her. She took to it immediately, even prefers to sleep in it at night as long as I keep my bedroom door open so she can check up on me from time to time.

It's nice, having her around.

Nice finally having Mel around too.

Feeling pretty good, I listen with half an ear as the women chat while I eat my dinner. From the living room I hear soft growling and I notice Cookie's head up. She's staring at the front door. Then I hear it too, the deep rumble of a bike approaching.

Shit.

"It's all right, girl," I try to calm Cookie, who just jumped down and is barking furiously.

I manage to snag her up off the floor moments before my front door slams open and Honon marches in.

The first thing he sees is the snarling dog under my arm.

"What the fuck is that thing?"

"That's Cookie," Lindsey says, stepping up beside me

and plucking the dog from my arms.

"Hey, Lindsey. Cute dog." Then he glances over my shoulder. "Hi there, Mel." Finally his eyes come back to me. "Sorry, brother, but when you don't show up at the clubhouse for dinner four nights in a row, and you don't answer your goddamn phone—pardon my French—you know Ouray's gonna eventually send out the troops."

"Jesus. I had shit to do."

"I can see that." His comment is delivered with a smirk on his face. "Sorry to interrupt, but we're riding out first thing tomorrow morning. Heading back to Moab. They think they may have found the kid's mother."

"I can't."

Haven't quite thought through what the hell I'd do with a dog when I'm out on a run.

"What do you mean you can't? Since when?"

"If you're worried about Cookie, we're happy to take care of her while you're gone," Lindsey offers.

"Hey, speak for yourself," Mel pipes up. "What about when we're at the office?"

"Easy," her daughter smiles at her brightly. "We'll just bring her with."

Honon looks confused. "But isn't that your dog?"

"No. She's Paco's little princess."

Mel snickers behind me.

Yeah. Never gonna live that down.

PACO

"DOES THIS LOOK like him?"

Ouray lifts up a plastic bag holding a picture of a toddler sitting on a tricycle. I take it and have a closer look.

"I think so."

Three days ago a hiker found the body of a woman caught on a rock on the bank of the Colorado River, just south of Moab. Police had no reports of someone missing who would fit her general description and she wasn't carrying any identification. She'd apparently been in the water for a while.

Then yesterday, they got a call from a camper who reported a van in one of the disbursed camping spots, not far from where the woman was found, which looked to be abandoned. The cops checked it out and in the van they found evidence of someone living in it. Some of the stuff they found suggested the van's inhabitants had been a woman and a kid. Their thoughts immediately went to the child we picked up five miles upriver.

Ouray mentioned when they called him yesterday, they'd wanted him to bring the kid back to Moab for them to interview. That request didn't go very far since the boy still hasn't said a word, but even if he did, there's no way Ouray would've let them grill a little kid for information.

Our trip here was to satisfy his own curiosity.

With the help of his contact at the local CPS, he was able to convince the cops to let us have a look at the contents of the van.

"This was the only picture you found?" I ask the evidence tech, who's been keeping a close eye on us.

"Yeah. Found it underneath the front passenger seat. There was nothing else, just some receipts for gas and groceries tucked in the driver's side door, a small cooler with rotting food, two sleeping bags, a few toiletries, and the clothes. Oh," he adds. "And that stuffed toy."

He points at the threadbare rabbit.

"Can I take a picture?" I ask, already pulling out my phone.

The guy shrugs. "Be my guest."

I snap a quick shot and send it off to Trunk, asking him to show the boy the picture.

"Smart," Ouray mumbles, catching on quickly.

"Any luck?"

Yelinek, the detective in charge, comes walking into the department garage.

"Could be him," Ouray volunteers. "Clothes look the right size and we just had a look at the picture. Possible it's the same kid."

I hear my message alert and check my phone. Trunk already got back to me.

It's his. Bunny, first word the kid said, now he's crying.

Be good if you could bring it.

"It is him. The boy recognized the rabbit. Trunk wants us to bring it back for him."

"I can't do that," Yelinek states. "It's evidence."

"Maybe so, but it'd do more good if it could help get the boy to talk than getting dusty in your evidence room," Ouray points out.

"No chance for prints and I already checked it for fibers or hair," the tech unexpectedly pleads our case. "Found one long blonde hair that matches the victim's and is consistent with the ones we recovered from the brush. The only fibers I found are consistent with the carpet in the van."

Yelinek seems to mull on that. "It's been photographed?" he asks the tech.

"Yup. And the findings have been recorded."

"Fine. Take the thing, but make sure you let me know if the kid says anything."

He pulls a card from his wallet and hands it to Ouray,

who slips it in his pocket.

"Any news on the woman?" he prompts the detective.

"Preliminary report from the coroner indicates asphyxiation. There was also fresh bruising on the body, suggesting she'd fought. This was murder. She'd been in the river for maybe a week, which unfortunately took care of any of her attacker's DNA we might have found under her fingernails. Everything suggests she's the same woman from the van, we just don't know who the hell she is." He takes off his glasses and rubs a hand over his face. It's clear he hasn't had a lot of sleep since catching this case. "The van comes back registered to a Harlan Farrell of Blanding, Utah. Local law enforcement tried to contact him, but it turns out Mr. Farrell is currently on week two of a month-long Panama Canal cruise, which suggests the vehicle may have been stolen, but we can't confirm 'til we get hold of the man."

"Gotta be frustrating," Ouray commiserates.

"You've got no idea."

It's another two hours before we're back on the road heading home. The detective asked us to show him the area we'd covered when searching for the boy. At this point he's assuming they were together in the van, but the kid somehow ended up five miles upstream from where the woman was discovered. I guess he hopes to find some clues by retracing the boy's steps.

I wonder if the kid saw something. Maybe he witnessed the attack and ran off. What if the victim was his mother? That kind of trauma can scar you for life. No wonder he won't talk.

The rabbit is safe in my saddlebag and I'm curious to see what his reaction will be. Maybe I should swing by Mel's office and pick up Cookie. She seems to be able to put anyone at ease. Even Honon.

Their initial contact was rather hostile, and Honon may have likened her to a hairy rat, but before I was able to get him a beer from the fridge he was sitting beside Lindsey on the couch, Cookie loving all over him.

Mel came to stand beside me in the kitchen, watching them.

"See? That dog has talents. She's managed to seduce not one badass biker, but two."

I grinned at her. "And don't forget a hard-nosed lawyer."

"Fair enough. Her feisty character packed into to all that fluffy cuteness is pretty irresistible."

I almost told her that's exactly what attracts me to her, but luckily had the presence of mind to swallow it back. Something told me being compared to a dog and being called fluffy might not come across the way I intended.

We ride into Durango and at the first traffic light, I roll up so I'm level with Ouray.

"Gotta make a quick stop in town."

"Picking up your dog from Mel?"

Honon and his big fucking mouth.

"Yeah. She's little and friendly, I'm thinking maybe she can help with the boy. Put him at ease or something."

"Worth a try, but how are you gonna take the dog on your bike? Why not see if Mel can drop her off at the clubhouse? There's a few things I'd like to talk to her about anyway."

Both Mel's new SUV and Lindsey's RAV4 are parked behind the office when I pull around. When I open the door, Cookie is right there, her whole body wriggling in her excitement. I have to go down to my haunches to greet her.

"Hey, girl, did you miss me?"

"You're back sooner than expected."

I look up to find Mel leaning against her office doorway, glancing down at me. She's wearing those worn jean bib overalls again, an old Eagles concert T-shirt, and her feet are bare. My guess is she had no client or court appointments today. I let my eyes drift up, catching the tattoo I've been curious to explore peeking out of the neck of her shirt.

"Couldn't stay away."

MEL

I SUPPRESS A shiver.

Those eyes of his stroked up my body and woke every nerve in their path.

I watch as he gets to his feet, Cookie tucked under his arm.

"Don't tell me you've come to take her already."

I try for a light tone but my raspy voice betrays me.

His lips twitch.

"And so the truth comes out; you only want me for my dog."

I lift my chin in challenge.

"Who says I want you at all?"

Apparently, the wrong thing to say because his eyes darken and he suddenly leans close, his lips just a fraction from mine.

"I do."

I'm not sure who moved, but it was probably me.

His lips are surprisingly soft and pliant, the facial hair he keeps neatly trimmed tickling my cheek. In my fantasies I've imagined that coarse hair brushing other sensitive parts of me and again my body shivers.

He's passive this time, letting me control this kiss. I'm tentative at first, too aware I'm standing in the back hallway at the office, but then I taste him deeper. It's like a switch is thrown, turning off my mind, allowing instinct to take over. The need to touch and feel is overwhelming.

"Whoa, Darlin'," he rumbles, lifting his head. "As much as I like the direction this is going, I'd recommend a change of venue."

It's not until he straightens up, I notice I have my hand shoved down the back of his jeans. I immediately yank it back.

Oh my God, how embarrassing.

"Mom! Is Cookie with you?"

Like a cold shower, Lindsey's voice drifts from the front of the office.

"Yeah," I croak and quickly clear my throat. "She's right here."

"Hey, Lindsey!" he calls out.

"Paco? Don't tell me you're picking her up already!"

Lindsey's face appears at the end of the hallway.

"Actually I've come to ask your mom a favor." He turns to look at me. "Would you be able to drive up to the clubhouse after you're done here? Ouray has some stuff he wants to discuss with you and I was kinda hoping you could bring Cookie with you."

My embarrassment is instantly forgotten and my curiosity is piqued.

"Did something happen in Moab? Did you find the boy's mother?"

"Looks like it," he says, and then he drops a bombshell. "Police found the murdered body of a woman in the river we think might be her. It's a long story, most of it guesswork at this point, but it's possible the boy was a witness to what happened to her."

"Oh, that poor tike. And he still isn't talking?"

Paco shakes his head.

I feel a pang in my chest at the idea of that little guy watching his mother get killed. He must've been so scared.

"Linds? Were there any messages I need to follow up on?"

I spent most of the afternoon working on Jessica Huberfelt's motion for a modification of child custody. A task I'm not particularly enjoying, which is why I've been dragging my ass, but she is my client and it's my job to represent her the best I can. So I had Lindsey take messages while I put my nose to the grindstone.

I was almost done when Paco walked in.

"Nothing pressing." Lindsey walks up and hands me a couple of messages. "Detective Evans called but said he'd catch you later."

I quickly flip through them. I can tackle these tomorrow morning. I'm curious to know what Evans was calling about, though. Maybe I'll try to get a hold of him.

"Okay, then I just need half an hour to finish what I was working on and I'll be there," I inform Paco.

"No rush," he says, handing Cookie to my daughter, who immediately disappears with the dog down the hall.

As soon as she's gone he turns to me, catches a strand of hair between his fingers, and tugs it lightly.

"Later, Darlin'."

I'm having a hard time concentrating and have to force myself to finish the work before I make a quick call. I end up getting Evans's voicemail and leave a brief message. Then I grab the Huberfelt file and walk into the front office.

"It's done?"

"Yes. My notes are in front."

At least my work on it is done, Lindsey has to type it out in the proper format. I bend down to pick up Cookie, who is curled up under the desk.

"What time is Jessica coming in again?"

"Noon tomorrow."

"Good. I'll tackle it first thing. I want to get out of here too."

She shuts down her laptop and shoves it in her bag.

"Where are you off to?"

"The Chop Shop. Anika was able to fit me in for a keratin treatment."

My daughter has the same wavy hair I do, but opts to

have it smoothed out regularly. She prefers the groomed look. Luckily for her, there's no sign of the premature gray I was cursed with.

She locks the front door and follows me to the back, where I set the alarm and follow her outside.

"I don't know how long I'll be," I call out to her as I set Cookie on the passenger seat.

"Don't worry, Mom. I caught that clasp you had on Paco. I don't plan to wait up for you," she yells back, and I just catch the cheeky grin she wears as she gets behind the wheel.

Brat.

9

MEL

"HEY, MEL."

"Mel!"

I feel a little like Norm in *Cheers* when I walk into the clubhouse, closely followed by the prospect who was behind me the entire way here.

Or maybe the dog I'm carrying is drawing all the attention. Either way, our arrival has clearly been noted.

"He's so cute!"

Kiara, Lisa's granddaughter, is rushing this way.

"It's a she, and her name is Cookie," I tell her when she greets the dog.

"Can I hold her?"

Behind Kiara I notice a little boy, his blond hair a little too long as it flops in his eyes. He's standing by the big dining table watching carefully.

"Tell you what, let's first find Paco. It's his dog so it should be his decision."

"Really?"

I smile at the disbelief on her face.

"Yeah, really. I was just dog sitting her."

"Huh," she says with a shrug before turning around and scanning the clubhouse.

"Mr. Paco! Your puppy's here!" she hollers, and every head in the clubhouse turns this way.

The kitchen door swings open and a stern-looking Lisa walks out.

"Swear to God, child, use your indoor voice," she scolds her granddaughter. "One of these days I'm gonna staple your mouth shut."

The little boy hovering by the table startles but Kiara—not at all impressed—turns and smiles at her grandma.

"Nana, look! Mr. Paco got a puppy. She's sooo fluffy!"

I catch movement on the far side of the clubhouse where Paco emerges from the hallway leading to Ouray's office, Trunk's office, and a bunch of bedrooms.

"Fine-looking dog you've got there, brother," Brick comments from his perch at the bar.

Paco glances in his direction without saying anything but I can read the "Fuck off" in his expression. These guys are not in the habit of checking their language but they're careful when the kids are around. One of the many things I appreciate about this rugged band of brothers.

"Hey, Darlin'," he mumbles when he reaches me and

before I realize his intent, he presses a hard kiss on my lips.

A few whistles go up around the clubhouse, which Paco pointedly ignores as he plucks Cookie from my arms. My face is burning.

"Is Mel your girl, Mr. Paco?" Kiara asks, observing us with great interest.

"Yup."

I'd like to give him a piece of my mind for putting me on the spot like this, but what I have to say would not be appropriate in the presence of children. I resort to glaring at him and silently vow to never admit a small part of me enjoyed being claimed so publicly.

"Mel, guess that means you're staying for dinner, yeah?" Lisa says, a sparkle in her eyes.

"She is," Paco answers for me and I jab a sharp elbow in his ribs.

"I can speak for myself, you oaf."

"What's an oaf?" Kiara asks, not missing a thing.

"Never you mind," Lisa intervenes. "You and Bunny come eat in the kitchen."

I find out who Bunny is a moment later when Kiara walks up to the little boy and takes his hand.

"Bunny?" I mouth at Paco as the kids follow Lisa to the kitchen.

"It's the only word he's uttered since we found him," he explains. "Why don't you come on back. Ouray is in his office."

He sets Cookie down on the floor, and she is immediately crowded by Ouray's dog, Jake, who is about five times her size.

"Is she gonna be okay?"

"She'll be fine," he says confidently.

As if to illustrate, Cookie snaps at the big dog when his nose is a little too invasive to her liking. Jake jumps back and whimpers.

Good girl.

"Appreciate you popping in, Counselor."

Ouray is sitting at the large conference table in his office, with his right-hand man, Kaga. He invites me to take a seat.

"Don't know how much Paco told you, but I want to get you up to speed on our newest guest."

"Pretend I don't know anything," I tell him as Paco takes the seat beside mine.

For the next twenty minutes, he takes me from the initial call for the club's help to what they've found out today. Although, right now, evidence the dead woman discovered in Moab is the little boy's mother is highly circumstantial, my gut says it's her. The fact he recognized and emotionally responded to the stuffed rabbit they found in the van is enough to convince me.

Ouray's main concern is if he can refuse police access to the child with only the temporary guardianship papers. If the two are related, the boy may have been witness to what happened to her. Possibly the only witness.

"Legal guardianship is not the same as legal custody," I explain. "It covers your day-to-day decisions about the child's welfare. In a case where legal decisions need to be made, it's likely CPS would have to jump in and the court may have to get involved." I lean my elbows on the table. "That being said, I don't think anyone will argue with you. The child isn't speaking and is clearly traumatized. At worst I'd imagine law enforcement might call in the help of a child psychologist or therapist to question a child his age. But since he's not even talking, that's a moot point."

"We're hoping that may change," Ouray indicates. "We brought back the stuffed animal. After dinner, when Trunk gets here, we plan to give it to him."

"Earlier today I sent Trunk a picture of the rabbit and Trunk showed the boy," Paco explains. "He clearly recognized it. It was the only time he said anything."

"You're hoping it'll prompt him to start speaking," I deduct.

Ouray hums a confirmation.

"Could backfire as well," I suggest. "What if he did witness something and the animal triggers memories?"

"That's why I wanted you to bring Cookie. She's small, nonthreatening, and may be a good distraction. Something safe to comfort him?"

Paco has barely finished speaking when a loud dinner bell rings from the clubhouse. I snicker when all three men get to their feet at the same time at the promise of food. So predictable.

"Come on," Paco prompts me. "Trust me, these guys will decimate the dinner table like a bunch of locusts."

It wasn't quite that bad.

Lisa reserved me a spot beside her at the table, while Paco joined Nosh and Honon at a smaller table.

Nosh is the club's former president and born deaf. His wife—who passed away a few years ago—used to rule the clubhouse before Lisa. The old man now has a room in the clubhouse and is looked after by Lisa and the brothers. I remember being surprised when I discovered almost every adult and most of the children were able to communicate with him in sign language.

Paco's hands are flying now, his lips forming the words at the same time.

I'm not aware I'm staring until Lisa whispers beside me.

"Don't stare too hard or the pretty'll wear off and that'd be a cryin' shame."

When I turn my head, I find her wearing a grin.

"You're happily married. You're not supposed to notice that."

She huffs, shrugging her shoulders as she starts loading lasagna on my plate.

"I may be married but I ain't blind. Glad to see you've finally opened your eyes too."

"Me?"

Thick strings of cheese stick to the plate as she sets it in front of me. My mouth instantly waters.

"Paco. That man's had it bad for you for a long time."

I swallow a snort and glance up at her. "He sure didn't give me that impression."

"These men aren't much for sweet-talking, but you give 'em a chance, learn to read the actions instead of waiting for the words, you won't regret it."

For lack of a response—mainly because I figure she

may well be right—I focus on my plate instead.

I moan out loud at the first bite, the food is so good. Lisa chuckles beside me but when I glance over at Paco, he's observing me intently.

PACO

EVER SINCE THAT kiss in her office I've been having a hard time thinking of anything other than her blunt nails digging into my asscheek.

My attraction to Mel has suddenly turned into something very physical. No longer a fantasy teetering on the edge of reality, but something more tangible, more concrete, in a way I can imagine how it would feel to have her naked underneath me.

Even seeing her obvious enjoyment of the food Lisa dished out earlier became sexual. The bliss as she closed her eyes on the first bite, the sounds I imagined her making, gave me a glimpse of how she'd respond when I finally slide inside her lush body.

"Paco? The toy?"

Trunk, who just walked into the clubhouse, leans over my chair.

"Yeah, let me grab it. I left it in my saddlebag."

I head outside to where the bikes are parked just as Wapi comes rolling through the gates. I collect the rabbit and wait for my younger brother to park.

"Lindsey?"

"Fucking sat outside the hair salon for two hours," he grumbles. "She's home now, tucked in for the night."

Mel already had a decent security system on her house that didn't need upgrading—a better one than she had at the office anyway. I just hope Lindsey remembered to set the alarm.

I shoot off a quick message to remind her and instantly get one back.

Yes. You're as bad as my mother!

"Any dinner left?" Wapi asks, as we head for the clubhouse.

"We had lasagna, so my guess is no, unless she put some aside for you."

"Fucking Lindsey. Who spends two goddamn hours at the hairdresser?"

I almost remind him he volunteered to keep an eye on Mel's daughter but keep my mouth shut. If there's one thing I've learned it's that we all have to find our own way. Wapi will find his, eventually.

"Here." Mel shoves Cookie in my hands and nudges her head toward the back hallway. "Lisa just walked the boy to Trunk's office."

"You gonna come in?" I ask her.

"No. He's never even met me. Best to keep the numbers to a minimum."

She's got a point. Even Ouray apparently opted to stay out and is sitting at the bar.

"All right. Mind sticking around so I can see you home?"

She pauses for a moment, and I can see an internal

struggle playing out on her face. She eventually settles on, "Fine, I'll wait."

Lisa just slips out of the room as I'm about to enter.

"Not staying?"

"No. The child seems to trust me. If this turns out to be too much for him, I can be his safe place."

Inside the boy is perched on the edge of a couch, watching Trunk play *Mario Kart* from a safe distance. I know my brother sometimes uses a game system to connect with the older boys and it seems to work on this little guy as well.

"Bunny," the child whispers when he spots the rabbit I'm holding.

"Is that his name?"

I may have imagined the small nod, but take it as a good sign and take a step closer, holding out the stuffed animal. He suddenly charges at it, snatching it right from my hand before he retreats to the far corner of the couch, clutching the threadbare thing to his scrawny chest.

"Is this your bunny?"

I get another faint nod and his eyes drift to the dog.

"This is my dog. Her name is Cookie. Can she come say hello?"

This time there's no mistaking his agreement. I put the dog down on the couch and she darts to the other side, her entire body wagging as she almost crawls to the boy. One of his hands comes away from the stuffed animal and tentatively reaches for the dog. Beyond excited at the attention, she flips on her back.

"I think she wants you to rub her belly," Trunk

suggests in his deep rumble, observing the scene with mild amusement.

The moment the little guy touches her, she starts to squirm and a giggle escapes the boy, startling even him.

We're quiet for a bit as the two seem to bond. Cookie snuggles as close as she can before eventually putting her head on his leg.

"My name is Paco, what's your name?"

His eyes shoot up at me, and then swing over to Trunk before he lowers them to the dog again.

Fuck, maybe I shouldn't have put him on the spot. I wince as I glance over at Trunk, who just shrugs. The man can have a temper but has the patience of a saint when he's working with the boys.

"Mason."

For a moment I think I imagined it, his voice is barely audible, but Trunk reacts as well.

"Mason. That's a good name," he tells the kid. "I have a little boy at home, his name is River. He's four years old, but I think you may be a little older. Are you five?"

Almost instantly the boy responds.

"Six."

A sharp knock on the door is immediately followed by Ouray poking his head in. His eyes fix on me.

"Need you out here."

The urgency in his voice makes the hair on my neck stand up. Leaving Cookie with the boy, I follow Ouray into the hallway and pull the door shut behind me.

"What's wrong?"

"I just got a call from Luna. They went to arrest Carlos

Mesina tonight but it looks like he was expecting them. There was an exchange of gunfire and he escaped."

"Is Luna okay?"

"She is, but Gomez wasn't so lucky. He got hit in the shoulder. Luna wanted to make sure we had an eye on Mel and her daughter."

Lindsey. Fuck.

Ouray reads my expression and immediately follows it up with, "I sent Wapi and Honon to get the girl, but I haven't told Mel yet. Figured I'd get you first."

Mel will go ballistic.

"We're gonna have to hold her back."

Ouray nods.

"That's what I figure."

10

MEL

"GET OUT OF my way."

I glare at the three bikers blocking my exit.

"Darlin'…"

Paco puts a hand on my shoulder I shrug off.

"Are you kidding me? Mesina's out there somewhere, my daughter is not answering her damn phone, and you guys are just standing around. I have to go!"

Anger is fueling me right now, masking the fear I feel deep in my gut. Unfortunately, none of these fucking Neanderthals seem impacted by my yelling.

"And do what?" Paco points out calmly, which only serves to piss me off more. "Wapi and Honon will be at your place soon. They'll let us know if anything's wrong. For all we know she put her phone on silent and went to bed early. Or her phone died. Tons of plausible reasons I can come up with why she's not answering." I hate that he makes sense when panic is closing my throat. "Going off half-cocked does no one any good."

Except it would make me feel better to do something, to take control of the situation. Of course that would only be an illusion because I have no control at all. None.

I growl my frustration, but then I catch a glimpse of Kiara, shock and even fear etched on her little face as she looks at me from behind Lisa. *Jesus*, I'm scaring the kids.

"Fine," I concede grudgingly. "I need a bathroom."

What I need is a few moments by myself to get a grip, or maybe let myself lose it.

"Use the one behind my office," Ouray offers.

Paco puts a light hand on my elbow. "I'll show you."

I don't object as he leads me down the hallway and into the office. Then he opens the door at the far end, revealing a complete bedroom suite.

"I've got it from here," I mumble, and without looking up I aim for an open door to the attached bathroom.

Shutting the door, I immediately turn on the faucet and splash cold water on my face. Then I lean my hands on either side of the sink and let the water drip down.

I'm a family lawyer for fuck's sake. It's not like I represent career criminals for a living, yet here I am, scared out of my wits because, somehow, I managed to land a client married to one. He already threatened my daughter and he's out there, armed, and clearly not afraid to shoot to get what he wants.

My eyes burn and I douse myself with cold water again, just as the door opens a crack and Paco peeks in.

"Wapi called. They have Lindsey, she's fine."

"Ooof," escapes my lips as my knees buckle under me.

The next moment my face is pressed against Paco's shirt as his strong arms hold me up.

"She's fine. The boys will bring her here."

I lift my head.

"She'd better get ready for a piece of my mind for not answering her damn phone," I sputter.

"That's a given."

He plucks at his shirt and I spot a few wet blotches I left behind on his chest.

"That's just water. I was splashing my face," I hurry to explain.

"Of course it is," he mumbles, suppressing a grin as he takes my face in his hands and brushes the pads of his thumbs over my cheeks.

Ten minutes later, the door to the clubhouse I've been staring at almost as long swings open. Honon is the first one through with Lindsey wedged between him and Wapi, who is in last.

I barely remember getting off the barstool I'd been perched on when my daughter is in my arms.

"Easy, Mom. You're choking me."

"Good," I mumble, overcome by emotion. "Since I gave you life, I'm the only one who can take it back. Answer your damn phone!"

I release her and take a step back so I can check her

head to toe to make sure she's in one piece.

"I had it on the charger in the kitchen. It ran out of juice. I told you I need an upgrade." It's a repeat discussion we've had since the latest model iPhone came out. Nothing but the newest is good enough for her—especially when it's available in Pink Champagne—and I happen to think it's all just a waste of money.

"If you'd remove even half of the three-thousand apps you constantly have running on that thing, you wouldn't run the battery down in half a day," I reiterate my argument.

She opens her mouth for what I'm sure is some smart comeback but seems to change her mind.

"Have you been crying?" she asks, narrowing her eyes on my face.

I snort, shoving my chin in the air. "I don't cry. You know that."

Lisa is snickering as she steps close and drapes an arm over Lindsey's shoulder.

"Have you had dinner?"

"I grabbed something at home," Lindsey answers, giving my face one last look before focusing on Lisa. "But the tub of Ben & Jerry's Chunky Monkey I was enjoying for dessert is currently melting on my bedside table, so I wouldn't say no to some ice cream. If you have it."

"Chocolate Cookie Dough okay?"

Lindsey weaves her arm around the older woman's waist.

"Perfection. Lead me to it."

I notice Wapi shaking his head and I swear he mutters something under his breath that sounds like, "Princess." I don't disagree. I love my daughter to distraction, but sometimes it feels like we're from different planets.

"Where's their stuff?" I hear Ouray ask from behind me and my antennae vibrate.

It's Honon who answers.

"Back of the truck. I'll go grab it."

I swing around to Paco and lean in.

"What stuff are they talking about?" I hiss.

"Probably an overnight bag. Safer to stay somewhere other than your place, at least until they catch the guy."

My knee-jerk reaction is to protest but that'd be stupid. I have no doubt Mesina knows where I live. Instead I nod.

"Good. We can check into a hotel."

I pull out my phone but Paco covers my hand with his.

"Here's safer."

"In the clubhouse?"

"Surrounded by a ten-foot fence, state-of-the-art security, and a small army of men to protect you? Yes, in the clubhouse."

Well, when he puts it like that.

"Oh, Mom?" Lindsey calls from the kitchen door. "Don't worry, I packed your good undies."

PACO

"ANOTHER ONE?"

Wapi picks up my empty bottle and shakes it in front of my face.

I'm tempted, knowing the girls are safe in the back, but decide against it. It's already after midnight and only Wapi and Honon are still up. Ouray walked out of here half an hour ago—his place is two minutes away—and the other guys either went home as well or are in their rooms in the back.

Lisa put Lindsey in my old room and her mom is in the bedroom behind Ouray's office. She protested at first, but Lisa—in no uncertain terms—told her to suck it up. I gladly stayed out of that one.

There are two available rooms left for me to choose from, but I know I won't sleep a wink on the other side of the hallway from Mel.

"Nah. I'm turning in."

I jerk my chin in Honon's direction, who responds in kind, and make my way to the back. I turn to the second door on the right, the first one past Trunk's office and the closest available room to Ouray's office. My hand lingers indecisively on the knob for a moment before I swing around and head across the hallway.

The office is quiet.

There are no sounds coming from the bedroom but then Mel went to bed a few hours ago. She's likely been asleep for a while. I'm pretty sure if I were to slip into that room, she'd be awake in a flash. And likely pelting me with the bedside lamp.

I glance around the darkened room and my eyes land on the old lumpy couch against the wall. Guess that'll have to do.

Kicking off my boots, I grab a throw pillow to stuff behind my head, and try to stretch out on the couch that is at least ten inches too short for my body. It'll be a long fucking night.

Over the next few hours, I drift in and out of sleep until the sound of a door opening has me shoot upright.

"Jesus!"

Mel stands frozen in the doorway to the bedroom, her hand clutched at her chest. Her hair forms a wild halo around her head and backlit by the bedside lamp behind her, the nightie she's wearing leaves absolutely nothing to the imagination. My body is instantly wide awake.

Then she disappears for a moment and returns with a blanket wrapped around her. I didn't mind the view before, but this is probably for the best.

"What's wrong?"

She ignores my question and asks one of her own.

"What are you doing here?"

"Trying to get some sleep," I respond dryly, wiping a hand over my face and through my hair.

"Out here? Isn't there a bed you can use?"

I grin at the sharp edge in her voice. I'll bet good money she's not a morning person.

"I sleep better here," I lie. She knows it too, but what is she going to say? "But you didn't answer my question," I prompt. "Are you okay? Can't sleep?"

"I'm fine." She pulls the blanket tighter around her and walks into the room, taking a seat at the table. "Where is Cookie?"

"With the boy at Lisa's."

The child had clammed up with all the commotion in the clubhouse and hadn't said another word. Truck said he ended up falling asleep in his office with the dog by his side. Brick carried him to the cottage, but showed up at the clubhouse just as Ouray was leaving.

"He had a nightmare and they couldn't calm him down so Brick took him to see if Lisa could quiet him down. Haven't heard anything else so I hope it worked."

"That poor boy."

She tries to tame her hair with her hand but that causes the blanket to slip off one shoulder. My eyes lock on that bare stretch of skin.

"Yeah. Ouray left a message with the detective in Moab with the boy's name and his age. It's not much but it's a start."

Abruptly she tugs the blanket back in place, throwing me a stern look. But I'm not about to apologize for looking my fill.

"Any more news about Mesina? Did Luna call?"

"Not that I know. When Ouray went home at around eleven thirty, she hadn't called yet."

She turns her head to the window where faint morning light is visible between the blinds. I check my phone to see it's twenty to six. Hardly worth trying to get more sleep.

I reach for my boots and pull them on. When I get to my feet and move toward her, she's watching me.

"I'm gonna put on some coffee. Wanna join me?"

I put a hand on the chair's backrest and one on the

table in front of her, leaning down.

"I should probably get dressed," she whispers, her eyes lingering on my lips.

"Personally I like what you're wearing under that blanket just fine, but I don't wanna risk any of my brothers getting an eyeful. I may end up having to hurt one of them."

Her grin is instant, reaching all the way to her eyes.

"You would?"

I bend my head and kiss her smiling lips.

"Damn right. I don't share."

"To share something you have to have it first," she teases.

"Sounds good to me. Coffee can wait," I threaten.

"That's not what I…I'm getting dressed."

She ducks from under my arms and rushes to the bedroom, the blanket trailing behind her.

"Make it strong!" she calls out right before she shuts the door.

Turns out, I don't have to make coffee since Lisa is already in the kitchen, a large pot already made.

"You're up early," I observe.

"So are you," she fires back. "Did you sleep?"

"Some. You? Did the boy settle down?"

She grins as she pours me a coffee. "Yeah, that princess of yours has the magic touch. Hope you don't mind? Brick will bring her over when he gets the kids up."

"It's all good. Glad she helped."

I take a sip of my coffee just as Ouray walks in, his

greeting a grunt.

"Luna never came home, for fuck's sake," he grumbles when Lisa hands him a mug as well. Doesn't matter how often we tell her we can get our own, when she's in the kitchen, she pours.

"I'm guessing they haven't found Mesina then?"

"No. They're running down a few leads, but with Gomez out of commission they're spread thin."

Fuck. Almost forgot about the agent.

"Any news on Gomez?" Mel must've caught part of that conversation as she walks into the kitchen.

"In surgery this morning to repair some damage the bullet did, but he should be okay," Ouray shares.

"Thank God."

Lisa hands Mel a mug as well and directs her to the sugar and creamer before turning to us.

"Okay, you're all loaded up, now I need you out of here. I've got breakfast to cook."

Lisa shoos us out of the kitchen and we sit down at the big table. Ouray just starts updating Mel about Mesina when Luna comes in the front door. She looks exhausted and makes a beeline for her husband. He immediately turns sideways and pulls her on his lap.

"Long night?"

"You have no idea," she tells him, stealing his mug from the table and taking a deep swig. Then she turns her eyes on Mel. "We may need your help."

"Mine?"

"I've just spent the last two hours trying to find out from Shauna where her husband might be heading, but she's so scared she's totally shut down. I need you to try and get through to her."

"No."

The refusal comes flying out of my mouth without thinking.

"Excuse me?" Mel turns to me looking mighty annoyed. "Did you just speak for me?"

Fuck.

Ouray starts to chuckle and looks at his wife.

"Sounds familiar, eh, Sprite?"

"Of course I'll help, if I can," Mel addresses Luna, pointedly ignoring the rest of us.

"Appreciate it. I'm quickly gonna head home, grab a shower and a change of clothes, and I'll be back to pick you up."

I wisely keep my mouth shut this time, but I intend to be right behind them.

No way I'm letting Mel out of my sight.

11

MEL

HE'S STILL OUT there leaning against his bike when I glance out the window.

"They're all the damn same," Luna mumbles as she follows my line of sight. "Protective streaks a mile long."

I don't have a chance to react because the door opens and Luna's colleague, Dylan Barnes, leads Shauna into the room.

I have no idea where they've been keeping her, I didn't see any other vehicles pull into the parking lot. For all I know, she's been held right in this building.

Shauna's eyes dart around the room before landing on me. Then her face crumples. Luna sighs, grabs for a box of tissues from the table, and holds it out to Shauna, who immediately plucks a few and starts dabbing at her eyes.

"I can't," she snivels without prompting.

Looks like she clued in to the reason for my presence and it makes me wonder if the tears are an attempt to avoid talking.

"He's gonna kill me," she adds.

"Not if we can find him first," Luna comments.

"Shauna," I draw her attention. "If there is anything you know, anything at all, you need to tell us. The only way to guarantee your safety is with Carlos behind bars. You know this."

She shakes her head. "What if he gets out on bail?"

"He won't. Trust me, there isn't a judge who would grant bail to a man who not only shot a federal agent, but was already on the run. He poses too big a flight risk."

"You don't understand, he has friends everywhere."

"They can't help him," Luna responds. "His is a federal case, with a lot of eyes on it. There will be too much publicity for anyone to want to risk sticking their neck out for him."

Shauna turns questioning eyes on me.

"She's right. As your lawyer I'm advising you to cooperate the best you can. The sooner they can pick him up, the safer it'll be for you."

She plucks nervously at the wad of tissues in her hand and I can feel tension radiating from Luna. I'd be ready to explode too if I were her. She was in a shootout, in which one of her fellow agents was shot, their suspect managed to get away, she's been up all night trying to find him, and now the only person who might be able to give them a lead is refusing to talk. All on no sleep. Hell,

I'd have lost my shit already.

Time to pull the guilt card.

"Shauna…" I wait for her eyes to meet mine. "You do realize that you're not the only one potentially in danger, right?"

Apparently she hadn't, judging by the confused look on her face.

"Remember Lindsey?"

She nods. "Your assistant."

"Right, but what I don't usually share is she's my daughter as well. But Carlos knew. He called my office, made it clear he not only knew about our family connection, but he'd also been watching her. What if he comes after one of us? Is that something you can live with?"

That launches a fresh waterfall of tears and Luna shoves the Kleenex box at her again.

"You're the only one who can help us put a stop to this, Shauna," Luna says surprisingly gently. "We've kept you safe for over a month, why stop trusting us now?"

She's quiet for a long time and I'm about to throw in the towel when she finally speaks up.

"Can you keep them safe too?" she asks Luna.

My eyes are automatically drawn outside, where Paco is still leaning against his bike. I have a feeling we're covered.

"Only way I can promise you that is if we can find Carlos."

"His father's old hunting cabin up near Overlook

Point. I've never been there, but Carlos would go hunting with friends sometimes."

She speaks so softly it takes me a second to realize she's just given us what we were after.

"Can you be more specific?" Luna asks.

Behind her I notice Dylan is already on his computer. I can't see what he's looking at but my guess is he's pulled up a satellite view of Overlook Point.

"Like I said, I've never been there, but I heard him mention Tank Creek a few times."

"Forest Road 682 crosses the creek not far from Overlook," Dylan shares. "I can't see any structures but the tree cover is pretty thick."

"Call Greene. See if we can get a drone up," Luna orders. "Let's confirm he's there before we call in reinforcements."

The younger man already has his phone out.

"If he gives you the slip again, I'm done for," Shauna says, her face tight.

"He's not getting away this time. We'll plan this carefully and cut off any possible escape before he even knows we're there."

I hope to God Luna is right.

IT WAS ALMOST ten by the time we got to the office.

"I can't work with you glaring at me."

Lindsey's annoyed voice drifts into my office.

Luna had taken me back to the clubhouse, with

Paco's bike stuck to her bumper like glue. My daughter had been up, finishing her breakfast when she reminded me Jessica Huberfelt would be dropping in at noon to sign her affidavit. That caused a bit of a stir since Paco wanted us to stay in the compound, and he and I had a heated argument on the subject until Ouray intervened. He ordered Paco to load us in his SUV and told Wapi to follow us to the office.

Lindsey had not been happy when the younger man sat down in the waiting area, across from her desk, to keep an eye on the front door. Paco said he'd have the back door covered. I assume he's out in the parking lot because I haven't seen hide nor hair of him since we got here.

I can't quite make out what Wapi says in that low rumble, but I hear my daughter's disgruntled huff. She'd better hustle with those documents, my client could be here any minute.

The cell phone on my desk starts buzzing with an incoming call. I don't recognize the number, who'd be calling me from Utah? I contemplate letting it go to voicemail when it suddenly remember there *is* someone I know in Utah, but if they're calling me it's cause for concern.

"Morgan," I answer the call.

"Melanie Morgan, family law?"

It's a male voice, and not the client I was thinking of.

"This is she."

"Ms. Morgan, my name is Frank Yelinek. I'm a detective with the Moab Police Department in Utah."

"Detective, what can I do for you?"

I try to keep the growing unease from my voice.

"To be honest, I'm not sure, but in the course of an ongoing investigation we came across your business card."

"Okay…"

"I was hoping you might give me some information."

"That depends, Detective, I'm sure you understand I'm bound by attorney-client privilege."

"I wouldn't ask you to break that. This is a matter of identification only."

Goosebumps rise on my skin.

"Maybe you should explain yourself," I say a bit more curtly than I intended.

"Sure. The person we are trying to identify was in possession of your business card. She's about five seven, slim build with dyed-brown, shoulder-length hair, and hazel eyes. We estimate her to be in her early to mid-thirties. Anyone by that description you know who might carry your card on her person?"

I'm freezing cold. All kinds of possibilities and scenarios run through my head, and I don't like any of them.

I'm hesitant to give voice to any of my thoughts right now. This man could be anyone and there's no way for me to know.

Or maybe there is.

"Detective Yelinek, are you at your office?"

"Yes."

"Could I call you right back?"

"I guess," he grumbles, clearly not happy about it, but that's too bad.

Before I'm willing to divulge any information, I need to be sure.

"I'll give you my number," he adds.

"That's not necessary, I'll find it."

I hang up and run to the back door. I've barely opened it when Paco gets out of Ouray's big SUV.

"What's wrong?" he asks as he approaches.

"Do you know a Detective Frank Yelinek?"

He looks startled.

"Yeah. He's with the Moab PD. He's lead on the murder of that woman they found in the Colorado River. Why?"

I have to swallow a few times to release the lump stuck in my throat.

Mason, oh no. The pieces are starting to come together.

"I think I may know who she is."

PACO

"WAIT."

I grab for her arm as she spins around and heads back in.

My head is trying to catch up with what just happened.

"I've gotta call him back."

I release her and follow as she heads back to her office. I lean against the doorpost and watch as she types something on her laptop. Then she grabs her phone.

"Yes, it's Melanie Morgan calling for Detective

Yelinek." Her gaze lifts and she locks on to me. "I'll wait."

I can feel the charged energy in the office.

"Detective. Yes, your description reminds me of a former client, but she was blonde."

Holy shit.

"Is it possible to see a picture first? Oh…I see."

I watch her wince. I assume he just explained to her, given the state the body was reportedly found in, it would make visual identification difficult.

"My former client's name is Kelly Forbes—"

"Mom?"

Lindsey's voice sounds behind me and I step to the side to let her by.

"Can you hold on one second?" She presses the phone to her chest and turns to her daughter. "Yes?"

"Jessica is here."

"Put her in the conference room and tell her I'll be right there."

"Detective? I'm sorry, but I have to go. I have a client. Could I call you back after?"

She hangs up the phone, gets up from her chair, and walks straight up to me. My arms automatically reach for her.

"You're shaking," I observe, tightening my hold.

"This is too bizarre," she mumbles against my shirt but then goes silent.

"Talk to me," I prompt her.

She shakes her head.

"After. Let me deal with my client first. She just needs

to sign some paperwork. I won't be long."

Just signing paperwork takes over an hour, most of which I spend pacing the short hallway trying to make sense of this. Bizarre is right. It would be a weird fucking coincidence if the little boy I left my dog with this morning turns out to be the child of Mel's former client.

By the time she shows her client out, I've already made up my mind the odds are strongly stacked against that being a possibility.

"Come with me."

She grabs my hand and pulls me into her office, closing the door.

"Five years ago, Kelly Forbes walked into my office, although, stumbled is a more appropriate description, I guess. She had a black eye, was bleeding from a large gash in her scalp, had three broken ribs, a dislocated thumb, and was frantic."

"Fucking hell."

"Yeah. It was ugly. Abusive marriage, young child at home. Husband found out she was planning to leave him and take the baby. He beat the tar out of her and locked her out of the house. Luckily she came straight here."

"Tell me she filed charges against the asshole," I growl.

"She did, but a lot don't. They're too afraid of the consequences, even if they can get away. Some of these women never stop looking over their shoulder."

She plops down in her chair and leans it back, grabbing her head with both hands.

"I feel guilty I can't remember all the details. The

stories are often so similar. Anyway…" She sits up and shakes her head. "Long story short, Zack Forbes was tried and convicted and Kelly and her son relocated to Utah, starting a new life there. She's the only person I know in Utah who fits the description he gave me, except for the hair."

I sit down on the edge of the desk and lean toward her.

"Darlin', it could be anyone. Just basing it on a vague physical description and the fact she had your card on her is not enough."

"I know, that's why I asked to see a picture. I guess they'll have to confirm with dental records or DNA or something. Maybe they still have the tissue sample from the—"

I interrupt her rambling by putting my palm against her warm cheek. "Mel, slow down."

"But you don't understand," she pleads, her pretty eyes swimming with tears as she looks up at me. "Kelly's little boy? He would be about six now. Guess what his name was?"

It only takes one guess.

"Mason."

12

MEL

THE MAN WHO walks into the clubhouse is not what I expected.

The mental image I had formed of Frank Yelinek based on the sound of his voice and the way he spoke was one of a much older, stuffier individual. Certainly not the tall, handsome man in jeans and a pair of Chucks, much like the ones I have.

Ouray meets him by the door and leads him to where Paco, Lindsey, and I are sitting at the bar.

I spoke to the detective this afternoon and gave him some of the background on Kelly. It interested him enough to announce he wanted to talk to me in person and would drive down.

Since we hadn't heard anything from Luna yet, I

didn't balk when Paco drove us right back to the Arrow's Edge compound. To be honest, this whole thing with Mesina is a bit unnerving the longer it's drawn out. Add to that the possible murder of one of my clients, and yes, I'm a little shaky.

In my twenty-year career, this is the first time I've actually felt unsafe. So I'll take the club's offer of protection if not for me, then for my daughter. I'll even put up with Paco hovering, because I'm sure the FBI has their hands full keeping an eye on Shauna and tracking down Mesina.

Then there's the boy, Mason. Something in me wants to stay close to him. He was only a toddler when I saw him and his mother last, but I feel a sense of responsibility.

"Ms. Morgan?"

"Mel, but yes." I slide off my stool and shake his hand. "Detective Yelinek."

"It's Frank."

The disarming smile which follows is pretty lethal, however, it's not directed at me but at my daughter. I'm pretty sure the low growl I hear behind me comes from Wapi, who is behind the bar.

Oh my.

I quickly make introductions.

"Why don't we take this in my office?" Ouray suggests.

The kids, sprawled all over the huge sectional facing the TV, eye the newcomer with curiosity when we pass. Except for Mason, who's sitting on the floor, Kiara beside him on one side and Cookie curled up against him on the other. He keeps his head down.

Ouray leads us to the table and I'm surprised when Paco follows us in and takes a seat beside me.

"Maybe we should ask your daughter to join us?" Yelinek asks.

"She wouldn't know anything. She wasn't working for me yet when Kelly was a client."

"Very well," he says easily, taking in the space and in particular the large plaque on the wall behind Ouray's desk, sporting the Arrow's Edge crest. "If I can be honest, I'm surprised you asked me to meet here."

It's Paco who answers.

"The husband of one of Mel's clients is wanted by the FBI. Recently, Mel's office was broken into and she and her daughter were threatened. He escaped his arrest, shooting an agent, and is currently on the loose. Mel and Lindsey are safer here until he's caught."

Yelinek nods his understanding before turning to me.

"You certainly see a lot of action for a family lawyer."

"Trust me, it's not a situation I'm accustomed to."

Paco drapes his arm over the back of my chair and when I glance at him, he's focused intently on the detective.

"Did you have questions?" he asks Yelinek.

"Yes," he confirms with a grin as he pulls a small notebook from his pocket.

"You mentioned Zack Forbes was serving an eight-year sentence?"

"Yes," I confirm. "At Centennial near Pueblo. At least that's where he was transferred, to my knowledge. I was

Kelly's divorce lawyer and as such had no part in his trial."

I explain the only part I had was finalizing the actual divorce and encouraging her when she announced she wanted to make a fresh start somewhere she could feel safe. She wanted to leave Durango and the life she'd had here behind.

"Did she leave a forwarding address?"

"I probably have it at the office. I can't remember the name of the place, but I'm sure it wasn't Moab," I add with my last attempt at hope.

"Does Blanding sound familiar?"

His eyes are sympathetic. Too much so.

"It's possible," I tell him, even though the town sounds uncomfortably familiar. I'm just not ready to accept we're talking about the same woman. "It would be in her file."

He scribbles in his notebook, his pen scratching on the paper, which gets on my nerves. When he looks up, he tosses out a question that knocks the wind right out of me.

"Were you aware Zack Forbes was granted parole at the end of August?"

"That's impossible." There is four years left on his sentence. "He shouldn't even be eligible until seventy-five percent of his term is served," I point out.

"The system is overcrowded with serious offenders," Yelinek explains with a shrug. "Murder trumps assault, what can I say?"

It takes me a second to process and I realize any

lingering doubt the body they found is Kelly's vanishes. There's a reason she wanted to disappear with her son; he'd threatened to kill her, given the chance, and she took him seriously. It would appear with good reason.

"But how did he find her?" I mumble mostly to myself.

"Anyone other than you who might've known where she was?" the detective wants to know.

I shake my head. "I don't know. I don't think she had any family. Maybe a friend, but I seriously doubt she would've risked that."

"The break-in at your office," Paco suggests, his hand squeezing my neck. Any other day, I'd have probably shrugged him off but right now that hand anchors me.

"But that was Mesina."

"We thought it was because it seemed most likely at the time."

I never even checked my inactive files to see if anything was missing, I was so convinced it was Carlos Mesina who broke in.

Yelinek pulls out his phone and looks for something. Then he holds it up for me to see. It's a picture of what looks like a four-leaf clover tattoo.

I take in a sharp breath. The last time I saw Kelly in my office, she showed off the new tattoo on her ankle. It was after Zack's conviction and right before she left for Utah.

"Where on the body?" I want confirmation.

"Her right ankle."

I nod and my eyes sting. "She had it done after the trial. Said she hoped it would bring her good luck since she hadn't had much of it in her life."

"Sounds to me you might wanna pick this Forbes guy up," Ouray suggests.

"Looking for him as we speak." Yelinek runs a hand through his hair. "He settled in Cortez after his release, so we contacted the Montezuma County probation office who has his file. He says he was gearing up to do a home visit tomorrow since Forbes missed his appointment this week."

"Mason…" Everyone turns to me. "He'll be looking for his son."

"No one knows he's here," Ouray supplies.

"No, but Forbes knows Ms. Morgan. And it wouldn't be unreasonable for him to think she might know where the boy is." Then the detective turns to me.

"Until we have him in custody, you need to be careful. Be alert. I'm also concerned for Mason. If the boy saw anything, he might be in danger."

Jesus, I hadn't even considered that.

"And I think we should have a look at your office."

PACO

WE'RE ABOUT TO head out when Luna's SUV pulls up to the clubhouse.

She looks like death warmed over when she gets out of the vehicle, but the smile on her face more than makes up for it

"We've got him."

"Mesina?"

138

"Was holed up in that hunting cabin with an arsenal of weapons, so we had to wait for reinforcements and it took a little, but we have him. Of course he won't talk, called for Redfern right off the bat, but it doesn't matter. He's going down."

Then she notices Yelinek and suspicion replaces the smile.

"Detective, this is my wife, Special Agent Luna Roosberg. Sprite, meet Frank Yelinek with the Moab PD."

"The woman?" she asks right away. "Why are you all the way out here?"

Yelinek nods. "The victim turns out to have been a client of Ms. Morgan."

Her eyes dart to Mel and back at the detective, and she pulls herself up to her full five foot two.

"If you think Mel has anything to do with this, you're barking up the wrong tree," she snaps.

"Easy there, tiger," Ouray intervenes, wrapping an arm around her. "The man's just following a lead. They're heading to Mel's office to look at the file."

"I'll come with."

"You've been going for forty-eight hours and are dead on your feet. You're going nowhere but bed," he tells her.

"I'm too wired to sleep," she complains, to which Ouray has a ready answer.

"Who said anything about sleep?"

Yelinek follows my truck in his own vehicle. Lindsey wanted to come but her mother made her stay at the clubhouse where she'd be safe. Beside me, Mel is wringing her hands in her lap and I cover them with one of mine.

"Relax."

"Don't tell me to relax," she snipes. "I may have led that man right to Kelly."

"You didn't do anything."

"No, and that's the problem, isn't it? I should've checked up on him. I could've warned her."

I can tell her it's not her fault until I'm blue in the face but knowing Mel, she's going to have to come to that realization herself.

"At least Mesina is no longer a concern," I offer instead, but that makes her snort.

"Until he's let out on bail," she scoffs.

"Not after shooting a federal agent," I point out.

Once we get to her office, it doesn't take Mel long to locate the file labeled Kelly Forbes.

"Don't touch," the detective cautions Mel, who rolls her eyes.

"If you're concerned about prints, mine will be all over it already."

"Indulge me."

He opens the bag he took from the trunk of his vehicle and pulls out a pair of latex gloves.

"They already checked for prints and found none."

"On this particular file?"

"Well, I'm not sure. I'd have to check with Lindsey but I can't remember her file being on the floor when I got here."

"He may have done that to divert attention from this one," Yelinek suggests. "Either way, there is plenty of other trace evidence he may have left behind: saliva, sweat, epithelial cells, hair."

He flips open the file folder. On top is a yellow-lined sheet of paper.

"Wait," Mel stops him. "It's out of order."

"What do you mean?"

"We are meticulous about the way we file. A printed sheet of the client's particulars—full name, age, phone number, address, email, etcetera—is always on top. Then a sheet with docketed hours, after that come copies of documents filed or letters written on behalf of the client, and my handwritten notes are always on the bottom." She points at the opened folder. "My notes are on top."

The detective pulls out his phone and takes a few pictures. Then he slowly starts flipping through, page by page, until he comes to a white sheet with the woman's name at the top.

"That's her pertinent information," Mel indicates. "He didn't take it."

"He wouldn't have to," I point out. "He could've taken a picture and left the sheet behind so it would look like no one messed with it."

"Blanding, Utah," Yelinek says, his finger pointing to the address only showing a post office box. "No phone number," he observes.

"No. I remember she was supposed to call me with her new number but I guess she never did."

Half an hour later, we're standing in the parking lot.

"I'll contact your local PD tomorrow morning. Let them know what's going on."

"You'll want to talk to either Detective Tony Ramirez or Bill Evans."

"Appreciate it. And you stay vigilant," he says to Mel. "I'll be in touch."

After we watch him drive off, she turns to me.

"I guess I'm not sleeping at home again tonight."

"Pays to be careful."

"Yeah, but what if this drags on? What if they don't find him? A night or two is fine, but I'm not about to move into the clubhouse permanently."

Maybe not into the clubhouse, but I can see her moving into my place. Permanently.

"One day at a time."

"I'll be going back and forth to the office, what if he follows me? What if he finds the boy because of me?"

I give her knee a squeeze and repeat, "One day at a time. Let's head back to the clubhouse, talk it over, and come up with a plan."

"Okay, but I need some clean clothes from home."

"We can swing by there on the way."

Mel ends up calling Lindsey to see if she needs anything which turns out to have been a mistake, judging by the two suitcases standing by the front door.

"Is that all?"

She catches the sarcasm and roll of my eyes.

"Don't get me started. When she went off to college, I had to rent a U-Haul. Even when she went on vacation last year to the Dominican to spend a week at the beach, she brought two full suitcases. Who needs that many clothes when you're just going to spend your days in a bathing suit? I'm telling you, it's that I distinctly recall giving birth to her or even I wouldn't believe she was my daughter."

I grin at her rant and take the opportunity to tag her behind the neck, dragging her close for a quick kiss.

"So is that all?" I repeat.

"I just need to grab a few things for myself. It won't fill more than a tote."

Like I care if she wants to pack a trunk. As long as it's ending up at my place—which is my plan for tomorrow—I don't give a flying fuck.

"While you do that, I'll get these loaded up."

Christ, it feels like she has bricks in these things. I end up taking them one at a time, and curse under my breath as I heave them into the bed of my truck. Then I secure them with some bungee cords.

A strange sense of foreboding has the hair on my neck stand on end and I immediately turn to the house. The light is on in what I assume is Mel's bedroom, and I catch her shadow crossing in front of the window.

I suddenly feel the need to get the hell out of here and head for the front door.

I've taken a few steps when something hits my shoulder and I find myself flying forward.

It's not until my face hits the pavement the sound of a gunshot registers.

13

MEL

I'S LOUD.

My first thought is a car backfiring. My second far more ominous, and I cautiously peek between the blinds. Halfway up the walkway to the house I see Paco, facedown on the pavers. I don't think, I react, and start running for the front door.

I've barely set one foot outside when he lifts his head.

"Get back inside! Now!" he yells as he scrambles to his feet.

Fuck, I need my phone.

Right when I turn to head back in, I hear another two shots and I hesitate. But a rough shove in the middle of my back propels me inside. Behind me I hear the door slam.

"9-1-1, Mel. Now," Paco snaps.

I dive for the bag I dropped on the couch and with shaking fingers hit the digits. I already hear him on the phone, barking orders.

"9-1-1, what is your emergency?"

"Shots fired at…" I give him my address when I notice Paco's left arm hanging down, blood dripping down from his fingertips onto my white rug. "You're shot!"

"Get down, Mel."

"Who is shot?" the dispatcher asks.

"You're bleeding."

I vaguely register the man on the line speaking to someone, but I'm focused on Paco.

"I'm fine, now get the hell down!" he barks, just as the narrow window beside the front door shatters.

"Ma'am, are you still there? Ma'am?"

Paco drops his phone and lunges toward me, taking me down to the ground with him. He pulls me behind the couch, his hand pressing my head down.

"Stay put."

The next moment his weight is off me as he crouches in front of me, shielding me from the front of the house as he pulls a gun from an ankle holster.

"Ma'am? Are you okay?"

Somehow, I still have my phone pressed to my ear.

"No, I'm not fucking okay. Some idiot is shooting at us."

"I have police and fire and rescue en route, ma'am."

I feel like my head is about to explode and I take it out on the poor guy doing his job.

"If you call me ma'am one more time I will scream."

I feel like I'm teetering on the edge of reality. This is chaos on top of chaos. Paco is bleeding and some lunatic is out there shooting up my quiet neighborhood. Everything is happening at once and I've never felt so out of control.

"Yes, M-uh…of course. Are shots still being fired?"

"Yes. No, I don't know. I counted four. The last one came through the window beside the front door."

"Stay on the line with me until help gets there, okay?"

I nod my head before realizing he can't see me.

"Okay."

Paco glances over his shoulder.

"You okay, Darlin'?"

"Stop asking me that," I grumble, and he has the gall to wink at me.

The five minutes it took for sirens to sound in the distance seemed a lifetime. If I weren't already gray, this would've done it for sure. It's another ten at least before there's a knock at the door and Detective Ramirez announces himself, fire and rescue right behind him.

"I recommend you let us take you to Mercy. Get an X-ray to make sure you—"

"Not gonna happen, brother," Paco tells Sumo.

I know Sumo well, helped him out with a custody case, and I was glad to see he was one of the EMTs who showed up. Unfortunately, not even Sumo's professional opinion will sway that stubborn mule to get himself checked out.

The bullet apparently went straight through the soft

tissue, and according to Paco, no damage was done and there's no amount of talking that'll change his mind.

"They're just gonna flush, put a stitch or two in, and send me on my way. You can do all that here."

I throw up my hands and climb out of the ambulance where a few of his brothers are waiting.

Ouray walks up and drapes an arm around my shoulders.

"It's just a flesh wound. He's had worse."

I pivot on him and explode, "If that was meant to make me feel better, you failed!"

That's it. I've officially lost it. The last of my marbles.

In front of Paco's brothers, half the Durango police force, and the entire crew at Station 3, I burst out in tears. Not just a few. No, a deluge. Years of carefully checked weakness is leaking from my eyes like there's no tomorrow.

In a last-ditch effort, I slap my hands over my face but it's no use, there's no stemming the flow.

"Is she crying?" I hear Paco behind me, and then, "Mel, get your ass up here!"

I don't usually respond well to orders, but I just don't have it in me to put up a fight. Besides, the back of the rig doesn't sound bad right now, it'll give me some privacy while I have my emotional breakdown.

Paco pulls me down on the stretcher beside him and with a hand cupping the back of my head, shoves my face in his neck.

"Give us a few," he mumbles over my head, and I hear the back door slam shut. Then I feel his lips against my ears. "We're gonna get through this."

He doesn't let go until the tears dry up.

"I look like hell."

"You look fine," he says, which is manspeak for *'Yes, you sure do, but I value my life.'*

"I hate crying," I share.

"Thank fuck. I hate crying too. Never know what the hell to do with that."

I sit back so I can look at him.

"Are you kidding? Do exactly what you did. Hell, now that I know you're that good at comforting, I might actually let myself cry a little more," I tease.

The grimace on his face is priceless.

"We good in here?" Sumo sticks his head in the door.

"Yeah. Stitch the man up," I tell him.

This time when I step out of the rig, all the brothers have dispersed. Also not fans of emotional displays, I gather. Detective Ramirez doesn't seem to share that problem. He walks up and with gentle eyes asks me if I'm okay.

"I'm good now. Did you find anything?" I rush to change the subject.

He'd spoken both with me and Paco earlier, getting each of our statements, but I don't know if we were much help. Neither of us ever saw the shooter.

"No sign of the shooter. We found at least one bullet lodged in the wall above the mirror in your entranceway and we're still looking for more. A neighbor gave a vague description of a vehicle seen circling around the block a few times. We're canvassing the neighborhood and checking for security cameras. Hopefully, we can catch an eye on the shooter or his vehicle."

He glances over my shoulder and tilts his chin at the ambulance.

"How is he doing?"

"You mean aside from the stubborn streak that may require an exorcism to be removed? It's just a *flesh wound*."

I make air quotes for emphasis and Ramirez chuckles. His grin is easier than Paco's but no less devastatingly handsome. Where have all these men been my entire life? It's not like I'm exactly new to town.

"As soon as that shoulder is stitched up, I'm sure he'll be back in the saddle playing knight in shining armor."

Another flash of those pearly whites and then he's all business again.

"I'd just gotten off the phone with Frank Yelinek when this call came through. He filled me in on his murder investigation and the connection to you. I agree with him that it puts the break-in in a slightly different light. We've agreed to compare notes, which I'll do as soon as I get back to the office, and I'm sure he'll want to know what happened here tonight as well."

He pats my shoulder.

"If I could give you some unsolicited advice? Stick close to the brothers. We've got men out there looking for this guy, but it may take some time. Have you got somewhere to stay?"

I open my mouth to answer but Paco—who steps up beside me—beats me to it.

"She's staying with me."

"Weren't you getting stitched up?" I fire at him.

"All done."

"How are you all done already?"

"He insisted on butterfly bandages," Sumo answers for him as he steps into sight.

I make a frustrated sound, which the guys seem to think is funny.

Dear Lord, give me patience.

PACO

I WASN'T KIDDING either, she's staying with me.

I think the shooter may have been watching her. Maybe lying in wait for her. Clearly, he wasn't happy she didn't show up alone. If this is Forbes and he's out for revenge, he could have harmed Mel. He had opportunity to shoot her, but other than the round that hit me, his shots seemed intentionally high. It's possible he thinks Mel knows where the boy is and is looking to catch her alone and vulnerable. I'm gonna make sure that doesn't happen.

"I don't see why this is necessary," she grumbles beside me.

We're in the back seat of Ouray's vehicle, with Honon behind the wheel.

"He could be watching."

This was Ouray's idea. Out of all the brothers, he is the closest to me in size and looks so he's driving my truck all over Durango and plans to drop it outside of the gym, hoping the asshole is watching. He can catch a ride home with Bubba, the guy who manages the boxing gym for the club.

In the meantime, Honon is driving us to my place, which shouldn't be on anyone's radar. There we're supposed to meet with Brick, who is planning to bring not only Cookie, but Mason as well.

It's not only for Mason's safety—there's nothing the club wouldn't do to keep that boy out of harm—but he's not the only kid the club is responsible for and we don't want any of the other children ending up in the crossfire, so to speak.

My house is far enough back from the road it's almost hidden, and as an added bonus it has a back way in from my brother Tse's house up the road. A trail runs through the woods from the back of their property to the back of mine. I use it all the time with my ATV, but you could also travel it with a four-wheel drive vehicle, as long as you have enough clearance.

My freezer is well stocked, we've got plenty of vegetables in the garden, so we should be fine for a while. If we do need supplies, one of the brothers can pick them up.

The only issue had been Mel's office. She can't just disappear and leave her clients hanging, so Lindsey will keep the office open and tell clients Mel is away for a family emergency but will continue working remotely. The only time she'd have to appear in person is for a court date in a week and a half for one of her custody cases, but for the rest of it she just needs her laptop and a phone.

Mel hadn't been happy about Lindsey staying behind but, since her daughter only came back to Durango to work for her mother two years ago, Forbes wouldn't know who she is. Besides, she'll be well looked after by the club.

"No one on our tail?" I ask Honon.

"Nope, I think we're good. I'm taking the back way in, just to make sure."

A dense thicket of trees blocks the property from view of the road, and with the house in the middle of a clearing you can always see someone coming. In addition to that, the place has a state-of-the-art security system. Mel and Mason will be safe here.

Brick's truck is already parked in front of the garage when we drive up.

"Word of warning," he says when we get out. "The kid's a bit spooked."

I peek in the back seat. Cookie's whole body starts wagging when she catches sight of me, but the boy has a death grip on her.

"Hey, Mason," I say gently when I open the door. "I see you've been taking good care of my dog."

I reach in and scratch the pooch under her chin.

"This is where Cookie and I live. She has her own bed by the fireplace and lots of toys, do you wanna come see?"

The child glances past me at the house, and then his eyes slide to Honon and Mel, who are standing at a distance. Then they come back to me and he nods. I hold out my good arm and he lets me lift him out. Propping him on my hip, I reach back in and scoop the dog under the other arm, wincing at the pull on my shoulder. Mel notices and steps up, taking Cookie from me with a pissed-off look I choose to ignore.

"Hey," I turn to the boy. "What do you say we find Cookie something to eat? She looks hungry. Do you wanna feed her?"

I continue to mutter nonsense to the kid as we make our way inside. Honon and Brick stay long enough to haul some stuff in before they take off.

Then it's just the three of us. Well, four of us, if you count the dog.

Mason hasn't said a word to either of us but I can hear him softly speak to the dog inside. Mel and I are in the kitchen discussing sleeping arrangements since it's well after midnight.

"For now let's put him down in the guest room and you take my bed. I'll sleep out here so I can hear him," I suggest. "We can figure out what stuff goes where tomorrow."

"You're hurt, you should take the bed. I'm fine on the couch," Mel protests.

Of course, I wouldn't have expected anything else. Still, I shoot her a stern look, at which she rolls her eyes.

"Oh, fine. It's that I'm beat and I'd really like a shower or I'd fight you harder on that," she grumbles.

Mason doesn't make a fuss when I show him the spare bedroom and when I bring in the dog bed a minute later and put it beside him, he actually smiles.

"Think you can keep an eye on her for me?"

An enthusiastic nod is my answer.

I turn off the bedside lamp but leave the door open a crack and the light on in the bathroom. That way he can find his way there if he needs to, and I can hear him from the living room.

"You're good with him."

Mel startles me when I walk into the darkened living room. She's sitting on the couch, a towel wrapped around her head. I figured she'd go straight to bed after her shower.

"I like kids."

I shrug as I sit down beside her and kick off my boots.

"Yet you don't have any."

"Just wasn't in the books for me," I tell her what I've been telling myself. "Wasn't ready for the longest time and when I thought I was, I pinned my hopes on the wrong woman."

"Sounds like there's a story there," she observes.

"Yeah, but let's save that for another time. I'm beat."

My shoulder is sore as fuck, I can count the hours of sleep I've had these past few days on one hand, and the smell of Mel's shampoo is getting my dick hard. Now's not the time to dig into the train wreck that was Britney.

"Of course," she scrambles to her feet and I realize she probably thinks I'm blowing her off.

"Darlin'…" I soften my voice as I grab her hand. "I'm not chasing you away, but that part of my life is gonna take a while to explain, and I'm not sure I'll do it right if I try now."

"I get it. I have some history myself. I didn't mean to pry."

"You're not prying. I've got nothin' to hide from you."

She unexpectedly leans down, dropping a kiss on my lips.

"That's good," she says. "Now get some rest. You look like hell."

I'm grinning as I watch her walk away.

ARROW'S EDGE MC

14

MEL

"WHAT DO YOU want on this one?"

I carefully form another pancake on the griddle, while Mason tries to decide whether he wants the blueberries I found in the freezer or the chocolate chips that were a surprise find in Paco's pantry.

If I didn't know any better, I'd never have guessed this house was designed and built by a bachelor. I mean, I'd noticed the kitchen was well-outfitted but I figured he enjoyed cooking, which isn't that unusual for a single man. Last night though, when I snooped around the master suite, I noticed other things. The walk-in closet was clearly not added for his sake. It's not even half-filled; mostly jeans and T-shirts haphazardly tossed on a few shelves, and only one dressy shirt and a flannel one on hangers. And then there was the bathroom; double-sink vanity with enough room to spread out, plenty of cupboard space, and—next to the glass-enclosed, multi-head shower I wasn't having any trouble visualizing Paco in right now—a beautiful freestanding soaker tub.

Aside from the big stuff there are plenty of small touches throughout his place that appear to be catered to a woman. Including his pantry. I wonder if he built the house for that woman he referred to last night. If so, she's an idiot. Not only is the man hot as sin, he obviously has a soft spot for animals and kids, is smart, loyal, and despite his earlier incidents of foot-in-mouth disease, he seems to have gotten better at using his words. He's a catch and this house is a dream.

"Blueberries," Mason—who is sitting on the counter beside me—says softly.

I try not to show my surprise at hearing him talk, he hasn't said anything since we got here last night.

"Think you can put them in yourself?"

"Uhuh."

"Okay, grab however many you want and drop them on top of the batter."

"Like that?" he asks.

"Perfect," I declare. "Now are you sure you'll be able to eat all three of them?"

He nods enthusiastically, his longish, blond hair flopping in his eyes. I have to resist brushing it off his forehead.

He'd already been up, sitting on the couch watching cartoons, when I walked in this morning. Paco had been in the kitchen working on coffee—thank God—so I offered to make breakfast. He disappeared to the master suite to have a shower and get cleaned up, and I asked the little guy if he wanted to help.

"Time to flip. We'll do it together, okay?"

He grabs the spatula from the counter beside him and I cover his small hand with mine. Together we flip and a minute or two later they look about done.

"Almost ready. Wanna sit at the table or on a stool?"

"Stool." The answer is firm.

I wipe my hands on a towel and lift him up by his waist and intended to put him down, but his little arms sneak around my neck, holding on, so I do too. I turn toward the kitchen island, with the boy perched on my hip, when I see Paco leaning against the doorway to the master.

He's hard to miss, with worn jeans hanging low on narrow hips, and his broad chest on full display.

Yowza.

"You got hurt," Mason says, noticing the angry red wound on his shoulder.

"It'll heal," Paco assures him with a smile before turning to me. "Kinda tough to bandage myself though. Give me a hand? Kit is in the bathroom."

"Right, of course. Let me get Mason his breakfast quick."

I plop the boy on a stool and avoid looking at Paco while I scoop the pancakes on a plate.

"Want me to cut them for you?" I ask when I set it in front of the kid. "Or are you gonna use your fork?"

"Fork."

He demonstrates right away, chopping off a sizable piece and shoving it in his mouth.

"I'm just gonna give Paco a hand, okay? We'll be right in there."

I point behind Paco, who hasn't moved. I could offer to do it in here, but I don't want to do it in front of the boy.

I watch the muscles flex in his back as Paco leads the way to the bathroom, taking a seat on the toilet. A first aid kit sits open on the counter with a box of Steri-Strips beside it.

"You probably should've waited a bit before taking a shower," I comment, keeping myself busy by rummaging through the first aid kit for some gauze.

"It's fine."

I turn to look and find him eyeing me intently.

"What?"

"I like you in that."

I check myself with a quick glance in the mirror. I pulled on an old concert T-shirt and my bib overalls this morning. Only one clip of my bib is done up. I look like a cross between Jed Clampett and Daisy Moses of the *Beverly Hillbillies*.

"To each their own," I mutter, tearing the envelope with the gauze.

When I turn back to Paco, he spreads his legs in an invite for me to step between.

The wound in the front is easy to get to, but for the one at the back of his shoulder I need to reach over him, and every cell in my body is aware of our rather awkward proximity. It's a struggle to keep my hands steady as I dab the skin around the wound dry. Even more so when his warm hands grab on to my hips.

I've never considered the oversized overalls sexy, but when Paco's rough fingertips brush the exposed skin between my shirt and the button closure on the side, I quickly change my mind. All it would take is a quick flick of the one clip holding it up and I'd be standing here in my undies.

I try to apply the strips as best I can, but Paco makes it hard when he spreads his fingers and the pads of his thumbs start stroking the stretch-marked swell of my belly.

"Soft," I hear him mumble and then, "Kissable."

My fingers trace over his skin as I slow down my movements to match his. It's subtle; light touches, small movements, but enough to have the air charge with electricity. My body sparks alive with perhaps the most erotic discovery I've experienced and our lips haven't even touched.

My mistake to think a man like Paco would be the hard, up against the wall, kind of guy. Not that I would object to it—that is, if he can get me off the ground—but it would be a hard race to the finish line. This lazy exploration keeps me in the moment, needing nothing more than what the next sensation brings.

"I'm done."

Mason's voice drifting from the kitchen has me mumble a curse. I almost forgot about the kid.

To my surprise Paco doesn't release his hold.

"Be right there, bud," he calls out, even as he bends forward and with one hand pulls aside the bib and presses a hot open-mouth kiss on my belly.

I nearly come on the spot.

PACO

"You GOTTA PULL it hard. Use both hands."

The boy repositions his feet, wraps both little fists around the greens, and pulls hard but the carrot still won't budge.

"I've got an idea. Hold on tight, yeah?"

I wrap my good arm around the kid's narrow chest, lift him abruptly, and the carrot slips free of the packed soil.

"I did it," he says, triumphantly holding up the decent-sized carrot.

He's been out here in the garden with me most of the morning. Ever since I showed Mel the office and suggested she set up there to work.

Probably better for both of us not to share the same space for a while. I, for one, would have a hard time keeping my hands off her after this morning.

"Good for you. Let's see how many more we need. How many carrots do you think you'll eat for dinner?"

"Ten," he answers right away and I chuckle.

"Bud, these are big carrots. I don't think I'll be able to eat ten of them. Remember those potatoes we dug up earlier? We have to eat those too."

When I asked him earlier what his favorite vegetable was—often a loaded question when dealing with kids—he told me carrots were. So I figured we'd do one of my quick meals on the grill: carrots, potatoes, onions, and sausage tossed with everything-but-the-bagel seasoning, wrapped altogether in a tinfoil package.

"How about we get five more?" I suggest.

We're just rinsing the vegetables under the garden hose when Mel calls from the back porch.

"I've got Evans on the phone."

I turn off the faucet, help Mason dump the vegetables back in the bucket, and herd him inside.

"Here." She holds out her phone and grabs the bucket from my hand. "Take it in the office, he wants to talk to you. I'll get Mason settled in."

"Thanks."

I ruffle the boy's hair, shoot him a wink, and head toward the office with the phone to my ear.

"Evans, you wanted to talk to me?"

"Heard from Ramirez what happened last night. You okay?"

I take a seat at the desk. Even though I've been using the other side, my shoulder hurts like a sonofabitch.

"Yeah. Didn't hit anything vital."

The other man chuckles. "Good to hear. I was going to see if we could meet up somewhere. I have a few follow-up questions my partner didn't get to last night, but Mel tells me to check with you first?"

For some damn reason, the fact she'd trust me with that decision makes me feel good.

"I assume Ramirez filled you in on the murder in Moab, as well? Detective Yelinek's visit?"

"He has."

"Well, then you know this guy may be after Mel. Or rather, information he may think she has. Either way, we're keeping a low profile."

"In a secure location?"

I have no reason not to trust the guy but it still costs me to spill where we are.

"So to speak. We're at my house, which is pretty much off the grid. Made sure no one followed us but that's an ongoing concern if people go in and out."

"I hear you. If it makes you feel better, we can do this over the phone."

"That depends; what kind of vehicle do you drive?"

"Old department issue Charger, why?"

"There's a back way in here, but you won't get far with anything but a four-wheel drive."

From the corner of my eye, I see Mel stopping outside the door. I wave her in.

"I've got better things to do than get stuck in the boonies. Over the phone it is," he decides. "Is Mel there too?"

"She's right here. I'll put you on speaker."

I gesture for her to take the chair but she shakes her head, scooting a hip on the edge of the desk instead. It's encouraging all kinds of mental images I shouldn't be having right now. Not with the cop on the phone or the boy in the other room.

"Not gonna take up much of your time. You took the

Moab detective to your office, Mel?"

"Yes, to have a look at my client's file."

"And from what I understand, he left straight from your office to head back to Moab?"

"That's what he said he was doing. He wanted to get the file sent to their lab as soon as possible."

"Said he needed whatever evidence he could find to get a judge to sign a warrant for his arrest," I contribute.

Yelinek pointed out all he had so far was a theory, but what he needed was some piece of concrete evidence linking Zack Forbes to the death of his ex-wife.

"Yeah, makes sense. So you saw him leave?"

I'm puzzled with the direction these questions are taking.

"Walked him out and watched him get in his car and drive off," I respond curtly.

When I look at Mel, she has her eyebrows raised in question too. Evans catches my tone and chuckles. "Bear with me. I have a suspicious mind and it spares no one. Not even fellow law enforcement."

"Wait," Mel says, shaking her head. "You suspect Yelinek?"

"I'm naturally suspicious," he states calmly. "And when it involves people getting shot, no one is exempt. Not even law enforcement."

I don't know Evans's history—he's pretty new to town—but something tells me there's a story there. Possibly involving crooked cops.

"In any event," he continues. "Assuming Forbes is behind this, he may have followed Yelinek from

Moab, hoping he'd lead him to his son. Which he did, technically, but there would've been no way for Forbes to know the kid was right inside the MC clubhouse when Yelinek met you there. Instead he followed you home, Mel, hoping to get the boy's whereabouts from you, but Paco was in the way."

That's pretty much what we figured.

He has a few more questions about the shooting before he lets us go. We find Mason in the living room. A cartoon is playing on the TV but the boy is fast asleep, Cookie curled up beside him on the couch.

"You tired him out," Mel observes, as she starts pulling the vegetables we picked from the bucket and dumping them in the sink.

"I was trying to tire myself out," I comment, leaning against the counter beside her. "Been wired all morning."

"Is that a fact?"

I can tell she's teasing from the small twitch of her lips. She knows exactly what I'm talking about, which means it's been on her mind as well.

Pivoting, I trap her between my body and the counter, pressing my hips to her ass and dropping my chin on her shoulder.

"How long do you figure he'll be asleep for?"

I can see a vague reflection of us in the kitchen window, Mel with her head ducked low to hide the flush darkening her cheeks. Two silver heads of hair, with heat sparking between us I haven't felt since my much younger—and darker—days.

I brush her hair from her neck and press my lips

right there, where a rapid pulse is visible underneath her tender skin.

"Not long enough," she sighs, her body relaxing into mine as she tilts her head slightly, exposing more of her neck. "And I have an agreement I have to finish this afternoon."

"Then go finish it or I won't be able to stop," I mumble, giving her one last kiss before I release her. "I'll take care of this." I indicate the vegetables in the sink.

I watch her move toward the office.

"But, Mel?"

She stops and turns.

"Not sleeping on the couch tonight."

15

MEL

THIS IS RIDICULOUS.

I slap my brush down on the counter and give myself a stern look in the mirror. I'm on fifty's doorstep and I'm behaving like a nervous schoolgirl. Even my hair looks on end, although the fact I've been vigorously brushing it for the past five minutes may have something to do with that.

Work was able to distract me and I forced Paco's words from my mind while we cooked and ate, but when we settled in to watch some Disney movie with Mason, the nerves started setting in. I barely made it through the movie. As soon as the credits rolled and Paco picked up the boy—he'd fallen asleep on us again—to carry him to bed, I made a beeline for the bathroom.

I'm a coward. I've been killing time here for at least twenty minutes. Long enough to hear Paco's determined footsteps making their way to his bedroom.

Shit.

As much as I want this to happen, I also don't. It's stepping into uncharted territory with someone around whom I've allowed fantasies to build up. What if it turns out to be a disaster? *Yikes*, what if he's a disappointment? Or worse yet, I am?

I splash some cold water on my overheating face—again. What if I get one of my night sweats?

Argh. If I keep this up, he's going to knock down this door. Or…maybe he fell asleep already.

I run my hands down the Mickey Mouse nightshirt I defiantly grabbed and irrationally wish I had that shift nightie my daughter packed, which is still at the clubhouse.

I turn off the light before I open the door. Backlight is the devil at my age, I learned my lesson the other night.

Sparsely lit by the small lamp on the bedside table, I see Paco propped up against the headboard. One arm is folded behind his head, the other relaxed on his lap, which is as far as the covers reach.

Somehow my eyes get frozen there; on an unfairly perfect man—V pointing to the promise underneath the sheets.

And judging from what I can glimpse, what is down there looks very…promising.

"Darlin'?" His grumbly voice is soft and seductive. "I'm up here."

My eyes snap up, catching a smirk on his face. I struggle for a snappy comeback but my mind isn't as engaged as I'd like it to be.

"Cute nightie."

I roll my eyes. "It's a Mickey Mouse shirt," I point out stupidly.

"So it is. Gonna look great on my floor," he comments. "Which is where I'm gonna toss it right after I strip it off you but, Melanie, you're gonna have to get your ass over here first."

My feet are already moving before my brain has a chance to compute he called me by my full name. First time ever.

As soon as I'm within reach, he swings his legs out of bed, sits up, and grabs my hips, his eyes burning into mine.

"Stay right here," he orders, pulling me between his legs.

Not that I had any intention of moving.

But he does, his fingers dragging up the hem of my shirt until my belly is exposed. The next moment his hot mouth is there, right where he left off this morning. No longer concerned about any of the things I had swirling through my mind not five minutes ago in the bathroom, I slide my fingers in his hair and moan softly.

"Fuck," he mumbles against my skin. "You smell good all over. Soft and sexy."

He squeezes the flesh of my ass, pressing me closer to his mouth. His tongue takes a dip in my belly button before he drags it down to the edge of my panties. Good ones I packed myself last night. Even a girl my age needs her fantasies.

"These are gonna come off first," he announces, dragging them down my legs.

A full body shiver courses through me as he nuzzles my patch and hums against my mound. But then he lifts his head, looking up at me with a hungry glint in his eyes.

"I get one taste of you I'll be lost, but first I want to see all of you."

Without reservation, I take the hem of my shirt and whip it over my head.

"*Jesus*, Melanie," he hisses, his eyes tracking up and down my body.

Sagging tits, a belly pouch, and flabby hips, but you couldn't tell by looking at the expression on the man's face. Hunger, lust, adoration, and a hint of reverence.

I can't be sure who makes the first move, but the next moment we're a tangle of limbs in bed. Months of build-up after years of drought have need driving my hands and mouth. No thought goes into the way I touch him; every stroke, brush, or squeeze sheer instinct.

For once my mind is not involved, but my body is in charge and it is *really* enjoying the attention Paco pays it. His calloused hands map my curves with urgency, the delicious rasp on my skin making me feel desired. His mouth is hot and hungry, nipping and licking as he explores every inch of me.

I'm in a free fall, propelled by sensations so powerful I'm no longer sure where I am. Not until his hips wedge into the cradle of mine and I feel the blunt head of his glorious cock press against my entrance.

"Darlin'…" he mumbles as he lifts up on his arms.

My body is buzzing and my vision blurred, but I recognize his need for consent.

"Don't stop," I manage, and illustrate by grabbing on to his fine ass and wrapping my legs around him. "Don't you dare."

Pleasure is accompanied by a pinch of pain as he drives inside me with a deep groan, holding nothing back. The body remembers, even if the mind does not, and mine quickly accommodates the intrusion.

"You. Are. Fucking. Perfection," he growls near my ear, the words punctuating every thrust.

I'm not sure whether it's the words or the powerful strokes of his cock, but already my body is preparing for climax. My breath rasps, my legs tremble, and when he plants deep, grinding his root against my clit on the next stroke, I shatter.

He grunts deeply on his next two strokes before his full weight collapses on me, his body shaking with aftershocks. I hold him as close as I can, waiting for our breathing to return to normal.

He finally mutters, his lips against the skin of my neck.

"I think you've killed me."

PACO

"How COME I didn't know your real name is Nathan?"

I lift my head and look down at her.

"Who told you that?"

"Detective Evans asked for you by that name. I wasn't sure who he was talking about until he told me."

Asshole.

"Does it matter?"

It comes out a bit testier than I intended and I'm not completely sure why. My legal name isn't a secret, but it means nothing to me and I don't want it to mean something to her.

I roll onto my back and take her with me, tightening my hold on her by way of silent apology for snapping.

"I guess not. Maybe it's the lawyer in me, who'd like to know who I just had mind-blowing sex with."

The grin on my face is instantaneous, earning me an elbow in my ribs.

"You're such a guy," she mutters, as if that's an insult.

But I hear her. She's naked in bed with me, if anyone deserves to know it's her.

"My birth name is Nathan Philips according to my birth records. I don't know the people who gave me that name so I don't care for it. When the club took me in as a teenager, they named me Paco. It was given to me by people I care about—by family—so that's the name I identify with."

This time it's Mel who lifts her head. With her hair in a sexy tangle around her face and a satisfied flush on her cheeks.

"You never knew your parents."

It's not so much a question as it is a statement.

"Nope, but at fourteen I found Momma and Nosh at the Arrow's Edge, who more than made up for that lack, and I suddenly had more brothers than I could handle."

Her lush mouth spreads in a smile.

"I bet. I bet you guys were holy terrors growing up."

And then some, well into adulthood in fact, but I keep that to myself. Those days are far behind us.

I slide a hand in her wild hair and pull her close enough for my lips to reach her mouth.

"Let's get some sleep," I suggest, rolling her off me and curving myself against her back.

Tucking my face in her hair I inhale deeply, loving that shampoo she uses. In turn, she presses her soft ass against my crotch and hums softly. I love that too.

God knows I've been with more than my fair share of women in my lifetime—touched toned legs and firm breasts—but nothing has ever felt as real as Mel's ripe curves and soft skin pressed against me.

It takes me no time at all to drift off.

"Paco, wake up."

A firm hand pushes my shoulder as Mel's soft voice pulls me from a deep sleep.

I pry my eyes open.

"My nightshirt is on your side of the bed," she whispers.

I'm momentarily confused as to why she'd wake me up in the middle of the night to tell me that, when I spot movement by the foot of the bed.

Shit. The kid is standing right there.

I reach over the side and feel around for her shirt, handing it to her when I find it.

"Hey, Mason. Is everything all right?" I ask while Mel quickly makes herself presentable and flicks on the bedside light.

He looks like he's been crying, fat tears still clinging to his cheeks.

"I can't find Mommy."

"Oh, honey," Mel responds to the boy's thin little voice and swings her legs from the bed.

It takes me a moment to register this is the first time he's mentioned his mother, but Mel is already lifting him up on her hip.

"Did you have a bad dream?"

Mason nods as his spindly arms wrap around her neck.

"Good thing I know just how to chase those bad dreams away."

She throws me a pointed glance over her shoulder as she carries the boy out of the bedroom. I hadn't even noticed Cookie yet, but she trots out behind them. Then I quickly swing my legs out of bed, shrug into my discarded pair of jeans and a shirt, and follow them down the hallway.

I find them in the kitchen; Mason perched on the counter next to the stove, while Mel pulls a pot from the cupboard. Outside the sky is already turning gray. The clock on the stove says five fifteen. Close enough to morning, I guess.

"Can you grab the milk from the fridge?" Mel asks, one of her hands protectively on the boy's legs.

I grab the jug and place it next to her.

"What are we making?" I direct my question to Mason but he shrugs.

"Magic juice," Mel jumps in. "Otherwise known as chocolate milk. Best medicine for bad dreams there is."

The poor boy's eyes still look haunted and I'm not sure chocolate milk is going to chase those ghosts away.

"Did you know sometimes in the early morning deer stop by for a snack from the vegetable garden?"

He shakes his head and turns to look out the window.

"How about we grab a blanket to stay warm and go wait for them outside?"

There's no way the kid is going back to sleep so maybe the deer will make for a good diversion. I just hope they'll show up.

It'll also give Mel a chance to put on some actual clothes. What she's wearing now is far too distracting.

The boy nods and holds out his arms. I scoop him up and walk into the living room to grab a quilt before heading outside.

I have a couple of Adirondack chairs on the back deck and sit down in one, Mason on my lap. I'd planned to wrap him warmly and let him sit in his own chair, but he tugs the quilt closer and snuggles in against my chest.

We sit like this until I hear the sliding door open behind me and Mel steps into view, now fully dressed, and carrying three steaming mugs.

"Let them cool off for a few minutes."

She sets two of them down on my armrest before sitting down in the second chair with her own cup.

"I don't like bad dreams," Mason suddenly says.

"Neither do I," Mel responds.

"When Mommy goes in the water, I try to find her."

My breath sticks in my throat as my eyes dart over his head to Mel, who is looking right back at me. Was this really a bad dream or more of a memory? Was that why the boy was sticking close to the river when we found him? Looking for his mother?

I'm not sure how to respond, but apparently Mel does.

"I'm sure you tried really, really hard."

His little head bobs. "She floated away."

In my peripheral vision I see movement in the tree line.

"Mason…" I whisper, dropping my head next to his. "Look."

I point at the buck stepping into the clearing, thankful for the distraction. But twenty minutes later, when the hot chocolate is gone and the deer decimated a few more of my plants, Mason's last words still fuck with my head.

Whatever it takes, I'm going to erase that haunting image from the boy's mind.

ARROW'S EDGE MC

16

MEL

UGH.

'Doc' shows up on my screen.

I love Sara, I do, but right now I really don't want to talk to my friend because I know what she's calling about.

"You not taking that?" Paco wants to know.

He looks up from the dining table where he's working with Mason on reading. The homeschooling was something he'd come up with this morning over breakfast. I was surprised to find out Paco—with Lisa's help—apparently homeschooled some of the MC's younger wards. No wonder he's so good with the boy. It also adds a new and extremely hot layer to an already-hard-to-resist man.

Heck, who am I kidding? It's not like I bother trying to resist him anymore. It's the one part of this new reality I'm living that actually makes me feel good.

I spent the morning in the office, getting some work done, but the need for more coffee drew me to the kitchen, where I was just pouring a fresh cup when my phone started ringing.

"I'll call her back," I tell him, and like the coward I am, immediately redirect the conversation. "Did you get hold of Trunk?"

After Mason's early morning revelation, we'd agreed it would probably be better to get a professional involved. This isn't new territory for Trunk, it's what he does; look after the mental well-being of the kids at Arrow's Edge.

"He'll be here around noon. Apparently, Lisa is preparing a care package for us."

He shoots me a shit-eating grin.

"Does she know you can cook?"

I start laughing when he shakes his head.

"You kidding? And miss out on all that good food? Nah, that's on a need-to-know basis only, and Lisa doesn't need to know. I wouldn't want to mess with her belief she's the only thing standing between me and starvation."

"Opportunist," I accuse him with a grin.

He just shrugs and turns his attention back to Mason.

Five minutes later, fortified by fresh coffee, I call my doctor back.

"I thought I'd have to physically chase you down," Sara says by way of greeting.

"Sorry, was in the middle of something. What's up?"

"You were supposed to set up a follow-up appointment with my assistant," she scolds.

"I was going to wait until after I get the mammogram done."

"And when is that scheduled for?"

Damn. The reminder is somewhere folded in with the pamphlets she handed me last time. I think I stuffed all of that in my knapsack when I cleaned out and returned the rental car.

"Well…"

"You haven't called yet, have you?"

"Life's been a bit busy, you know?"

"Tell me it involves a man," she jokes.

"Several," I snip back. "If you count the one who broke into my office, the one who threatened me, the one who murdered my client, and the one who was shooting at me just a few nights ago. Although, they could all be one and the same for all I know. I've had a few things on my mind."

"Jesus, Mel, I had no idea, I'm so sorry…are you okay? What's going on?"

Great. Now I feel guilty for making *her* feel guilty.

"It's fine. I'm fine," I quickly reassure her. "Police are investigating and I'm keeping a low profile."

"If you need a place to stay, you're welcome at my house. I have a wine fridge and everything."

"Glad to know you have your priorities straight, but I'm, uh, being looked after."

"Oh, good. Well, I guess that means I'm going to have

to forgive you for slacking, but I still want you to come in. I'd like to get you started on some treatment for those symptoms you have. Least I can do is make you feel comfortable."

"About that…" I start, not quite sure how the broach the subject. "You're definitely sure it's menopause, right?"

"No doubt."

"So no more periods, or worry about unwanted pregnancies?"

I had sex with Paco and we didn't use protection because I figured I was safe, but this morning it started nagging at me.

"Is that a concern?" Sara asks after a lengthy pause.

"I'm just curious," I lie through my teeth and she knows it.

"Oh my God, it is, isn't it? I was right, it does involve a man!"

As I was afraid it might, the remainder of the conversation consists of Sara fishing for information and me trying to be evasive. By the time I hang up, I not only have an appointment in her office next week, but a lunch date she arm-wrestled me into, which I'm sure will include further attempts to dig into my new and burgeoning love life. My favorite pastime—girl talk—*not*.

I'm about to dive back into the separation agreement I'm drafting for a client when I catch a shadow pass outside the window. I shoot out of my chair and lean forward to see, but whatever or whoever that was has disappeared around the corner to the back of the house.

I open the door, rush down the hall, and notice Mason still sitting at the table when I enter the kitchen. But there's no sign of Paco. I glance out the patio doors but there's no one out there.

"Where did he go?" I ask the boy, trying not to let my surge of panic show.

My heart is galloping in my chest when he points to the front door, which is wide open. Without looking away, I approach the boy as calmly as I can and reach for him.

"Let's play hide-and-seek," I whisper, lifting him out of the chair.

Then I hear Paco's voice yelling, immediately followed by the sharp crack of a gunshot. Mason jerks in my arms and I press his head against my shoulder, holding on tight as I dart toward the master suite. I hesitate for a moment, debating whether to hide in the walk-in closet, but opt for the bathroom instead. There's a lock on the door and a window we can slip out of if someone kicks down the door.

It's not until I crouch down, Mason's body feeling way too frail in my arms, that the full weight of the situation hits me.

Then I start shaking.

Paco

THAT SON OF a bitch.

I could see him coming toward the house through the

front window, sticking close to the cover of the tree line.

I mumble at Mason to stay put and rush to the front door, grabbing the gun I keep there on a high shelf over the coatrack. Then I ease open the front door and step out to see him just disappear around the side of the house.

Key is not to alert him until I have a clear shot, so I follow cautiously. I don't want a repeat of last time when he was able to run off unscathed or he'll just keep coming.

It's not until he veers toward the back of the property that I line him in my sights.

"Get out of my goddamn garden, you asshole!"

His big head swings around just as I hit my mark.

I'm feeling pretty fucking pleased with myself when I walk back in, only to find the boy gone.

Maybe he went to check in with Mel? I tuck the gun back on the shelf—hopefully I won't have to use it again—and head for the office.

That's also empty.

As are the guest room, the guest bath, and the laundry room behind the kitchen.

"Mel?"

I cross to the other hallway, checking the master bedroom before I try the bathroom door. It's locked.

"Mel? Are you in there? Is Mason with you?"

I hear scrambling on the other side, followed by the sound of the lock being turned. The next thing I know, I'm being pulled into the bathroom and Mel's hands are all over me.

"Are you hurt? Did you get shot?"

I realize my mistake instantly and grab her wandering hands, stilling them.

"I'm fine."

Glancing over her shoulder, I see Mason stepping out of the shower, where I guess they found refuge.

"I saw someone outside the office window. Mason said you went outside, and then I heard shooting, and—"

Letting go of her hands I cup her face. "Darlin', I'm fine, it's all fine, it was a bear."

"I forgot to grab my phone, I should've—" she continues to ramble but abruptly stops. "What? What did you just say?"

"The shadow you saw was a black bear. This guy's been dropping by every couple of days recently, pillaging my garden."

"A bear?"

"Yes, they're generally not dangerous unless they become too comfortable around people and this guy was getting there. I had to do something."

"You're the one who shot?"

"Yes, and I probably should've warned you."

"You think?" She takes a step back and shoots daggers at me. "I was scared shitless, you moron! And what is wrong with you killing animals when there are kids around?"

I notice Mason flinch behind her so I try to keep my voice calm.

"Beanbags, Mel."

She shakes her head. "What?"

"I wasn't killing him; I was scaring him enough so he

won't return. I hit him with a beanbag."

She grabs a handful of hair on either side of her head and lets out a frustrated growl.

Behind me I hear a deep familiar chuckle.

"Smooth, Paco. Smooth."

I turn around to find Trunk in the doorway, grinning ear to ear.

"Come right on in, why don't cha?" I snap sarcastically.

"Sheeit, brother, I was afraid there'd be bloodshed." Then he turns his eyes on Mason and holds out one of his shovel-sized hands. "Come on, kid, you can help me get lunch together. Lisa made tacos just for you."

The boy looks back and forth between Mel—who seems to have calmed down a little—and me. Trunk tries again.

"Let's go, bud. These two knuckleheads will sort themselves out, okay?"

Mason's mouth twitches at the big man's colorful language. Then he puts his little hand in Trunk's and follows him to the kitchen.

When I turn back to Mel, she has her arms crossed over her chest and the toe of her flip-flop is tapping the floor.

"If I end up with high blood pressure, I want you to know I'm blaming you," she grumbles.

She tries to stomp past me but one sidestep has her bump into me.

"Let me—"

The rest of her demand is cut off when I firmly kiss her open mouth. When I lift my head, she has a stunned expression on her face.

"I apologize, Darlin'. Getting a crash course in sharing my space with someone and clearly failed my first assignment. Not gonna happen again."

She nods stiffly.

"I should hope not."

This time when she tries to get past me, I step aside, but I'm grinning when I follow her to the kitchen.

She's gonna keep me on my toes, but fuck if I'm not enjoying the hell out of it.

"STOP EAVESDROPPING."

"Shhh," she hisses.

After we had Lisa's tacos for lunch, I grabbed my laptop and sat at the dinner table while Trunk took Mason outside. The boy's choice, he wanted to see if the bear would come back. Mel has been washing dishes for the past half hour and if her ear would reach, she'd have it plastered to the slightly cracked window.

I shake my head, put my reading glasses back on, and redirect my focus to the system upgrade I'm working on for one of the club's properties, the Riverside Apartments. The last few years we've been doing structural upgrades but we never touched the security system. It's long overdue.

"Don't you think one of us should've been out there with him?"

I peek up at her over the rim of my glasses.

"Darlin', the whole point of us staying inside was so we could be his safe place should this talk with Trunk upset him. And weren't you the one who suggested it?" I point out to her.

She rolls her eyes at me, clearly annoyed with the reminder.

"Maybe I've changed my mind."

No sooner have the words left her mouth when the sliding door opens and Mason walks in, Trunk right behind him. The boy appears a little shell-shocked as he looks around, spots Mel, and walks right up to her, wrapping his arms around her hips.

"Step outside with me," Trunk mumbles under his breath.

I glance at Mel, who waves me out before she bends down to lift Mason on her hip.

Trunk is waiting outside.

"This is fucked up, brother," he opens with, and I brace myself. "He remembers camping in a van and his mom waking him up and telling him to be quiet. Then he says she dropped him out of the window and told him to run. Except the kid was scared and hid in the brush. He watched his mom get dragged from the van and to the river's edge by some man, who then tossed her in the water."

"*Shit*." We'd already suspected this but having it confirmed is heartbreaking. "No wonder the kid has nightmares," I observe.

"May wanna keep him close tonight. Wouldn't be surprised if all this doesn't stir up more of those. I suggest you leave off the subject unless he brings it up himself."

I tell him we will and he promises to check in tomorrow. When he drives off, I head back inside.

Mel is sitting beside Mason on the couch watching something on TV, but Mel's eyes immediately come to me. I indicate the kitchen, where she joins me a few minutes later and I fill her in.

"That son of a bitch better not try anything, because I swear to God, I could kill him with my bare hands," she snarls while tears fill her eyes.

"You and me both, Mel. You and me both."

17

MEL

"SERIOUSLY, MOM, I'M surprised the guy's knuckles don't drag on the floor."

I stifle a snicker, because underneath all that indignation I detect a hint of fascination. I don't blame Lindsey; I suffered the same mix of emotions around Paco for the longest time. These Arrow's Edge boys have a way about them.

"Honey, he's just keeping an eye on you."

"An evil eye," she huffs. "He hates me, which is fine," she adds quickly. "Because I hate him too."

Keep telling yourself that, daughter-dear.

"Other than that, anything else I need to know about?"

Lindsey's been alone in the office—if you don't count Wapi—most of the week. Sounds like she's coming out of her skin a little as well. I know the feeling; I'm getting cabin-fevered myself. As much as I love this house, I miss being able to go to my office. I miss the freedom to just go where I want, even if I don't really want to go anywhere. It's really starting to piss me off our movements are being restricted by someone no one seems to be able to find.

We've heard nothing from Detective Yelinek since he left here with my file, and the last we heard from the Durango PD was Bill Evans's phone call the day after that. One of the things I want to do today is call for updates, right after I take care of whatever Lindsey has for me.

"Jessica Huberfelt called again this morning," she informs me.

"Great. Looking for her day in court," I mumble.

"Looks like she'll get it. I just heard from the court clerk there was an opening on Judge Micheals' docket this coming Tuesday. Ten thirty."

"Shit."

Judge Micheals doesn't like me much. Mainly because I blew off his advances about five years ago, right after his wife passed away. Micheals has to be nearing seventy. In my opinion, well beyond his best-before date, but mandatory retirement age in Colorado is seventy-five now, so he has a few more years to make my life miserable in family court.

He wouldn't have been my pick, but beggars can't be choosers and all things considered, we're lucky we were able to get in so quickly.

"Okay, I'll give Jessica a call. Can you pull the file and find a way to get it here? I want to review it over the weekend."

"I will. Oh yeah, before I forget, I fielded two calls from someone insisting on speaking to you in person but wouldn't leave a message."

"Who is it?"

"Says he's a former client but won't give me a name."

My antennae start vibrating.

"Do you have a number?"

"Comes up as 'private number' on call display."

"If he calls again, can you record the call?"

"Already done, Momma," she says smugly. "You didn't raise a fool."

I chuckle. No, I didn't.

"Send me a copy of that conversation?"

It might really be a former client—I'll know soon enough when I listen to the recording—but it could also be Forbes on a fishing expedition. In that case, I'll forward it to the police. They may want to put a trace on the phone, or whatever it is they do. I wouldn't mind an update either.

A few minutes after I hang up the call with Lindsey, she sends me a message with the recording attached. The voice doesn't sound familiar, I'm pretty sure whomever it is was never a client of mine.

"Who was that?" Paco asks, walking into the office.

"Not sure. Apparently, he called the office asking for me a few times. I'm sending it to Evans now."

He nods. "You're thinking it could be Forbes?"

"It's possible." I shrug as I type out a quick message. "Most people leave a name or a number, and apparently he does neither."

"I'll give Wapi a heads-up too." He slides a hand in my hair and tugs lightly, tilting my head back before dropping a kiss on my lips. "I need to meet up with a contractor at one of the club properties tomorrow morning for a few hours. Unfortunately, I need to do that myself, but I'll get one of the brothers to keep an eye out here."

"Is that really necessary?" I want to know. After all, the security in this place rivals Fort Knox.

"It is for my peace of mind."

He's dead serious. How the hell am I supposed to argue with that? Besides, I may be able to use it for leverage. I haven't told him about my upcoming appointments yet.

"Fine. I have a couple of places to be this coming week."

"Like?"

"Court on Tuesday."

"Okay. I'll be there. Trunk can keep an eye on Mason."

I give him a dubious look. I'm not sure how well it's going to go over with Judge Micheals when I walk in with my biker 'entourage.'

"What?"

I pointedly scan his well-worn T-shirt and threadbare jeans.

"You know I'm not one for fancy clothes, but—"

He grins at me. "You worried about the way I look?"

"Hey, the judge is an asshole and I wouldn't put it

past him to use it against me. Or rather, my client," I defend myself.

"I can clean up," he says, before adding. "A little. Where else do you need to be?"

Ugh.

"A few medical appointments on Monday."

I was able to get a time slot for a mammogram right after my doctor's appointment, since both offices are in the same complex.

"Everything okay?"

I wasn't going to go into specifics but his concern is immediate and I don't really want him to worry for nothing. Guess this is what being in a relationship means.

Fuck, I'm out of practice.

"It's fine, just some routine stuff. Mammogram and… uh…picking up a script for something to help with symptoms of menopause."

Might as well lay it all out there. Not like he hasn't noticed my hot flashes or the fact I throw all the covers off me in the middle of the night. Hell, my daughter pretty much announced it. Besides, guess that's my new reality now, and if he wants me, he'll have to take my mood swings and night sweats too.

"Good. Was wondering if you were gonna try and tough it out. Nosh's wife, Momma, did that and the entire clubhouse was on eggshells for a year until she finally went to the doctor."

"Glad it makes you happy," I snap, more than a little annoyed.

"Darlin', I don't give a fuck about me, I just don't

want you to be miserable if you don't need to be."

Well, that took the wind out of my sails.

"Mel?"

I swing around to find Mason standing in the doorway.

"Yeah, bud?"

"I'm hungry."

"Then let's get some lunch going."

I push up out of my chair and as I pass Paco, I place a hand on his chest and lift up on my toes to brush a quick kiss on his jaw.

"You're a good man."

Paco

"Enough?"

Mason nods.

I pick up his soup bowl and plate, along with Mel's and mine, and take them to the sink.

Soup and grilled cheese sandwiches, the ultimate comfort food. Mel turns out to be a pretty damn good cook, who knows her way around fresh produce. We've been sharing kitchen responsibilities these past few days and I'm surprised how easily we move around each other. I generally don't like people getting in my space and in my way, but Mel and I seem to be well-orchestrated. Almost effortless.

We've shared the same bed a couple of nights now too, although the last two nights we ended up with Mason between us. I initially took the floor beside the bed, but he slept better with Mel and me on either side of him. Mel thinks it makes him feel safer. Fuck, I want the kid to feel safe, but it sucks the woman I've dreamed of having in my bed for a year now is two feet away. She might as well be in another room.

"It's Yelinek calling," Mel says when her phone starts to ring.

She scoots her chair back and walks to the office, gesturing me to follow. We've made it a point not to talk about anything in front of the boy, so I install him in front of the TV. We really need to come up with some other ways to entertain him.

"You're on speakerphone, Detective," she tells him when I walk in.

"Evans forwarded that recorded conversation you sent him to the sheriff in Cortez. He took it to Forbes's parole officer, as well as the manager at the motel where Forbes prepaid for a room. They both said it sounded like Forbes but they couldn't swear to it."

"Any luck on locating him?" I want to know.

"Nope. Hasn't been back to the motel for the past two weeks and he prepaid for two months, it seems."

"Two months?" Mel exclaims. "Where the hell would he get that kind of money? He just got out of jail."

"Haven't been able to figure that out yet. It's one of the things we're trying to track down. According to the parole officer, he'd mentioned maybe having a job, but he doesn't know how that ended up, or where it was, because Forbes never showed up for his next appointment. Leads are thin, but…" He pauses a beat. "If it's him calling, we may be able to pinpoint his whereabouts if we put a tracer on your office phone."

Mel is already shaking her head.

"I can't do that. To be honest, I already thought about it but it's dicey since I'm bound by attorney-client privilege."

"But it would only be on your daughter's incoming line."

I lean over the phone. "Yelinek, can you give us a minute?" I don't wait for his response before hitting the mute button. Then I look at Mel. "What if I set up a tracer? One that Lindsey can engage when the guy calls. No one would be listening in, but the tracer would become active the moment Lindsey hits the button."

"Can you do that?"

"I can. Only thing is she'd have to keep him on the line for at least thirty seconds. Doesn't sound like much but it's actually quite a long time. If it's successful, we can forward the information to law enforcement right away."

I love the way she smiles at me. Like I'm the smartest person in the room when we both know that's far from the truth. Heck, I barely even graduated high school, I just happen to be handy with electronics.

"Do it. Beats feeling useless. I want this to be over," she says.

Not sure what to make of that, though. I want the threat to be over but I'm not looking forward to Mason going back to the club or Mel going home. This house finally feels lived in.

I unmute the phone and make the suggestion to

Yelinek. At first, he's not too enthusiastic about the alternative, but Mel makes it clear it's our way or not at all. I promise him I'll get it installed before Monday, which seems to appease him.

"Now, we haven't exactly been sitting still," Yelinek announces. "A few things to fill you in on. First off, we were finally able to connect with the owner of the van. We found out Kelly had been renting the apartment over his garage for three years. We were at his property yesterday and found an older model Mazda that was registered to Kelly in the garage. The apartment looked like someone grabbed a few things in a hurry."

Mel comes to the same conclusion I do.

"She was on the run."

"Would appear that way. Anyway, I have a couple of things I took from the apartment I thought the kid might want. Just some toys I found in his bedroom."

"That would be great," Mel says right away.

"I'll send someone to pick them up," I suggest.

"Sure. I can leave the bag at the station at the front desk."

After we end the call, I make a quick call to the clubhouse and talk to Ouray while Mel finishes up her work. He's going to send one of the prospects to pick the stuff up in Moab in the morning.

"Also, I'm gonna need to head into the Riverside Apartments tomorrow."

"You want someone at your house?"

"Probably not a bad idea. And is my truck still at the gym?"

"No, Brick picked it up with the tow truck the other day. He pulled it in the shop so it's out of sight. You can use one of the club's trucks."

"Fair enough."

"I'll see who's gonna be around tomorrow and let you know."

When I get off the phone, Mel is bent over her laptop and I drop a kiss to the back of her neck before I leave her to check on Mason.

The boy is on the floor, playing tug-of-war with the dog and ignoring the TV. I grab the remote and turn it off.

"How about you and me fix dinner tonight, bud?"

"Okay."

"Do you like fish?"

His little face scrunches up a bit but he follows me into the kitchen.

"I don't know."

"Never had fish? Trout?" He answers with a shrug. "Boy, are you in for a treat."

I open the freezer and pull out the whole fish I caught, cleaned, and froze earlier this summer.

"Ever been fishing?"

A shake of the head this time, but he looks engaged.

"Well, we're gonna have to fix that too. Soon you and me are gonna go fishing. I know a great spot."

"Mel too?" he asks, climbing on a stool, his eyes fixed on the large trout.

"Why not?"

She just might be game for that.

ARROW'S EDGE MC

18

MEL

I STUFF THE second load of laundry in the washer.

It's been years since I've washed clothes other than my own—even longer since I've washed a man's clothes—but I need something to do to feel useful. Housework wouldn't be my first choice but my options are rather limited.

Mason is sitting at the dining room table with an educational game I pulled up on my laptop. I figure it's a better option than planting him on the couch with the TV on again, and I promised Paco we'd stay inside.

That boy needs to socialize, he needs to hang out with other kids, be stimulated. Being cooped up in this house with a couple of adults and a dog for company can't be healthy for him in the long run.

I've also had some concerns about our sleeping arrangements. It's a bit of an adjustment going from sleeping alone in a queen at home, to sharing a king-sized bed with a large man, a boy, and a dog. But more so, I'm worried having Mason share a bed with us every night is going to become a hard-to-break habit.

Let's be honest, the situation is unconventional at best. We're not the boy's parents—we're not even really a couple—and yet we're living as if we are. We may be sending the wrong signals to Mason. The lawyer in me worries it's inappropriate, but the mother in me disagrees.

All I know is when this is over and we go back to our normal lives, that child is left with nothing. No one.

I turn on the washer before returning to the kitchen.

"Hey, Mason?"

The boy looks up.

"We still have some chocolate chips left. Wanna bake some cookies?"

I'm guessing the answer is yes, judging by the speed he gets up from the table.

Okay, so the mother in me wins. For now.

THE KITCHEN LOOKS like a war zone and Mason is covered in flour as he tries to lick the last crumbs from his fingers. Yeah, I know it's not good for him to eat raw dough, but every kid should experience the joys of cleaning the bowl.

I slide the two trays of cookies into the oven and am

just setting the timer when I hear the crunch of tires on gravel.

Paco's only been gone for a couple of hours and said he'd probably be gone most of the day. He'd been hesitant leaving since Tse—who was supposed to be babysitting us today—had to take care of his family. The twins and Sophia came down with something and had to stay home. I'm the one who told Paco we'd be fine, even if someone knows where we are, they'd have a hard time getting through Paco's security system.

Still, I don't want anyone to spot Mason until I know who it is.

It takes me a moment to react, but when I do, it's with lightning speed.

I swing around, scoop the boy under one arm, and shove him into the laundry room, which is closest.

"Do you think you can be really quiet?" I ask him, doing my best to smile reassuringly at the startled child.

When he nods, I put a finger to my lips and wink before closing the door on him.

Then I ease along the wall to the front door, trying to catch a glimpse of the vehicle outside. It's a pickup truck I don't know, but when the door opens, I see a familiar figure getting out.

I disarm the alarm like Paco instructed me and pull open the front door.

"A little heads-up would've been helpful," I toss out.

"Tried calling three times and you didn't answer, so I left a message," Wapi fires back as he walks in, carrying a bag and a large manila envelope.

Shit. Left my phone on the charger in the office and it's set to vibrate.

"I'm sorry. That's my bad. Can I make it up to you with cookies?"

He stops and sniffs the air.

"Chocolate chip?"

"Good nose," I comment.

He drops his load on the kitchen island.

"Envelope is for you, from Lindsey, and the tote is for Mason." He looks around the room. "Where is the kid?"

Crap.

I rush to the laundry room door and pull it open. He's still standing in the same spot I left him, with the same startled look on his face.

"Good job hiding, bud. We've got a visitor," I chirp like this was all supposed to be a game. "Looks like we're gonna have to share our cookies."

He doesn't say anything to Wapi's casual greeting but rewards him with a little smile.

"So how come you're not shadowing my daughter?"

A muscle in his jaw jumps before he answers.

"She's at your office with Paco. I just dropped her off. Told Paco I'd stick around here until they're done."

"Does that mean he's bringing Linds back here?"

Haven't seen her in person for days, it'd be nice. Maybe I can cook something and she and Wapi can stay for dinner.

"I assume so." He hands me the manila envelope. "She wanted me to give you this."

I quickly confirm it's the file I asked for before putting

it aside. I'll look at it later.

"And Mika, one of our prospects, picked this up in Moab this morning."

He indicates the bag, which I assume holds the stuff Detective Yelinek left for Mason. I'm not sure how he's going to react to it. I think maybe I should wait until Paco is here before I give it to him. I grab the bag and dump it in the laundry room for now.

The oven timer goes off, which means cookies first.

"Do you know how to operate this?" I point at the coffee machine I still haven't got the hang of.

"How many cups?" Wapi wants to know, already busying himself.

"However many you're gonna have plus one for me."

With coffee brewing and the cookies cooling, I send off a quick message to Paco.

Are you bringing Linds here?

Instead of messaging me back, he calls.

"Want me to?"

"Yes," I say eagerly. "Tell her I'll make stuffed peppers. You have ground beef in the freezer, right?"

"Should be. Plenty of peppers in the garden, but if you need anything else, let me know. I can pick it up on the way home."

Jesus, we sound so domesticated. It makes me grin.

"I will. Thanks."

He must've heard the smile in my voice because he chuckles in that deep rumble of his. I can feel the sound down to my toes.

"All right, gotta get back to it. Later, Darlin'."

"Yeah, later…Paco."

PACO

"YOU ARE SO gone for her."

I turn to Lindsey, who is grinning ear to ear.

"You're coming for dinner," I abruptly change the subject.

"I am?"

"I think your mom is missing you. She wants me to tell you she's making stuffed peppers."

"Yum. But, uhm, is that safe?"

She suddenly looks worried.

"Yeah, we'll be careful."

In the next forty-five minutes, I finish installing the tracer and show Lindsey how to use it. Just as we're locking up the office, my phone rings.

"Where are you?"

It's Tony Ramirez.

"Downtown, why?"

"Tell me Mel is with you?"

My blood runs cold. Surely Wapi would've called if anything happened.

"What's wrong?" Lindsey asks, looking at me.

"She's at my place. Why?" I tell Ramirez.

"Thank God, I'm on my way to her address. We just received a call about an explosion."

"What?"

Lindsey jumps at my bark and I put a hand on her shoulder.

"Look, I'm about to roll up. I'll call you when I know more."

He promptly hangs up.

Like hell I'm gonna stand around and wait for him to call.

Grabbing Lindsey's wrist, I start moving toward the truck, but she pulls me back.

"What the hell, Paco? What is going on?"

"There's a problem at your house. We've gotta go."

"A problem? What kind of problem?"

Her heels click on the pavement as she tries to keep up with me.

"Get in, Lindsey."

I wait until she gets in the seat and slam the door shut. As I round the hood, I'm already dialing Wapi's number.

"Talk to me," he answers as I get behind the wheel and start the truck.

"Mel and the boy there?"

"Yeah, sittin' right here."

My relief is instant. I quickly tell him what I know and tune out Lindsey's gasp beside me.

"Make sure the alarm is set and stay sharp. Not sure what is going on, but be careful anyway."

"Will do."

"Tell Mel I'll call her when we get there."

I'm not getting a good feeling. It's been quiet—maybe too quiet—and I can't help think this explosion, or whatever it was, is not an accident.

"Our house?"

I briefly take my eyes off the road and glance over at Lindsey.

"We're almost there, sweetheart."

Flashing lights from emergency vehicles are visible from two streets over. When we turn the corner the road is blocked by a couple of patrol cars. I pull off to the side. A crowd of people has formed on the sidewalks on either side.

"Wait for me."

I get out and help Lindsey out of the truck. Only an idiot would try something when half of Durango's finest is lining the street, but I don't want to take any chances. I'm keeping her close.

I hold on to her as I make my way through the curious neighbors. Then I run into yellow tape and the officer standing behind it to make sure no one crosses it. Glancing over his shoulder, I can see the front of Mel's house, the garage nothing more than rubble and every window is blown out. The fire department is dousing the still smoking shell of Mel's brand-new SUV, crumpled and halfway down the driveway.

"Oh my God, is that Mom's new car?"

Before I can stop her, Lindsey ducks under the caution tape and scoots past the officer.

"Hey!" he yells after her, and I use his distraction to duck under the tape myself. "Sir!"

"I'll go grab her," I call back over my shoulder as I jog after her.

Up ahead I see Ramirez break away from a group

standing at the end of Mel's driveway. He manages to intercept Lindsey, just as I catch up.

I get Mel on the phone and with her listening, Ramirez tells us what he knows, which turns out to be not that much.

"Neighbor called it in. The blast blew out her front window. When the fire department got here, the garage was a burning pile and the vehicle was on fire. The fire department is in the house now to turn off utilities. Once that's done, we can start looking into what happened."

"Uncle Scottie!" Lindsey suddenly yells.

One of the firefighters turns his head and spots her, immediately making his way over here.

"Linds! Jesus. Where's your mom?"

When he gets closer, I recognize him; Captain Scott Beacham, or Cap as his crew calls him. I watch as he wraps Lindsey in a bear hug and put the phone to my ear.

"You still there?"

"Oh God, just my luck, my brother-in-law is on call," Mel responds.

"She's safe," I tell Scott and his eyes dart my way.

"Safe? What does that mean?"

"Might as well hand him the phone," she says in my ear.

"She's on the line."

I hold out my phone. He throws me a suspicious look before putting it to his ear and turning his back.

Ramirez excuses himself after promising to get in touch when he knows more. Lindsey sidles up to me, the gravity of the situation suddenly visible on her face.

Shit. She's gonna cry.

I drop my arm around her and she immediately turns her face against my shoulder.

"Gonna be okay, sweetheart. That's what insurance is for."

"I know," she sniffles.

A few minutes later, Scott walks up and hands me the phone back. Then he looks at his niece.

"Police and the fire inspector are gonna be all over this place. You won't be able to get in. You got a place to stay?"

She nods.

"Good. Nothing you can do here, Linds. The boys and I will make sure the house is secure before we go."

"Thanks, Uncle Scottie."

She gives him a hug but over her head his eyes are on me.

"Mel tells me you're looking after her, but she won't tell me where she is."

Good girl.

"You're gonna have to trust me there's good reason for that," I inform him, leaving it at that.

IT'S ALMOST SEVEN by the time we get to my place.

Mel has clearly been on the lookout because she has the door open when we walk up. I stand aside while the two women hug and I hear Mel tell her daughter, "It's only stuff."

Then she lets go of Lindsey and turns to me.

"Let's have dinner and we can talk after Mason is in bed."

"Sounds like a plan to me."

I bend down and brush her lips before I follow her inside.

If you don't count this afternoon's events—or the armed standoff between Wapi and Lindsey hanging heavy in the room—dinner is great. I can't believe how Mason is starting to become more animated, clearly feeling at ease with the group around the table.

Family. I've only ever felt this sense of belonging at the clubhouse.

I catch Mel's eye and shoot her a smile she returns.

After dinner, I clear off the table and Mel follows me to the kitchen.

"I need to show you something," she says, motioning for me to follow her into the laundry room where she shows me a tote bag. "This is Mason's stuff Yelinek collected. I wanted us both to be here before I gave it to him."

"You wanna do it now?"

I take the bag and look inside. I spot two books, a couple of small cars, a box of Lego, and a framed picture of a young, blonde woman smiling at the camera with a younger Mason on her lap.

"That Kelly?"

Mel nods, swallowing hard.

"I was surprised Yelinek thought to put that in there," she comments.

"Yeah. You think seeing it will upset him?"

"His last memory of his mom is not a happy one, so I think it may help to remind him of happier times? If that makes sense?"

It does.

I grab the bag and reach out a hand to Mel.

"Let's do this."

Mason is in the living room, sitting on the floor, at the coffee table across from Lindsey who is drawing something on a piece of paper. It looks like an animal of some sort, but it's clear as capable as Mel's daughter is, drawing isn't one of her talents.

"Dog!"

"Nope. Bigger. Much bigger."

"Elephant?"

"Nooo, silly. Where's his trunk?"

Mason points at an appendage on the drawing.

"That's a tail," Lindsey explains.

I'm with the boy, it actually looks more like a trunk.

"Horse," Wapi says, sitting back in a chair observing the scene.

Lindsey's eyes snap to him as she drops her pen on the table.

"Mason was supposed to guess. Not you."

My younger brother shrugs. "Wasn't ever gonna happen."

"Well, *you* did," she points out.

"Lucky guess."

Before they get into it, I put the bag on the table in front of Mason.

"Hey, bud. Remember when we brought you your bunny?"

His eyes are big, looking from the bag to me.

"Well, we found a few more things I'm pretty sure belong to you. Have a look."

He darts a look at Mel, who nods and takes a seat on the couch behind him.

One by one he pulls the toys and books out, lining them up on the table without saying anything, but his little fingers seem to linger on each item. The last thing he pulls out is the picture frame. He stares at it a long time, his head bent low. Then he turns to me.

"Mommy's not coming back."

I crouch down in front of him.

"No, buddy, she's not."

"Did she go to heaven?"

Shit. Clearly this conversation is way out of my league and I suddenly wish Trunk was here to navigate.

"Absolutely," Mel assures the boy. "And I'm sure she's still looking out for you."

She leans forward and touches the little guy's chest.

"And she will always be in your heart. Right here."

He clutches the picture where Mel's hand was.

"I'm tired. Can I go to bed?"

"Sure, honey," Mel says easily, getting to her feet. "Want me to read to you from one of your books?"

He nods and points at a book titled *Love You Forever*.

"Mommy likes that one."

19

MEL

I CAN'T BELIEVE Mason is still in bed. His own bed at that.

It was his idea.

Saturday night he still slept in Paco's bed with us, but he was gone when I woke up yesterday morning. I found him in the guest bedroom where he was in the process of lining up his cars on the dresser. The two books were already neatly stacked on the nightstand where he'd also placed the picture of him and Kelly.

Damn near broke my heart when he asked if that could be his room.

He only has one drawer in the dresser in use with the few clothes Lisa pulled together for him and even with the few toys added, the room is sparse and impersonal.

I know this is just a temporary situation, but I don't give a shit. Like I told Paco yesterday, that boy needs more than what fits in one measly bag and I fully intend to make that happen. The first of my online orders will start coming into the office today.

"Morning."

I'm waiting for my toast to pop when Paco walks up behind me and brushes the hair aside, kissing the pulse in my neck.

"Where's the boy?"

"Still sleeping, believe it or not."

His eyebrows shoot up to his hairline. "And you didn't come back to bed?"

"We've got to be out of here in an hour," I remind him. "And I want a shower."

He snakes his arms around my waist and drops his mouth to my ear.

"I'm all for conserving water…"

"Can we have pancakes?"

Paco groans in my neck as I turn my head to see Mason shuffle into the kitchen, his bunny hanging from his hand.

Last night when we went to bed, we didn't go any further than snuggle and kiss, convinced Mason would show up in the doorway at some point, that same bunny in hand. But he didn't. He actually slept through the night.

"Cereal today. Okay, bud?" I untangle myself from Paco's arms, who thankfully heads straight for the coffee maker. "We have a few errands to run, so there isn't time today."

"Okay," he mumbles, climbing up on a stool.

Paco decided he felt better bringing the boy with us after what happened on Saturday. Tomorrow, when I have to appear in court, it's going to be a bit more complicated, but today he can stay in the truck with Paco while I'm at my appointments.

I spent so much time on the phone yesterday I had to recharge it twice. Insurance, the fire inspector, Tony Ramirez. Heck, even my sister checked in with me, and that rarely happens, even though we live in the same town. We're not particularly close and months can go by between phone calls, in-person visits are even more rare. It's not that we don't love each other, but we were very different as children and that never really changed.

Beth was always the good daughter. She married a man in a respected profession, had kids, and devoted her life to taking care of them. I, on the other hand, have always been considered the rebel in the family. I ran off with a race car driver—and that was the big one that got me cut off—got pregnant and raised a child as a single woman, while studying and working full time. Even now, at almost fifty with a successful law practice, I still elicit the same head-shaking reaction from my family. Like I'm somehow personally responsible for whatever misfortune lands on my path.

Which is why I never considered telling them what's been happening. Why bother?

My one saving grace in the family's eyes is my daughter. Of course they don't know her like I do. They don't realize in a lot of ways she's as single-minded as I was—*am*—but only see what Linds wants them to see.

I totally expect a rare phone call from my parents at some point today—I'm sure Beth will have informed them by now—full of concern for my daughter and some head-shaking for me.

"Not sure I wanna know what's going through your head right now," Paco says, as he slides a coffee in front of me.

"Trust me, you don't," I confirm, taking a sip of my mug.

Damn. That man knows how to do coffee.

My prediction comes true when we're on our way to Sara's office. Of course there's no way to take the call privately and I know from experience if I don't answer immediately, they'll just keep blowing up my phone until they get me.

Paco shoots me a questioning glance.

"My parents. Not looking forward to this."

I haven't talked about my parents with him, other than to say they currently live in Scottsdale, Arizona. Well, he's gonna get an earful now.

"Hey, Mom."

It'll be her on the phone, with Dad providing background commentary. That's the way it's always been.

"Oh for Pete's sake, Melanie, what have you gotten yourself into now? Your sister tells me you managed to get your house blown up."

Her shrill voice is loud enough for Paco to hear and

his face goes slack. Yeah, welcome to Morgan family bliss.

"We weren't even home, Mom."

"Well, you must've done something. Did you leave the oven on? I know how distracted you get when you're working."

Dad mumbles something in the background but luckily, I can't make out what. It would only piss me off more.

"No. Neither of us left the oven on. The explosion was in the garage, not the kitchen."

"Well, you should've called us," she changes her approach while Dad says something about old paint cans. "Your father isn't the healthiest, you know, his ticker is bad. He could've had a heart attack. You could show a little consideration."

"Nothing wrong with my ticker."

This time I hear him clearly. I close my eyes and take in a deep breath.

I'm not about to inform them that the preliminary verbal report I received from the fire inspector indicated evidence was found of a rudimentary explosive device. If that bit of information wouldn't send them through the roof, the conversation I had with Detective Ramirez after would've. He suggested perhaps the objective of the explosion had been to draw me out of hiding.

Unable to come up with an appropriate response other than 'fuck off,' I opt for silence, but that doesn't last long.

"And how is Lindsey? Does she have a place to stay? She can always move in with her aunt Beth, or better yet, she can come here for a visit."

"She's fine, she has a place to stay. I'll ask her to give you a call herself, but I've gotta go, Mom."

I don't even wait for a response and just hang up. It's all I can do not to permanently block their number from my phone.

"She never asked about you," Paco noticed.

"I know. I love my parents, and I'm sure in their own way they love me too, but they mess with my head. I can only take so much at a time."

"Honestly," he mumbles. "Not sure what is worse; no parents, or parents like that."

PACO

HOLY FUCK.

I'm relieved she doesn't talk to or see her parents that often because I'm going to have a serious issue with them if this is the way they treat her.

Pulling up right in front of the entrance to the medical building, I watch Mel walk in by herself. Her mass of hair is tucked into a ball cap I loaned her, and the sunglasses cover half her face. Even I'd have a hard time recognizing her. It's just a precaution, there's no way anyone could possibly know about her appointments. Still, I'd rather go in there with her, but I don't think that would've been an option, even if I hadn't decided to bring Mason along. I'm sure Mel would've shot me down.

Today a few of my brothers will be at Mel's house cleaning up the mess, fixing the broken windows, and the front door the fire department knocked down to get in. Mel doesn't know yet, but I wanted to at least take that load off her shoulders. Her brother-in-law said he'd be there first thing in the morning to deal with the insurance adjuster and the boys can get to work as soon as he's gone.

Tomorrow will be a bit more of a challenge when Mel has to make an appearance in court. There's no way I can bring the boy for that, it's too public, and besides, I'll have my hands full making sure Mel stays safe. Trunk will be keeping an eye on Mason, and Tse will tail us from the courthouse to make sure no one is following us back.

As much as I enjoy being around Mel twenty-four seven, I wish they'd catch the sonofabitch. For the boy's sake too, being cooped up inside can't be good for him.

"Are you okay back there, Mason?"

I glance in the rearview mirror where he's strapped into a booster seat Wapi was able to drum up for us at the clubhouse. Cookie is curled up beside him. Mason insisted she come too.

"Why can't we go inside?"

"Because Mel needs to talk to her doctor alone. She won't be long, though."

"Is Mel sick?"

"No, bud. It's a regular checkup."

"Oh," he mumbles, his eyes snapping back out the window.

I wonder if he's always been a quiet child or if that's purely a result of the trauma he suffered. I'm sure lots goes on in that head of his and I wish I could help him make sense of it.

"Wanna play a game on my phone?"

All I have is Sudoku but I'm sure I could download something for him. Maybe I should get him a Gameboy or whatever those little gaming systems are called these days.

He shakes his head but his eyes stay locked on the door Mel disappeared through. It's not until she finally appears, forty minutes later, that I see him relax. He's scared. He lost his mom, it's no wonder he's latched on to Mel, who is so easy with him.

"Phew," she huffs as she gets in the truck. "Glad that's done with."

She twists around in her seat to see Mason.

"Sorry it took so long, kiddo. How about I make it up to you with a milkshake and some tater tots at Sonic?"

"Crispy tenders," he responds, now smiling.

"You bet. Crispy tenders it is." Mel sits back and buckles up. The laugh lines around her eyes deepen when she looks at me. "What about you? Can I buy you lunch?"

"Haven't even bought you dinner yet," I grumble, putting the truck in gear. When I turn in the direction of town I add, "But I'll have a bacon double cheeseburger combo with unsweetened tea."

When I glance over at her it's not just her eyes smiling.

"Are you sure he's sleeping?"

I slide my hand under her shirt, cupping her breast.

"Out like a light. Are these tender?" I ask, as I press my hips against her ass.

"Mmmm. No, they're not."

My other hand slips behind the bib of her overalls and heads south. I fucking love this ugly old thing.

"Anyone could see us," she points out, but she makes no effort to stop me.

Instead she drops her head back against my shoulder when I slide my fingers along the liquid heat between her legs.

We're in front of the kitchen window, the only possible witnesses out there are of the four-legged variety.

"No one out there, Darlin'," I reassure her, before adding. "But I wouldn't mind moving this to the bedroom. I plan to take my time with you tonight."

True to my word, I'm in no hurry and by the time I have her naked and splayed out on my bed, she's almost cursing me.

"You enjoy torturing me," she hisses as she clamps her thighs against my ears.

I immediately lift my head, and she whimpers in response.

"Are you complaining? I can stop."

Her beautiful eyes glare down her body at me.

"Don't you dare," she growls in a low voice.

Damn. She's magnificent.

I love her deep passion, even when it expresses itself with a temper.

She props herself up on her elbows and I enjoy the entire view of her. Her silver hair wild and unruly draped over one shoulder, leaving the other naked. The stunning floral tattoo I discovered comes up her arm, covers her shoulder, and spreads with tendrils down her chest and one up the side of her neck.

My own are mostly black and pretty basic in comparison to the art that covers her.

"You're beautiful."

"And you need to wear your old-man glasses to bed. You're clearly losing your eyesight."

I burst out laughing. "Old-man glasses? I distinctly remember catching you ogling me when I was wearing them the other day. They turn you on."

"I don't ogle and they do not."

"Keep telling yourself that."

I push myself up and off the bed.

"Where are you going?"

I turn and lean over the bed, my face inches from hers.

"Be right back."

Then I drop a kiss on her mouth and walk buck naked out of the room.

"Are you kidding me?" I hear her behind me.

I'm only gone for a minute but when I walk back into the bedroom, Mel is no longer in bed. From the bathroom I hear water running.

She's in front of the mirror, her face pressed in a towel when I come walking in. I watch her body go rigid a second before she lifts her head, catching sight of me standing behind her in the mirror, wearing my reading glasses. For a moment her mouth goes slack, but then her head drops back, her eyes close, and her mouth spreads wide as she starts laughing.

I take it as a good sign and press myself against her naked backside. Feeling her body shake against me, I take a handful of her hair, lift it out of the way, and run the tip of my tongue from her ear to the top of her shoulder. When I look in the mirror her eyes are filled with heat.

"You're right," she says hoarsely. "They do turn me on."

"Thought so," I whisper against her ear. "Now tilt your ass and brace."

So much for taking my time.

After we roll into bed, still catching our breaths, Mel snuggles in against me.

"I like sleeping with you," she mumbles. "You're comfy."

I chuckle. "I like doing lots of things with you, but sleeping is definitely one of them."

She turns her head and kisses my chest. Not long after, I can hear her breathing even out.

Today was a good day, and after that impromptu workout in the bathroom, I'll sleep well tonight.

I let myself drift off, not realizing this'll be the last peaceful night I'll have for a while.

20

PACO

"WE WON'T BE too long, I promise."

I watch from the doorway as Mel crouches down in front of Mason, who is looking like he'll burst into tears any minute.

Trunk comes to stand next to me.

"He's bonded with you guys."

"Yeah. Especially Mel. I noticed it yesterday, he had his eyes glued to the front door of her doctor's office when she was inside."

"Separation anxiety. It's understandable given what that boy went through."

"I know, but what's gonna happen after?"

"Hmm, he'll be in the club's care for the foreseeable future. Unless someone comes forward to claim him, then the courts will get involved, but that doesn't happen overnight."

Knowing he'll have a place at the club is reassuring, but he seems so little compared to the other boys we've taken in over the years. Besides, he clearly needs a soft touch and Lisa has her hands full with her own three grandkids and the running of the clubhouse. Whatever way you turn it, the poor kid has a tough road ahead.

"We should head out," I announce in a louder voice, getting Mel's attention.

I walk up to Mason and ruffle his hair.

"Wanna take a ride on the four-wheeler when we get back?"

He lifts his head to smile at me and nods.

"Good. Trunk will take good care of you, okay?"

"Okay."

I help Mel to her feet, take her hand, and lead her out the door, which Trunk closes behind us.

We're taking Trunk's vehicle and leaving the club truck behind. Safer to use different vehicles in case anyone is paying attention.

"You look nice," Mel says when I get behind the wheel.

My black dress shirt and black jeans make me look like a grayer version of Johnny Cash. Not my choice, but it works for weddings and funerals. I don't own a suit—nor do I want to—but I'm glad I pass Mel's muster.

Ironically, Mel is dressed much the same. All black, with the exception of her shoes which are red Chucks. She can't quite let go of the rebel.

"So do you."

She does. She did something to her hair to make it stay up in a loose bun, not too stern but just the right side of professional. She also put something on her lips to make them look plump and shiny. Unable to resist them, I lean over the center console and kiss her softly.

"Ready?"

She taps the thick file on her lap.

"As ready as I can be."

The parking lot is busy, which means we have to park a block away and walk in. I keep my arm around Mel's shoulders, constantly scanning our surroundings. It's tough when you're downtown in the middle of a weekday morning, and I curse myself for not planning this better.

I let out a sigh of relief when we get to the courthouse. Plenty of people around here as well, but less likely for someone to try something.

Mel's client is sitting on a bench in the hallway, glaring at a couple of suits on the other side. I'm guessing the ex and his attorney. The woman gets up when she spots us, eyeing me suspiciously.

"This is Jessica, my client, and this is Paco Philips, my associate."

I bite off a grin at Mel's introduction and hold out my hand.

"Where's your fiancé?" Mel asks her.

"He's in Austin. He had to work."

Mel shakes her head, clearly annoyed.

"Like I explained to you, it would've been helpful

to your case if he could've been here. I could've called on him to testify to the fact his Austin business makes it impossible for him to relocate here. It also would've shown a united front, a family stability the judge will be looking for."

Jessica looks away.

"He couldn't get away."

Mel told me a bit of the backstory and I question whether the fiancé is as eager to have this woman and her children move to Austin as she appears to be. I know if it were me, and my future with Mel depended on it, I'd bend over backward to make it happen.

"I need to use the bathroom," Jessica says in the uncomfortable silence that follows.

"Don't be too long, we can get called in any moment," Mel cautions her.

The moment she disappears down the hall, Mel turns to me.

"She's expecting me to perform miracles, but her significant other can't even be bothered to show up," she grumbles.

"Are you sure she's even engaged?" I ask. I noticed a ring on her finger but who's to say it's a ring this guy gave her?

"Why would she lie?"

"I don't know. All I know is if the woman I'm about to marry is fighting for custody so she and her children could be with me, I'd damn well stand by her side while she's doing it."

A smile cracks through the annoyed look on her face.

"You would too, wouldn't you?"

"IT'S NOT FAIR."

Jessica has been sobbing since the judge indicated he did not find sufficient cause to change the current custody order on an emergency basis. She's not going to be able to take their children to Austin.

"I warned you it was a long shot. Philip's lawyer was able to show he's a good father. Maybe the judge will see things differently if you were to get married before this case goes to trial, but without anything showing the kids are at risk here, or that their life in Austin would provide a significant improvement on the current situation, chances are slim he will consider a deviation from the original custody arrangement."

Mel rubs the other woman's back.

"I don't know what to do now."

"It's not easy. You may have to content yourself with flying to Austin during the weeks you don't have the children. Perhaps your fiancé can come here and work from your house on the weeks they're with you."

"He'll never do that. He says he can't concentrate on anything with the kids around."

The guy sounds like a fucking prince.

I tune out the women and keep an eye on the street. We're standing on the sidewalk by the courthouse and a little too exposed for my taste, which is why I placed myself between the road and Mel.

A steady stream of vehicles drives by but my eyes catch on a black cargo van parked across from the courthouse. There are no markings on the side and there's someone sitting behind the wheel. Unfortunately the sun is reflecting off the driver's side window so I can't make out more than an outline. The license plate is just outside of my line of sight as well, but if I move, I leave Mel standing out in the open.

The sound of a motorcycle draws my attention. I'm relieved when I recognize Tse slowing down by the curb.

When my eyes snap back to the van, I just catch it pulling into traffic. I see a flash of a man's face, looking straight at me. A quick glimpse at the license plate, as the van rushes off, only tells me it's a black or navy and white Colorado plate.

"What was that?" Tse asks as he walks up to me, his head turned in the direction of the disappearing van.

"Probably nothing, but keep an eye out when we're heading home for a black Ford cargo van."

"Sure. You ready to head out?"

Mel hooks an arm in mine and when I turn to look, I see Jessica is already walking toward the parking lot.

"I am," she answers.

MEL

"How are the twins?"

Sophia looks a little the worse for wear but who could blame her? Ella and Wyatt are just six months old and were sick from what I gather.

I asked Paco to stop at their house so I could check in with her. I feel a little proprietary over those babies. After all, I came close to having to deliver them on the back seat of my Subaru.

"Sated but awake as you can see. They projectile spit all day yesterday."

"So did you," Tse comments.

"Thanks, honey. I'm sure they needed to know that."

Paco chuckles as I glance over to the twins, bouncing in two identical seats on the living-room floor.

"Come sit for a bit," Sophia says. "I'm glad I have some adults to converse with."

"Hey," Tse objects. "What about me?"

His wife doesn't even bother looking at him when she repeats, "Like I said, I'm glad for some adult conversation."

We stay for twenty minutes or so before driving the trail along the side of the A-frame to the back of the property. Two minutes later, I see Paco's house through the trees, the club truck parked on the far side of the garage.

The house is quiet. No TV on and no sign of Trunk, Mason, or even Cookie. Maybe they're in the boy's room but when I open the door to his bedroom, it's empty.

When I get back to the kitchen, I see Paco standing on the back porch, checking the garden.

"Can you see them?"

I peer out in the yard before scanning the tree line at the back.

Paco already has his phone out and is dialing.

"Where the hell are you?"

I lean forward, my hands on my knees as I let relief wash over me. Paco's starts gently rubbing my back.

"A what? You wanna build a fucking tree house? Here?"

"Mel!"

I shoot upright. Mason's voice is faint but I can see Trunk's large shape coming out of the trees to the left of the yard. A minute later, the boy pushes through some brush and runs onto the grass, the silly dog bouncing around his feet.

I'm down the steps in a flash when he runs up to me, wrapping his little arms around my hips.

"I thought you weren't coming back," he says, his head tilted way back to look up at me.

I brush the hair flopping down his forehead away from his eyes.

"I told you we'd be back."

"I wasn't sure."

Bending down, I press a kiss to the crown of his head. Trunk walks past us and up the steps to talk with Paco.

I'm in trouble. In very short order I've lost my heart to this boy, this place, and am well on my way to losing it to that man as well, which is perhaps the most troubling of all.

"So…a tree house?" I say to Mason as I take his hand and lead him inside.

"We found a good tree. Right, Trunk?" he calls out to the large man just stepping into the kitchen.

"Perfect, kid."

"I just finished building this house, now you want me to build another one?" Paco grumbles, but I can tell his heart is not in it.

"We'll help, right, Trunk?"

"Right, kid. My boy, River, can help too, but he's a bit younger than you. You may need to show him."

"I will."

It's by far the most animated I've seen Mason.

Even if I have to pick up a damn hammer myself, I'll see to it the boy gets his tree house.

I glance over at Paco, who's already looking at me. His eyes are liquid and warm, the hint of a smile playing on his lips. Don't think I'm the only one falling in love with a six-year-old.

Trunk stays for a bite of lunch but when he gets ready to leave, Mason convinces him to show Paco the 'perfect' tree. I opt to stay here, clean the kitchen, and do a little work until they come back.

My notes from this morning's hearing take longer to process than I expected. I make a few notes for Lindsey and shoot them off in an email. Maybe I should give her a quick call to let her know what happened this morning in case Jessica calls the office.

The phone rings and rings, until Lindsey's disembodied voice invites me to leave a message. Probably on the other line. I check the time on my laptop, it's too early for her to have left.

That reminds me, I should ask her to bring the stuff I ordered online for Mason to the clubhouse. I'm sure Tse wouldn't mind bringing it home so we can pick it up from his place, or maybe Paco is willing to pick it up.

I may have gone a little crazy. I got him clothes, of course, but also picked up some more Lego, a big dump truck he can play with outside, a child-sized wheelbarrow and gardening tools, and my biggest splurge was a bicycle. Every kid needs a bike and there's enough driveway outside for him to ride on.

Maybe I've gone overboard—Paco certainly seems to feel that way—but the boy has lost so much, is it that bad to want to spoil him a little? Fine, a lot.

To be honest, it's as much for me as it is for him. When Lindsey was his age, I was either working or studying, and I definitely didn't have the money for any splurging. Linds ended up with hand-me-downs and secondhand toys. Anything new she had was bought by my parents, which I hated. I wanted to get her all those things myself. Part of me has always suspected it was their way of showing me how inadequate they felt me to be.

Anyway, I have the money now—it's not like I spend a whole lot on myself—and I can put a smile on that little guy's face.

I dial the office once more, but am bounced to voicemail again. I'm about to try her cell when I hear shouting outside.

I get to my feet and lean over the desk to look out the window. Paco is running toward the house, Trunk right behind him carrying Mason.

Jesus, has something happened to him? Did he fall?

I rush through the house to the back door just as Paco storms up the steps.

"What happened?"

Paco doesn't answer but pushes me back into the house.

"Trunk's staying here with you, I have to go."

The large man follows us inside and my eyes automatically scan Mason. He doesn't appear injured, but the moment Trunk puts him down he rushes me, pressing his face in my belly. My arms automatically come around him.

"What on earth is going on?"

"Wapi called. Something happened at the office," Paco says, his eyes concerned.

My heart suddenly feels like a rock in my chest, cold and unmoving.

"Tell me," I force out, my voice strangled.

"Lindsey is missing."

21

Paco

"I'M COMING WITH you."

I grab her upper arms and drop my face to her level.

"Not smart, Darlin'. Remember the explosion? Getting you to come running may well be the intent."

"That's my daughter."

"I know," I try to calm her, "which is why it's important for you to stay here and available. Look, I've got to go. I'll let you know right away if I find out anything."

I press a hard kiss on her mouth and turn to Mason.

"It's gonna be okay, kiddo."

Feeling some guilt, I head outside. I haven't told her everything. Not yet, I want to get as much information as I can first.

Wapi explained he'd gone to pick up lunch for them

just down the street and told her to lock up behind him. When he got back to the office, the front door was locked but the back door was open a crack. At first, he'd thought she was messing with him. She'd been giving him a hard time all morning. But when he noticed her purse and phone were still where she left them behind her desk, he got worried.

As soon as I get behind the wheel, I open the app on my phone and pull up the video feed for the office. I select the one at the rear of the building and rewind it forty-five minutes. Wapi said it was almost two when he left to get lunch.

I fast forward through the first few minutes until I catch sight of a dark vehicle driving into the rear parking lot. It's hugging the fence at the back of the property which is lined with trees. Even though it looks like they're actively trying to avoid the camera, I can clearly see it's a dark cargo van. The same one I saw outside the courthouse this morning.

Whoever is in there did some casing of the office and knows exactly in what direction the camera is positioned. I see the van disappear from view but a minute later what looks like a delivery guy, wearing a ball cap low over his eyes, comes walking up to the back door with a large box in his hands. With the camera aimed down, it's impossible to see the guy's face.

The timestamp on the video says three minutes past two.

At two-oh-four I see him stepping back from the door, gesturing at the box he left leaning against the wall.

Then I see Lindsey stepping into view, leaning down to look at something—maybe a label—on the box.

It's five minutes after two when I watch as the guy steps close behind Lindsey, holding something to her back. I see her body jerk up and the next moment she's walking in front of him, heading in the direction I saw the van disappear.

Two minutes after that the van speeds by before disappearing off the other side of the screen. It all happened within the fifteen minutes Wapi was gone. Someone had been watching. Waiting for an opportunity.

I save the feed and forward the file to both Ramirez and Evans.

Then I tear out of there, throwing caution to the wind as I head straight for the road, already dialing Ramirez's number.

"What the hell did you just send me?"

"That's the back of Mel's office, and the woman being abducted is Mel's daughter, Lindsey."

"Shit!"

"That same van was parked in front of the courthouse this morning. A white male, my guess thirties, watching from behind the wheel. Tore out of there when Tse pulled up on his bike. Looked straight at me as he drove off. Couldn't make the license number but it looked like a dealer plate. Black Ford cargo van. Looked new."

"Where are you?"

"On my way to the office. Wapi is waiting."

"I'll meet you there."

"She's been gone for near half an hour."

"I know. I'm putting out an APB right now."

I keep my eyes peeled on the road, scanning for a black cargo van on the off chance our paths cross. Wishful thinking.

Wapi looks wrecked when I pull up to the back door of the office, making sure not to cross the path I remember the cargo van taking.

"I just walked down the fuckin' street. The damn grilled chicken sandwich Lindsey wanted took forever. I should never have listened to her. *Fuck!*"

He slams his fist into the brick wall beside the door, busting his knuckles open.

"Hey!"

I grab him by the shoulders and pull him toward me.

"Lock that shit down," I hiss in his ear. "No one seriously thought Lindsey might be a target or we would've handled things differently. There was no reason to. Last thing she needs right now is you going off the deep end, brother, so keep it together."

He drops his head and nods.

"Ouray is on his way," he mumbles.

"Good. So is Ramirez. An APB has gone out, the cops are already looking. Let's not go off half-cocked and do this smart."

I let go of Wapi and take a step back. "Now go inside and clean up your hand."

The words are barely out of my mouth and two unmarked Durango PD vehicles turn into the parking lot. The first one out is Bill Evans, who stalks in my direction.

"That the box?" he asks without preamble.

He points at a large Amazon box leaning against the wall about eight feet from the door. I hadn't even noticed it.

"I guess."

He pulls latex gloves from his back pocket and covers his hands before he carefully touches a corner of the box. Then he studies the label as Ramirez steps up beside me.

"Box feels empty," Bill shares. "Address is East 10th Street."

"Garbage pickup was this morning," Ramirez contributes.

"Mel ordered a bunch of stuff online she was having delivered here. He's been watching."

Tony nods. "Makes sense, he sees deliveries being made, finds an empty box, pretends to be delivering it."

"I noticed on the video this is about the same distance he left the box at before he went to knock," Evans observes.

"A way to get her away from the door? He could've asked her to confirm the address," Ramirez suggests as he takes a few steps into the parking lot and pans around. "We need to start knocking on doors. See if we can find other businesses with security cameras that may have picked up a different angle of the van. Anything that shows even a partial plate. The van is the only concrete lead we have, and he could have ditched it already."

"Why Lindsey?" Wapi asks when he joins us.

Ramirez turns to him. "A bomb caused the explosion in the garage. Only reason I can think of is to draw

Mel out of hiding. Following that logic, whoever was watching may have caught some of the interaction when Paco showed up with Lindsey. Put two and two together and figured out she's Mel's daughter. Maybe he thinks she has information."

Evans strips off the gloves. "Or maybe he wants to use Lindsey as leverage to get at Mel. We need someone with her, in case she gets a call."

I swing around at the squeal of tires as Ouray's Yukon pulls into the parking lot. Behind him three bikes follow.

But it's Luna who is first out of the vehicle, marching up with an air of authority despite her short stature.

The FBI has arrived.

MEL

"I DON'T UNDERSTAND."

Luna leans forward with a sympathetic expression on her face.

"Lindsey knows you and the boy are here, Mel."

"She'd never tell."

"Can't take that chance, Mel, we have to assume the worst. If you stay here, we'd have to pull men off the search to secure this location and we need all the manpower to look for her. It's easier at the compound, it has more security features in place, plus there's always protection around." She grabs my hand. "It's no longer about staying out of sight; this is about safety."

Luna and Ouray showed up a few minutes ago with the announcement I have to pack our things because they're moving us. Trunk took Mason into his bedroom, but the boy's been upset since Paco tore out of here.

I'm so torn. Moving him again is going to further traumatize him, but staying here might put him in danger.

I wish Paco was here so I could discuss it with him, but he's out there, looking for my girl.

My God, Lindsey.

"I'll go, but Mason stays with me," I compromise, hoping at least that consistency will make yet another transition easier on the boy.

I'm so fucking scared I'm not sure I'm thinking straight enough to make that decision, but I have no choice.

"Absolutely."

It doesn't take me long to pack my bag. When I walk into Mason's room, he's sitting on the floor with Trunk, building a pirate ship with Lego bricks. It reminds me of all the stuff I ordered online, now sitting in my office. After hearing how someone managed to lure Lindsey out of the building, I wish I'd never ordered any of it.

I force down the hysteria I've been struggling to keep in check since finding out she's gone. I need to control my emotions, especially in front of Mason.

"Hey, buddy. Guess what?"

The look he throws me is a little uncertain.

"What?"

"We're going to stay at the clubhouse for a little while. Would you like that? You can visit with Kiara and see Lisa."

"Is Paco coming too?"

"He's a little busy now, but I'm sure he'll come see us when he can."

He needs to think on that for a moment before he nods.

"Let's pack up your things, okay?"

"Are we coming back?" he asks me worriedly.

"Yes, honey. We'll come back. It's just for a little while."

I hope to God it is.

I can't bring myself to think about what happens after, so I shove that to the back of my mind.

The phone in my pocket starts ringing, just as I carry Mason's bag into the living room. Panic immediately seizes me and I drop the bag to the floor as I scramble to get to my phone.

"Easy. Check call display first," Luna says, walking up to me.

It's an unknown number.

My heart is hammering out of my chest.

"Shit," Luna mumbles. "We don't have a trace set up yet, put it on speaker."

She throws a look in Trunk's direction, who's just walking in with Mason. He seems to catch on immediately and swiftly steers the boy to the back door.

The moment the door closes she nods at me.

"Hello?"

There's a brief pause before I hear, "You have something of mine. Now I have something of yours."

The line immediately goes dead and my heart stops.

Through the rushing in my ears, I can barely hear

Luna talk to someone on her phone.

The voice was a man's, although clearly distorted, but his tone was menacing. He has my daughter. My beautiful, smart, stubborn daughter.

What am I supposed to do with that message?

"How does he know this number?"

"He doesn't," Luna says, tucking her phone in her pocket. "Remember I told you we forwarded your office phone to your cell? Did you hear that hesitation before he said anything? He didn't expect you to answer. I wanna bet he had a message prepared to leave on voicemail and was startled when he got a live person on the line."

"I don't even understand what I'm supposed to do now. What does he want?"

I feel even more lost now. Even on my best days, I'm not good at sitting and waiting. Especially now that my daughter is in danger.

If she's even still alive.

No. I can't let my thoughts go there.

"He wants you to worry. He wants you scared so that when he calls again—and he will call again—you'll be ready to do anything he asks."

I nod my understanding, grabbing a firm hold of myself. I won't be doing Lindsey any good if I lose it now.

"We should go," Luna insists. "My team is meeting us at the clubhouse."

She waves Trunk and the boy inside.

To my surprise, it's not only Ouray waiting behind the wheel of his SUV but three of Paco's brothers on their bikes.

Trunk takes his own vehicle and Mason and I are hustled into the back seat of the Yukon. The boy immediately scoots over, his small body pressing against my side.

I lift my arm around his shoulders and rest my cheek on his head.

"It's going to be all right," I promise, even as the convoy heads straight for the road.

I hope to God I'm right.

ARROW'S EDGE MC

22

PACO

"HE'S MADE CONTACT."

I turn to Wapi, who is getting into the passenger side of the truck with two coffees. Ramirez is behind him and leans into the door.

"How?" I want to know, accepting one of the cups.

"According to Luna, Mel got a call as they were about to move her and the boy to the clubhouse. Unknown number."

"What did he want?"

"Something about Mel having something of his and him now having something of hers."

"He's talking about Mason."

Ramirez nods. "That's more than likely."

"No demands?"

"Nope. Luna thinks he was thrown off when Mel answered. Was expecting voicemail."

Wapi and I were driving around, looking for any signs of the van—there's little else to go on right now—when we spotted Ramirez going into the coffee shop, so I sent Wapi in after him to get an update.

"He's gonna call back," I conclude.

"That's what we figure."

"What's our next step?" I ask. "Any luck finding more footage?"

"The hotel across the road has a glimpse of the van coming out of the parking lot and turning left on Main. It's blurry but maybe it can be run through some filters."

That's right up my alley. Something useful I can do instead of driving around town aimlessly. It also gives me a chance to check in on Mel, she must be out of her mind.

"Do you have a copy?"

Ramirez pulls out his phone. "Emailed it to myself and Jasper Greene."

Jasper is a colleague of Luna's, the FBI's resident techie.

"Forward it to me as well, will you?"

Tony lifts a questioning eyebrow.

"I know Greene is good, but he also probably has his hands full right now. This is something I can help with."

"Fine, but let him know you're working on it. We've got so many players in this game—fucking Yelinek is also wanting a piece—we at least have to communicate with each other on what the hell we're doing."

"Fair enough," I agree, and I immediately hear the ping of an incoming email on my phone. "I'm heading to the clubhouse."

"And I have about five dealerships I need to hit up." Ramirez mock salutes as he backs away from the truck. "Stay in touch."

"Yeah. You too."

Most of the parking spots are taken when I pull up to the clubhouse. I'm assuming the vehicles I don't recognize belong to Luna's two teammates. Gomez is still recovering.

Wapi gets out of the truck before me and leads the way inside. I spot Mel right away, sitting at the large family table beside Mason, who is playing some game with Kiara. Wapi beats me to her.

"I'm so fucking sorry," I hear him say.

Mel immediately gets to her feet and pulls him away from the table and the kids.

"Nothing you did, Wapi," she says softly, keeping a hand on his arm.

"I shoulda—"

"Nothing," she interrupts him. "Nothing you could've done. We'll find her."

Mel's strength shines through as she reassures him, even though I know she doesn't feel half as confident as she sounds.

"Brother," I call his attention. "Go have a beer and stop kicking your own ass. Let me talk to Mel."

He nods and turns to the bar; Mel gives him a little pat on the back. He looks dejected.

"He's blaming himself," she observes as she turns to face me.

I immediately fold her in my arms and hers slip around my waist. If we weren't in this fucked-up situation I'd be thrilled for the public show of affection.

"That boy carries a lot of guilt. None of which he deserves," I tell her. "He blames himself for not looking for his sister, even though he was just a kid when she disappeared."

A few months ago a car was found in the Animas River with the remains of a young woman inside, who turned out to be Wapi's sister. She'd gone missing twenty years ago.

"He takes everything on his shoulders, but the club will sort him out."

"He's not the only one feeling guilt," she mumbles.

I straighten up and look down at her.

"Don't, Darlin'. Guilt may be the single most unproductive emotion we can feel. No good comes of it." I lightly brush her lips. "Now, heard about the call, how are you holding up?"

"Still standing," she says with an attempt at a smile, but agony in her eyes.

"I can see that." I turn my head to check on Mason. "How about him?"

"Kiara is doing a good job keeping him distracted."

Just then Mason turns his head and notices me. He's out of his chair in a flash and runs over to clamp on to my side.

"Hey, bud."

I let Mel go and bend down to pick him up, setting him on my hip.

"You're back."

"Of course I am. I'll always come back."

The little guy puts his head to my shoulder.

"Dinner in five!" Lisa calls out from the kitchen door. "Kiara, child, clear the table. Istu and Ezrah! Get your butts over here. Kitchen duty."

Ouray and Luna come walking from the back hallway. I'm sure Luna has her team set up in Ouray's office.

"Mel, here's your phone back."

Luna hands her the cell. I'm sure Jasper put on a tracker of some sort. I notice Mel holds it like it might bite her. I almost offer to hold on to it for her, but think better of it. If she needs me to take it from her, she'll ask.

She doesn't, instead holding it in one hand as she hooks her other arm in mine, leaning her weight against me for another kind of support. I press a kiss to the side of her head.

None of my brothers are commenting on Mel's and my obvious involvement, when normally they'd have gotten a kick out of ribbing me. The mood is somber during dinner, even among the kids. Normally meals in the clubhouse are a lively event but any conversation taking place is quiet and subdued.

Mel eats a little when Lisa urges her, she needs fuel for energy. Had it been me she might've snapped, but from Lisa she takes it. I don't care, as long as she eats.

After dinner she gets up when Lisa does and starts collecting dirty dishes.

"You don't have to do that."

She glances at me but continues what she's doing.

"I want to do something."

"Of course you do," Lisa coos, shooting me a hard look.

I read Lisa pretty well. "Butt out," that look says.

I'm not saying another word as they disappear into the kitchen, but five minutes later when a phone can be heard ringing, I'm out of my chair like a shot.

MEL

I ALMOST DROP the stack of plates I was just about to load into the dishwasher in my hurry to get to my phone.

Unknown number.

Paco comes storming in, closely followed by Luna. I hold up the phone so they can see the screen.

"Go ahead," she says. "The guys are monitoring."

I take in a deep breath and seek out Paco, holding his eyes as I answer the call.

"Hello?"

"I can't believe it. She's dead? What happened? These guys won't tell me anything."

The last person I expected.

"Shauna? Why are you calling? What are you talking about?"

"Kelly Forbes! I saw a bit on the news just now that they're looking for Zack? I can't believe it."

My mind is reeling, trying to process the information. It's not making any sense.

"You know Kelly?"

"Of course I do. Who do you think referred me to you?"

Luna is gesturing wildly just as I hear the ding of another call coming in.

"Shauna, I have to go."

I don't wait for her answer and switch to the other call.

"Hello?"

"Mom?"

A sob breaks free uncontrolled.

"Honey, oh, honey. Are you okay? Where are you?"

"Mom…" Suddenly her voice is muffled and I can only make out a few words. "…not who…think it is—"

A blood-curdling scream tears through my ears and rips at my heart.

"Lindsey!"

I feel Paco wrap an arm firmly around my middle just as my knees give out.

"You know what I want."

It's his voice, the same man from earlier.

"…Mom, don't do it!" I hear my daughter scream in the background, then a scuffle and a thud.

"You want to see your daughter again?" The voice is back and my blood runs cold. "Give me the boy."

"I don't have him," I whisper. "I don't know where he is."

I'm not sure where the lies come from, but right now, I wish they were true. I wish I didn't know where he was. I feel like I'm being torn in two.

"You expect me to believe that?"

"I swear—"

"Well, that's your problem. You have twenty-four hours to find him. I'll call with instructions."

"My daughter, please…" I plead, but I hear nothing but dead air.

He's hung up.

I drop the phone away from my ear and look up at Luna.

"You did good," she says right before she darts out of the kitchen.

Paco turns me around and folds me in his arms.

"You did great, Darlin'. They'll find her."

My mind is churning, going over every word of the phone call. Something is nagging at me.

I abruptly push off his chest.

"Lindsey tried to whisper something. I only got parts of it and it didn't make sense, but it must've been important or she wouldn't have taken the chance."

Maybe Luna's team was able to make it out. They set up my phone so they could hear every word. I start out of the kitchen but bump into Ramirez.

"Mel. He called?"

"Just now."

"Did the feds get anything?"

"Ouray's office," Paco says from right behind me.

I catch sight of Mason, who is sitting beside Kiara on the couch. There's a movie on the large screen TV but his head is turned my way. Walking over to him, I crouch down beside him.

"You all right, Mason?"

He nods.

"Good. You watch your movie, okay? I just have to go have a talk with Luna's friends."

I give his hair a little ruffle and head to Ouray's office where Ramirez is already talking with Luna.

"What's going on?"

Tony turns my way. "Just updating Luna. I talked to Yelinek, they were able to match a partial fingerprint on the file you gave him to Zack Forbes. We compared it to prints we were able to pull off the tape on the box left at your office. No match."

"But wouldn't a ton of people have handled that box?" I suggest. "Plus, he may have been wearing gloves."

"Actually, we concentrated on the clear tape used to seal over the Amazon tape. We checked with the residents at the address on the label. They confirm they'd cut through the original tape and left the empty box at the curb. So whoever picked it up—"

"Would've sealed it with clear tape," I finish for him.

"Right. There was a clear thumbprint on the sticky side, right at the edge of the tape. It doesn't belong to Forbes, and we have nothing that matches in the system."

My brain starts spinning again. So if it wasn't Forbes, maybe he has an accomplice? Lindsey's muffled words come back to me: *not who…think it is.*

Is she talking about her kidnapper?

"What if it's not Forbes who has her?" I suggest.

Jasper Greene speaks up. "I was just replaying that part and was wondering if that's what she was getting at."

"He could have an accomplice," Luna agrees.

"Or we may have been barking up the wrong tree from the start," comes from Ramirez. "I found two dealerships who sell the Ford Transit Connect, which is the van Paco saw outside the courthouse and the same one visible on the surveillance tape. One doesn't have any black ones in stock and the other was already closed. We're trying to track down the manager." He turns to Paco. "Had any luck with that license plate?"

"I'll get on that right now."

I realize Paco has been busy keeping an eye on me when he could've spent his time more usefully. I can't lean on him; I need to be stronger.

"You gonna be okay?" he mumbles beside me.

"I'm fine. Go."

"Which dealerships?" Jasper asks Ramirez as Paco leaves the room.

"The one across from Walmart, I think it's Durango Lincoln Ford, and then there's the one by Oxbow Park, north of town."

"Capital Auto?" Dylan wants to know.

Ramirez swings around to him. "Yes, how'd you figure?"

"It's one of the businesses owned by CM Holdings."

A light goes up when he mentions that name.

"Carlos Mesina," I blurt out. "That call from Shauna earlier—"

"You need to call her back," Jasper interrupts. "I heard her say she knew Kelly. We need to know how."

Luna is already talking on her phone.

"Put Mrs. Mesina on the line."

I guess she's talking to whomever is guarding Shauna.

"Mrs. Mesina, it's Agent Roosberg. I have a few questions but I'm gonna put you on speakerphone for a minute." She puts the phone on the table so we can all hear. "Shauna, are you there?"

"I'm here," I hear her answer.

"How did you know Kelly Forbes?"

"She and I went to high school together."

"So you stayed friends?"

"Not really. We lost touch until her husband came to work for Carlos. We had lunch every so often."

My eyes dart around the room. Everyone seems surprised by that piece of information.

"What kind of work did Zack Forbes do for your husband?"

"Sold cars, I guess. He was hired on at the new car dealership."

"Capital Auto," Luna offers.

"Yes. I bumped into Kelly at the grand opening."

"Were your husband and her husband close? Did you ever socialize as couples?"

Shauna barks out a laugh. "Dear God, no. Carlos would never socialize with his employees."

"So it was just you and Kelly who were friends? Did she ever mention anything to you about her marriage?"

"Plenty," Shauna confirms right away. "We commiserated a lot, since I wasn't exactly in a dream marriage. But I didn't know he beat her until maybe a week before the shit hit the fan. She told me she wanted to leave him but she had to time it right. Next thing I knew, she was in the hospital and he was in jail."

"Is that when she recommended Ms. Morgan to you?"

"That was toward the end of the trial. She said she'd be leaving right after and wanted to start over. Told me if I wanted out of my marriage to give Mel a call. So that's what I did."

"Shauna, Agent Dylan Barnes here," he pipes up. "By chance did you ever discuss your suspicions around your husband's business dealings with Kelly?"

Great question, that might create motive for Mesina to go after Kelly. But if that's the case, then who the hell has my daughter and wants Kelly's son?

Mesina is locked up tight.

ARROW'S EDGE MC

23

MEL

"THAT WAS EVANS. He's bringing in Guillermo Peña, manager of Capital Auto," Ramirez announces after getting off the phone. "I'm heading to the station."

"Mind if I sit in?" Agent Barnes asks.

"Be my guest."

The two men walk out of the office, leaving Ouray, Luna, Jasper Greene, and myself.

"Did you get anything from the phone call?" I ask Greene.

He shares a glance with Luna and a silent conversation takes place before he answers.

"Not long enough to pinpoint a location. I'm sorry," he adds. "But I haven't had time to analyze the call yet. There might be some background noise I can lift out that could be helpful."

"In the meantime," Luna takes over. "Given what your daughter tried to convey, I think we should see if possibly someone other than Forbes was responsible for Kelly's death."

"How do you suggest we do that?" I ask, grateful to maybe be able to help. Beats sitting around and waiting.

The other woman's eyes are sympathetic and the pause is long—too long—when I finally clue in.

"Oh hell, no. He's been through enough."

Luna shakes her head. "He's the only one who could bring clarity on that question."

"He's only six. Who's to say he even got a good look?" I protest, every motherly instinct in me revolting.

"Or maybe he can eliminate one, or both, and we wouldn't be wasting time chasing down false leads. Valuable time Lindsey may not have."

Damn. That's below the belt, even if it's true.

And here I am, forced to choose between one child or another. It's impossible.

Paco already looked at Forbes's picture but all he'd been able to say was he couldn't tell for sure if Forbes was the guy in the van.

"We'll have Trunk sit in," Ouray suggests. "Let him guide the process. The boy seems to trust him as well and it would leave you as his safe place."

I press the heels of my hands in my eyes, rubbing vigorously. Damned if I do, damned if I don't.

"Okay."

The confirmation is barely audible but Jasper already

has the printer spitting up their pictures.

I go to fetch Mason who is still on the couch beside Kiara, both now snacking from a bowl of popcorn. I catch the time on the clock and am shocked at how much time has already passed. Dinner was earlier than normal, for me at least, but it's still already about bedtime for Mason.

"Hey, kiddo. Could you come with me for a minute?" He looks uneasily over my shoulder, almost as if he knows something is up. "I'd love for you to help me with something."

I feel so fucking guilty putting the kid through this, especially when he gets up immediately at my request. I try for a reassuring smile at him, even though I know I'm walking him into a situation where he has to relive the absolute worst day of his very young life.

It had been Ouray's suggestion to use Trunk's office, since the boy is familiar with that room, so I lead him there. Trunk is already inside, finishing the setup of a small camera, mainly so Luna and Jasper can see and hear Mason in real time without the need to be in the room.

"Hey, Mason," Trunk rumbles, giving the boy a wink before nodding at me.

"Come sit here with me." I tug Mason down on the couch beside me. "Do you know what's going on?"

"Lindsey is gone," he announces, confirming kids absorb information even when you think you're being careful.

"Yes. And we think maybe you can help us find out

where she went."

That seems to pique his interest.

"How?"

Trunk sits down across from us and takes over.

"Remember a few days ago when we were talking about your mom?"

Immediately Mason's back curves as he seems to make himself smaller. I scoot closer and lift my arm around him, letting him lean into my body.

He nods. "Mhm."

"You told me what happened to her and that was very helpful. But now I wonder if I showed you two pictures, would you be able to tell me if you ever saw the people in them before?"

Mason nods again, a little more eagerly.

Trunk handled that much smarter than I would've. He avoids asking the boy directly if the man who killed his mother was in either of the pictures, and instead simply asks if he recognizes them.

He grabs the pictures from his desk and puts them on the coffee table in front of the boy, who studies both images carefully.

Before he even answers, I already know neither of those men killed his mother or he would've reacted to them.

Trunk taps the image of Forbes first. "Have you ever seen him?"

Mason was little when his father was incarcerated so it's unlikely he remembers him and I'm convinced Kelly wouldn't have kept pictures of him around. Still, Mason hesitates slightly, but doesn't seem upset in any way.

"No."

Trunk flips the Forbes's picture upside down and points at Carlos Mesina.

"And him?"

A much more immediate reaction to that one with a firm shake of his head.

"That was great, Mason. Thank you."

Trunk nods at me and I turn to the boy.

"Did you want to watch the end of the movie with Kiara?"

"And popcorn?" he asks.

"Absolutely. But after the movie, it's bedtime and you have to brush your teeth really well."

"Okay."

He slips off the couch and heads for the door, not even looking twice at the pictures.

"Forbes's picture may have looked familiar to him. He seemed to look at that one more closely," Trunk confirms my own thoughts when Mason disappears down the hall. "But I'm convinced neither of those men killed Kelly."

I'd have to agree.

When I walk back into Ouray's office, my mood is gloomy and it doesn't get better the next twenty or so minutes, as I sit there feeling useless as a bump on a log while everyone else seems to be busy with something.

"Come on," Ouray says, holding out his hand to pull me out of my chair. "We're gonna have a drink."

I shake my head. "I can't, what if—"

"One drink," he insists. "Just enough to take the edge

off but not enough to impair your judgment."

I hesitate just for a moment before I give in and let him guide me to the bar. I notice in passing Mason is already half asleep on the couch. One drink and I'm putting that boy to bed.

Maybe I'll lie down with him for a bit.

Mason is so tired by the time I take him to bed; I don't bother making him brush his teeth. I quickly help him into his pajamas and then straight to bed.

"Mel?"

"Yeah, kiddo."

"Will Lindsey come back?"

I lie down beside him, still fully dressed, and pull him against me, brushing a kiss to his forehead.

"She will," I state firmly.

I wish I felt as convinced as I sound.

PACO

MY EYES FUCKING hurt from staring at the screen so intently.

I pinch the bridge of my nose and squeeze them shut for a second before focusing on the image I've been able clean up a little.

The three vertical letters on the left side of the plate confirm they're a dealer's. I've been able to clean up enough to make out the first two digits, but the camera angle makes it difficult to decipher the rest.

There's a knock on the door and Honon sticks his head in.

"How's it going?"

I'm in the basement of the clubhouse, in a fireproof room. Almost like a vault. Back in the club's old days different types of contraband would be stored here. We weren't choirboys and it wasn't uncommon for us to be involved in one club war or another.

This clubhouse has been firebombed, and shot up more than a few times. As recent as a few years ago someone launched a rocket into the building, injuring Tse and Momma, who almost died. But this room stood through all of that, which is why we keep anything important in here. Including a battery of computers and a wall of screens that access security systems not only of the compound, but for every business we own.

This is my domain.

"Come in here and see if you can make out more than I can. I don't think I can clean it up any better."

I roll my chair out of the way so Honon can take a closer look.

"Dealer plate. Seven, five, and I think that's a three. Or maybe an eight. Can't see the rest of it."

That's a bit more than I had.

"Are you going to run a check?" Honon wants to know.

"I'd have to have more than two or three digits. I'll take it to the guys upstairs; they can probably pull it right up."

I shove a key into the computer and copy what I have up on the screen. Then I follow Honon upstairs.

"You gonna come have a beer?"

I'd love a beer but more than that I want to check on Mel.

"Is Mel up there?"

"She had a drink, went to put the boy to bed, and I haven't seen her after. Not sure if she crashed as well, or is in with the feds."

"I think I'll keep my head clear," I tell him, opening the door to Ouray's office.

Mel isn't in here so I assume she's in the bedroom next door. Luna and Jasper are the only ones in here, both bent over laptops.

"I have a partial plate," I announce, handing the USB key to Luna, since Jasper has headphones in and seems very focused on his computer screen.

She sticks it in a port on her laptop and pulls up the cleaned-up image.

"Seven, five, and that looks like a three or an eight. Let me see what I can dig up."

I take a seat across from her and glance at the wall clock. Almost eleven.

"Where did Ramirez go?"

"Police station with Barnes. Evans found the manager of the dealership and pulled him in for questioning. Hoping to hear something soon."

The printer in the middle of the table starts spewing paper.

"It won't allow me to put additional filters on the search, so we'll have to go over them manually. I'm printing out both combinations. Don't bother looking at names at first, just look at city and if you find anything in

La Plata County, only check those. It's faster."

There are a lot of fucking dealer plates starting with those digits. She hands me a stack.

"I'm curious," I bring up as I start scanning the addresses using my finger as a guide. "What is Mesina going down for?"

"You mean aside from shooting a federal agent?" She's referring to her boss, Damian Gomez. "Money laundering, drug trafficking, we suspect him of murder but don't have sufficient evidence to charge him with that. Yet," she adds, her eyes peeking over her screen.

"So I assume you've investigated this CM Holdings?"

"Yep. And every business registered under that name. We spent months scrutinizing each one of them. Two of them we came up empty; the Silver Dollar in Hermosa, and—"

"Capital Auto," I fill in.

"Exactly. And if we can tie this van to Capital Auto, I'll be having a midnight chat with Carlos Mesina."

I've underlined three addresses and I'm down to the last two pages when I hit on another one in Durango.

"Bingo." Luna looks up at me. "License plate seven-five-eight-E-F-D, listed to Capital Auto."

She reaches out and takes the sheet from my hand, checking the information.

Then she grabs her phone.

"Dylan, how are things going there? …Really. That's interesting, since we didn't find a van on his property." She glances at me. "Oh he's into this up to his neck. I think it's time to ask Mr. Mesina a few questions. Wanna meet me there?"

When she hangs up, she taps Jasper, who takes his headphones off.

"Mesina took the van from the dealership about three weeks ago, according to the manager, claiming he needed to move some furniture, but he never brought it back. I'm meeting Dylan downtown now." Luna gets up. "Keep on the recording. Knowing Mesina he'll clam up and demand his lawyer be present."

With nothing else to do, I duck into the bedroom to check on Mel and the boy.

For a moment I think she's sleeping with Mason half-draped over her body, but then her eyes open and she looks straight at me.

"I thought you were out," I say softly.

She holds out her hand and I fit myself to her other side on the bed, slipping my arm under her head.

"I keep hearing her scream."

I press my lips to the side of her head.

"We've made some progress."

Her head tilts back. "Yeah?"

"Jasper is still working on the audio, but we've been able to tie the license plate on the van back to Mesina."

She shakes her head. "But he's been locked up, he must have someone doing the dirty work for him."

"Likely," I agree.

"But why? What's his motivation? I can't make heads or tails of it."

Mason moans a little and shifts restlessly.

Immediately Mel turns her attention to the boy, but

after a few moments he settles in again.

"Did Luna tell you?" she asks.

"What?"

"We ended up showing him pictures of both Forbes and Mesina. Trunk was there and handled it very carefully," she hurries to add when she catches the expression on my face. "He said he didn't recognize either of them, although he paused a little on Forbes's picture."

"So Forbes didn't kill his mother," I deduce.

"And neither did Mesina. Or Mason wouldn't have reacted indifferently to his picture."

There has to be a connection somewhere. Something that links Mesina to Forbes and to his ex-wife and child. I glance over at the boy, who has his bunny tucked under his chin and is snuggled up against Mel.

If someone other than Forbes is after the boy, it's likely because the boy can identify that person.

They don't just want the boy—they want the boy dead.

24

PACO

I SHOOT UPRIGHT at the soft knock on the door.

Mel is sleeping and Mason is still out too, but Cookie lifts her head from the foot of the bed.

I roughly rub the sleep from my eyes and swing my legs over the side of the bed, trying not to jostle them too much.

Luna is on the other side of the door.

"Sorry to wake you, but we've had a development I thought you'd wanted to be in on. We need all the manpower."

The office behind her is empty.

"We moved it to the main room. Ouray is getting everyone up."

"Should I wake Mel?"

She glances at the door I closed behind me and I notice the dark circles under her eyes. I bet she hasn't caught a wink of sleep.

"If she's sleeping, let her sleep for now. Nothing she'll be able to do anyway and I'm staying behind to coordinate, I'll explain when she wakes up."

I follow her through the clubhouse to find most everyone assembled. Even Lisa is already bustling around the kitchen, making a large vat of coffee, and Nosh is sitting at one of the smaller tables. A glance at the clock shows just past four in the morning.

Behind me Wapi comes stumbling in, looking almost green. He must've put away a few last night.

"You look like fucking hell," Ouray comments, catching sight of him. "Go back to bed."

"No," Wapi firmly defies him. "I'm fine and I'm in."

He gets a long hard stare from our president but to his credit, Wapi doesn't waver.

"Okay, now that I have everyone here," Luna calls out. "Jasper was able to filter out the sound of a train whistle in the background of the perp's call last night."

"The Durango-Silverton line," Honon suggests.

"Yes," Luna confirms. "The last train is scheduled to come into Durango at six. The phone call came in at five forty-five. Jasper did some calculations based on the volume, the speed the train travels, and the time, and figures the call came from somewhere within this area."

On the large table is an enlarged map of Durango, a section of the railroad marked with a highlighter.

"We think Lindsey is held somewhere within this

five-mile stretch running from approximately the turnoff for the River Bend Ranch, south to East 21st Street." She looks up. "Kaga, Tse, Yuma, and Trunk are on their way, and here we have Honon, Paco, Ouray, Lusio, Nodin, and Wapi. That's ten brothers. Plus my two guys and Ramirez and Evans, who are bringing two uniforms, makes for sixteen. Four groups of four. Nosh and Brick will stay here at the clubhouse."

With a marker she sets out a perimeter around the highlighted stretch of railway on the map. Then she divides it in four sections, two on either side of the Animas River, along which the railroad runs.

"Evans and Ramirez will be heading up these sections." She points at the northern two. "They'll meet you at the fairgrounds."

She continues to allocate Jasper and Dylan to the south sections and proceeds to split the rest of us into teams. It takes her less than five minutes to get us organized and instructed on what to look for. By this time my remaining brothers have arrived.

Not one single person questions the authority that seems to come naturally to Luna, and I catch Ouray observing his wife with a proud smirk on his face. She is certainly stepping up to the plate in the absence of SAC Gomez.

I estimate each of the stretches marked on the map is two-and-a-half miles long and covers everything between Highway 550 and the river on the west side and the river and County Road 250 on the east side. That's a fuckload of terrain to cover. Especially on the south end where it approaches the downtown core.

"What happened with Mesina?" I ask Luna as everyone starts filing out of the clubhouse.

"We grilled him. Confronted him with the van and he claimed it was stolen. When asked why he hadn't reported it, he shrugged. When we brought up Forbes working for him, he pretended not to remember him. Then he asked for his lawyer to be present if we had any more questions."

"So you didn't get far."

"Nope. But I'm hoping to go back in there later this morning, once I get hold of his lawyer. That is, if you guys haven't found her by then."

"Fuckin' hope so."

"Paco! Coming?"

I'd love to at least let Mel know where I'm going. I don't like the idea of her waking up with me gone, but everyone's already outside and Ouray is waiting.

"Go on. I've got Mel," Luna says, giving me a shove toward the door.

EVEN WITH THE four us searching, it's slow going.

This part of Durango is part residential and part industrial. We're looking for any sign of the van and check empty stores and houses, any kind of structure where Lindsey could be held with minimal risk of anyone hearing her.

It's getting lighter out here. Pretty soon people are

gonna start getting up and heading out. I'm thinking that won't make the search any easier. Still, being out here doing something beats hanging around the clubhouse twiddling my thumbs.

"What's down there?" Honon points to the end of the residential street we're combing.

"Playground," Jasper answers. "That building houses the bathrooms."

"I mean behind the playground. See that roof line? Can't see much more than that."

It takes me a minute before I see it. All you can see is the peak of a roof. It looks like the building is sitting lower than the playground where the ground dips down toward the river.

"Let's go check it out," Jasper announces.

Ouray, who is our fourth, comes walking out of an alley he was checking which runs parallel to the street.

The four of us cross over to the playground, which looks to be pretty new. A four-foot chain-link fence borders the far side of the park and beyond that is a pretty sharp drop off toward the water. It's easy to see what Honon was pointing at from here. It looks like a maintenance shed. Maybe it belongs to the railway. It's only about two hundred feet from the tracks.

The van doesn't look to be there, but when I sneak around to the other side of the shed, there's a dirt road running north along the tracks before it appears to veer left, back toward the main road.

I'm guessing the shed is maybe twelve by twelve feet and aside from the door, it has only one window. Jasper shines a penlight to try and peek through the blinds covering it. I step up behind him.

"I can't make out much," he says in a low voice.

Honon disappears around the corner. We follow him and watch as he examines the padlock on the door. Then he pulls a zippered wallet from his pocket and selects a couple of the slim tools inside.

"Jesus Christ," Jasper mumbles. "Only you guys would go on an FBI search with goddamn lock picks in your pocket."

Honon throws him a grin, not in the least concerned.

A few seconds later the lock clicks open.

The first thing we see when he eases back the door is a dirty mattress and some bedding on the floor.

MEL

"ANYTHING?"

Luna looks up from her laptop.

I'm probably a sight, I literally woke up, jumped out of bed, and ran into Ouray's office. My hair, I'm sure, is its usual bird's nest and I wouldn't be surprised if I have dried drool on my face.

Luna doesn't seem to care.

"A few things. Paco is out helping my team. Why don't you go grab a coffee and something to eat and I'll update you."

"Did you see Mason?"

Neither he, nor Paco, or the dog were in bed when I woke up.

"In the kitchen with Lisa."

Coffee would probably be good. I'll need something to clear my head. My mind is groggy, and I feel slightly disoriented. I didn't expect to sleep. Hell, I didn't really want to sleep, and now I feel guilty. I know everyone will say I'm of more use when rested—something I might've said myself to someone else—but it feels wrong when my daughter might be hurt out there somewhere.

I'm halfway out the door when the phone, still in my pocket, rings. My heart almost jumps from my chest. I scramble to pull it free as Luna rushes to my side.

The display says Beth.

"It's my sister," I tell her, as I silence the call and tuck the phone back in my pocket.

"You're not going to take that?"

"That would set off a chain of events I can't handle right now."

I shove it back in my pocket and make my way into the clubhouse.

"Mel!"

Mason sees me before I see him and comes flying toward me.

"Morning, kiddo."

"I was really quiet so I wouldn't wake you."

I kiss his forehead.

"That was nice of you. Have you been up long?"

"About half an hour," Lisa says from the kitchen doorway. "And he's already had breakfast. Come in here and I'll get you a coffee and something to eat."

She turns, fully expecting me to follow her.

"Coffee would be great, but I don't know if I—"

She glances over her shoulder and says, "You will eat," in a tone that dismisses any argument.

My phone rings again. Beth, *Jesus*. Silencing the call once more, I wait for Lisa to pour me a cup.

I feel a pang of guilt ignoring my sister, but I'm not sure I'd survive a round with my family. I'm barely standing as it is and I need to focus on Lindsey.

That first hit of caffeine is heavenly. Lisa shoves a plate with a muffin, which is still steaming, and a banana in front of me.

"Light fare. Easy to digest."

Thank God, I don't think I could've handled anything more than that. My stomach is in knots anyway.

"Thank you. Do you mind if I take it back with me?"

Standing at the counter, she waves her hand over her shoulder.

"Go. I've got the boy."

I turn to Mason, who has taken a seat at the kitchen table where he is coloring a picture of a dinosaur.

"You be good for Lisa, okay, Mason? I'm just going to get cleaned up a little."

He nods without looking up. His tongue peeks out from between his lips as he concentrates on staying inside the lines.

I catch sight of the clock on my way out of the kitchen. It's a little after nine, only eight and a half hours left.

Eight and a half hours to save my daughter.

"They're all out searching. We think she's being kept somewhere along the Durango-Silverton line in or just north of town," Luna says when I sit down across from her at the table.

She could be right under my nose.

"Can I do anything?"

"You can eat something while I get in touch with Guillermo Peña. He's the manager at the dealership. I want to find out exactly what the nature of the relationship between Forbes and Mesina is. Or if Forbes was close to anyone else working there at the time. If need be, we're going to call every last one of the employees."

"I'll help with that."

She smiles at me but I can see the fatigue etched on her face.

"Good, in the meantime you eat and listen in—two sets of ears are better than one—I'll put it on speaker."

"Peña."

"Mr. Peña, this is Special Agent Luna Roosberg. You spoke with Detective Ramirez and my partner, Special Agent Barnes, last night."

"Yes?"

"I have just a few follow-up questions for you, if you don't mind."

It's silent for a moment.

"Okay," he says hesitantly. Clearly, he doesn't like being put on the spot.

She starts easy; what kind of boss was Mesina, did he show his face often? She does the same for Forbes; was he a good employee, did he get along with his colleagues?

Then she asks him if he ever noticed his boss and Forbes interacting.

"I'm not sure what you mean."

"Did Carlos Mesina ever ask Zack to do any work outside of the dealership?"

"I just remember a couple of times he asked Zack to drive him somewhere."

"During work hours?" Luna probes, while giving me a thumbs-up. "What about after work?"

"I don't know about after hours. All I can tell you is I wasn't happy to have one of my guys 'borrowed' for the day."

"Understandable," Luna sympathizes. "One more question, after Forbes was incarcerated, did anyone else drive Mesina occasionally? Another employee who would chauffeur for him?"

"Not that I recall."

I hear the lie, just as Luna does.

"Well, I appreciate your time, Mr. Peña. We know where to find you if we have any further questions."

"Yeah, sure."

Mesina had Forbes drive him. Why? Was Forbes muscle or something? Like a bodyguard?

Still, there has to be someone else, someone who tossed Kelly's body in the water. Someone who has my daughter. We're still no closer than we were.

"I need more coffee," Luna says, getting up from the table. "And then I need to find a way to get Mesina to talk to me."

"I'm gonna quickly clean up," I announce, heading for the bedroom.

I feel a little more human when I've splashed some

water on my face, brushed my teeth, and tamed my hair. I'm just changing into clean clothes when Luna pokes her head in.

"Mel, you should…Shit. Sorry," she mumbles closing the door.

"It's fine," I assure her, pulling the shirt over my head. "What's going on?"

"You have visitors."

Oh, fuck no.

25

PACO

"RIGHT FUCKING NEXT to a playground."

Ouray shakes his head in disgust. A sentiment I think we all feel.

We're standing outside the shed, wasting valuable time while waiting for the Durango PD to arrive. Aside from the dirty old mattress, all we found inside was a three-legged old side table covered in drug paraphernalia. Burnt spoons, the stump of a fat candle, bits of tinfoil, used condoms and wrappers, and discarded needles. Someone's been using the shed as a place to shoot up.

We can't leave the shed unattended for obvious reasons and frustration wreaks havoc with my blood pressure. I want to be out there looking.

"Here they come," Jasper announces.

Two uniformed officers hoist themselves over the chain-link fence bordering the playground. Just as Jasper starts walking up to them, my phone vibrates in my pocket.

It's Brick.

"Yo, what's up?"

"May not be a bad idea to get your ass over here. We've got a bit of a situation at the clubhouse."

When I walk in twenty minutes later, Mel is in a standoff with her sister and brother-in-law, who apparently barged in looking for answers. I could hear Beacham's booming voice outside.

"Thought you were gonna look after them," Scott Beacham snaps when he catches sight of me.

Ignoring him, I place myself between him and Mel, who looks ready to lose it.

"Hey," I draw her attention. "You okay?"

Despite the stubborn set of her mouth, her eyes shine with barely contained tears.

"No," she says in a strangled voice. "They called my fucking parents."

Then she does a face plant against my chest.

Over her head I spot Mason peeking out from the kitchen, Lisa hovering behind him.

"Brick, you wanna show them to Trunk's office? We're not gonna do this in front of the kid. Mel and I will be right there."

My brother herds the couple to the back, while I tuck Mel under my arm and head for the kitchen.

"Hey, bud," I address the boy, who looks plain scared.

I let go of Mel and pick the boy up, setting him on my hip but he has his eyes on Mel.

"Is he a bad man too?"

"No, kiddo," Mel hurries to answer. "Those people are Lindsey's aunt and uncle. That man is a firefighter, he's not a bad man."

"He was yelling at you."

"Hey." I force him to look at me. "Sometimes grown-ups yell when they're scared, or worried."

"Or upset?" the kid adds.

"Yeah, or upset. It doesn't make them bad people."

"Oh."

"Do you think you can hang with Lisa for a bit longer? We'll just be down the hall."

"Okay."

As soon as I set him down, he heads to the table, climbs up on a chair, and picks up a crayon. Apparently, when you're six years old it's as simple as that.

"All right." I take Mel's hand and pull her out of the kitchen. "Tell me what happened."

"Beth tried calling a few times but I ignored her. Next thing I know, they're in the clubhouse. Scott somehow heard about Lindsey missing and when they couldn't get hold of me, they came looking."

It's not surprising he found out. The community of first responders is a fairly tight one. I can't really blame them for being upset, but they're going to have to get over that. To be honest, I didn't even think of contacting Scott, and I'm pretty sure Mel's had her mind on more important things as well.

"And what's this about your parents?"

Mel shakes her head. "They're supposedly coming here on the first flight they can get."

Lovely. We're in for some family drama.

"Okay, let's have a talk with Scott and your sister."

"You don't have to do this, you know?" Mel says, more mellow than I'm used to from her, but I can hear despair in her voice.

She's already barely hanging on.

I simply tighten my hold on her hand and start walking to Trunk's office. Brick is standing guard outside the door, only nodding as he steps out of the way.

Scott shoots to his feet when we walk into the room.

"I demand to know what's going on."

His wife has tear tracks down her face. I can see the familial similarities with Mel, but her sister has short, dyed hair, and dresses more conventionally.

"Yesterday afternoon, someone abducted your niece from the office," I start, trying to insert calm into my voice.

"Yesterday?" He turns to Mel with angry eyes. "And you didn't think we deserved notification?"

Mel opens her mouth to retort, but closes it when I give her hand a firm squeeze. Whatever the beef is in this family, this isn't the time for it.

"We've been a little preoccupied trying to find her," I point out. "That's been the focus, the *only* priority."

"But who would take her? Why?"

I glance at Mel, looking for guidance from her.

"Whoever it is wants a little boy we have in our care,"

Mel takes over.

"The little boy in the kitchen?" her sister pipes up in a timid voice.

"Mason, yes. He's only six and witnessed his mother's murder."

"Jesus fucking Christ," Scott mumbles, running an agitated hand through his hair. Then he turns to me. "That your kid?"

I shake my head but he still eyes me suspiciously.

"So why Lindsey?" Beth asks, as if her husband hadn't spoken.

"His mother was a client of mine. Whoever has her thinks I know where the boy is."

"Who has her?" Scott wants to know.

"That's what we're working on," I respond. "Mel got a phone call last night giving her twenty-four hours to produce the boy in exchange for her daughter."

"Oh no…" Beth mutters, wringing her hands in her lap.

"We've been out searching, hoping to find her before he calls again, but we don't have a lot of time left." I catch Scott's eyes and hold them. "No offense, but we really don't have time or brain space to deal with interruptions."

"Then what the fuck are we waiting for?" Scott says, moving to the door. "Let's go find her."

I glance over at Mel, who nods, and I bend down to brush a kiss on her lips.

"Call me if you need me."

"Go." She waves me out of the office.

I leave her to deal with her sister while I hurry to catch up with Scott.

Mel

BETH LOOKS AT me, her eyes red-rimmed.

I steel myself or I'll turn into a blubbering mess myself and I can't afford to right now.

"I need you to deal with Mom and Dad," I tell her. "Keep them away from here. They'll create more problems than they solve. Please," I add.

She nods, sniffing. "I'll call them now. See if I can keep them from getting on a plane, but you know how they are."

Unfortunately I do. All too well. For all their faults, they dote on their three granddaughters, Beth's two girls and Lindsey. So they'll want to come, for Linds, and they'll blame me for not notifying them right away. Another mark against the family's black sheep.

"Please," I plead again, mental exhaustion taking over. "I don't care how, but keep them away from me."

Beth leans forward and takes my hands.

"Don't worry about them, I've got your back. You just concentrate on finding your girl."

The uncharacteristic show of support sticks like a giant lump in my throat, making it impossible to speak, so I just nod.

"Let me know when they find her," she says, getting to her feet.

When. She said when, not if, a show of confidence I

desperately clasp on to.

"I will." I stand up as well. "Right away," I promise.

I suddenly find myself wrapped in a tight hug before she darts out the door. Taking a moment to compose myself, I find her already gone by the time I make my way into the clubhouse. I do a quick check on Mason, who seems happy enough in the kitchen with Lisa, and head back to join Luna.

"Did you get that sorted?"

"Yeah. Or rather, Paco did. Guess Brick called him right away when they showed up. He's off now with Scott, back to the search."

"That man loves you fierce."

My knee-jerk response is to deny, but the truth is I know he does. He's the only man I have ever trusted enough to hold me up.

"Yeah."

"I always hoped he'd find someone worthy. He's a good man. I'll wait 'til this is over before I grill you on your intentions with him."

She teases an unexpected smile from me. I love that he has people looking out for him.

"I'll be ready."

With a nod, she abruptly changes topics to tell me she's been trying to get hold of Redfern but according to his assistant, he'll be out of the office all day in meetings.

"He's stalling," I observe.

"I know. And Mesina won't say anything without him there. The best I could get from Redfern's assistant was that she'd let him know I need to speak with him urgently."

As if on cue, Luna's phone starts ringing. She gives me a hopeful look but then she glances at her phone and shakes her head.

She puts the call on speakerphone and sets it on the table.

"Roosberg."

"Agent Roosberg, Detective Ramirez told me I should give you a call. I understand you're dealing with an abduction?"

"Yes, so I would appreciate it if you could keep it short."

"No problem. I believe we found Zachary Forbes."

I lock eyes with Luna over the table.

"You think?"

"Well, the body isn't exactly fresh."

"He's dead?"

"Very. Found the body early this morning. The coroner says he's been dead at least a week but likely longer. Autopsy is scheduled for tomorrow morning and we'll get some more information and hopefully confirmation, but I've seen the body and I feel confident we've found Mr. Forbes."

I listen with only half an ear as Yelinek goes on to share the man was shot and left in a gulley on the side of the road about fifteen miles south of Moab. My mind immediately goes to Mason, who is now an orphan. Not that his father was any kind of parent.

Forbes couldn't have had anything to do with Lindsey's abduction. In hindsight, the whole thing seems a little too well-planned and clever for the likes of him.

"Then who is behind this?" I voice.

"I wish I could tell you," Yelinek says. "I'm about to drive out to Blanding shortly. Harlan Farrell—Kelly's landlord—is finally back from his vacation and I'm hoping maybe he can remember something helpful. It's not much, but it's all I have right now."

"Let us know?" This from Luna. "Anything you find out; I don't care how insignificant it seems. We're on a timeline here."

"Yes, I heard. That's why I'm heading out right now. I'll do what I can, Ms. Morgan," he solemnly directs at me.

"Appreciated," I tell him, swallowing hard.

After the call, I hang around the office for a little while, but waiting around with nothing to occupy me is getting on my nerves, so I head for the kitchen, hoping for something to do.

I find Mason on the big couch sitting beside Nosh. The two of them are watching some game show on TV and I take a moment to give the boy a hug. His little arms around my neck make me feel a little better.

Nosh taps my arm and I turn to look at him.

"They'll find her," he says in that monotone voice I've only heard once or twice.

I appreciate the words and mouth, "Thank you," before letting Mason go and heading for the kitchen.

Lisa is chopping vegetables.

"Have something for me to do?" I ask her.

She immediately hands me the knife she's holding.

"We're making a large pot of chili. Finish cutting these up while I rinse the beans."

By the time Luna pokes her head in, it's midafternoon and I'm having a cup of tea Lisa made for us. I feel like I have a gaping hole in my stomach, but I couldn't bring myself to eat anything. The more time passes without any news, the more nauseated I get.

"Yelinek called," she announces. "The landlord says he was about ready to head to the airport to fly to Florida for his cruise when two men came by the house. They were looking for Kelly, who wasn't home at the time. They didn't leave a name or a reason and he left a note up in her apartment to give her a heads-up someone had been by. He was able to identify one of the men as Zach Forbes. The second guy was better dressed, dark hair, about six two and fit, his guess is around forty to forty-five."

Carlos Mesina is dark-haired but balding, which is something I'm sure would've been noticed. He's also five ten at best and far from fit.

"Not Mesina," I point out.

"No," Luna agrees. "Does that description match anyone you know?"

Ha. It's not exactly much to go by. I come across a surprising number of dark-haired, six foot two, early to mid-forties guys.

"No one that jumps out at me."

"Cookie, no!" I hear Mason yell inside the clubhouse.

Luna turns to look and I slip past her to find Mason sitting on the floor, Cookie beside him wagging her tail.

"Did she bite you?" I ask, even though I have a hard time believing that fluff of a dog would ever harm Mason. She seems very attached to him.

"No," the boy says, his voice sad as he holds up his bunny.

One ear is missing.

"Oh, I can fix that," I tell him, taking the stuffed animal from his hand. "I bet you Lisa has a needle and some thread somewhere. I'll put him back together."

I look around him for the missing part.

"Where is his ear?"

Mason points at the dog and I can just see a few threads hanging from her teeth.

"Cookie, come here," I order the dog.

Unfortunately, she's not that eager to give up her prize and it takes the combined efforts of Brick, Nosh, a by now giggling Mason, and myself to corner the playful dog.

I manage to pry her small jaw open and fish out the slobber-covered bunny ear.

"There. Now let's fix this," I announce as I get to my feet and clench my hand around the appendage.

I immediately open my hand and study it, peering into the severed end.

"Luna!"

She comes running up. "What is it?"

I stick my finger inside the ear and pull out a USB key.

26

MEL

"MY LAPTOP ISN'T recognizing the key," Luna mumbles, frustrated. "I'm calling Jasper back."

I glance at the clock and note it's already getting close to four o'clock. Less than two hours left.

The moment I realized what I was holding in my hand, I knew we'd found the key, quite literally. The USB key clearly was put in the stuffed animal by someone hoping to hide it. It must contain valuable information, why else go to the trouble? It also makes sense to think it would've been someone close enough to have access to it. The most logical person to put it there would be Kelly, but who would she have had dirt on? And how would she have acquired it?

The bunny is pretty threadbare, Mason's clearly had

it for a while. What if he had it as a toddler? It could've been Zack who inserted it. If Mesina is as involved as he appears to be, perhaps Zack heard or saw or witnessed something.

Different scenarios play through my head, but I'm struggling to make all the pieces fit.

"I hope it's just dust or dirt that prevents my computer from reading this thing. God knows how long it's been in there," Luna observes after summoning Jasper back to the compound.

She blows in the USB slot and tries it again but nothing happens when she inserts it.

I glance at the clock as I feel every minute slip through our fingers.

"What do I do if he calls before we find her?"

I can hear the fear in my own voice.

Luna leans forward over the table and grabs my hand.

"You stall. Tell him you need more time. That you're close to finding out where Mason is. That you're waiting for information. Ask him for proof of life for Lindsey. Don't try to be cool and collected, it might make him suspicious. Just be the terrified mother you are. He'll be expecting that."

"What about the key? What if I tried to use that as leverage?"

She shakes her head. "Too risky. Especially since we don't know what's on it. Also, it would still leave Mason as a witness to his mother's murder. He could identify him."

"But..." My mind has been stuck on the edge of a

reality that's been in front of my face all this time, but I've been too scared to acknowledge. "So could Lindsey."

Luna doesn't have to say anything, I can read the truth on her face.

"He was never gonna let her go, was he?"

She gives my hand a squeeze. "We will get to her first. We have to. That's why stalling is important. Lindsey's the only leverage he has and for that he needs her alive."

Right. Acting terrified won't be hard to do, I feel it in every fiber of my being.

The temptation is great to give up my last thread of control and scream, give myself up to the blind hysteria that beckons. It would be a relief to numb the agony by letting madness take over.

How do people live with this? Parents who are missing a child, families missing a loved one, how are they able to breathe?

The room around me starts spinning and I'm getting light-headed.

"In through the nose, and out through the mouth," Luna says sternly, as black dots start appearing in front of my eyes. "You're hyperventilating. Slow down."

Forcing myself to focus on her face, I follow her example; in through the nose, out through the mouth. Slowly the dots disappear and the furniture stays in its place.

"Better?"

I nod.

"When's the last time you ate something?"

"Breakfast, a muffin and a banana," I admit.

I was in the kitchen for a few hours helping Lisa, and I even fed Mason but couldn't bring myself to eat.

Luna grabs her phone.

"Lisa? Is that chili ready? Would you mind asking Brick to bring Mel a bowl? Yeah. A pot of coffee might not be a bad idea. Thanks."

"I could've gotten something myself," I object when she gets off the phone.

"I'd rather you stay here."

I realize she wants me to stick close in case he calls. It's already four fifteen. The older kids should be back from school by now and Lisa will have her hands full.

There's only a little over an hour left.

Brick comes in carrying a tray with two bowls and some fresh bread and butter. He slides it on the table and gives my shoulder a squeeze in passing.

"Eat," Luna orders, once again leading by example.

I take a few bites—not really tasting anything—when Jasper rushes into the office.

Paco is two steps behind him and I fly out of my seat and into his arms. They bind around me tightly, as if he's trying to hold the pieces of me together. Gratefully I soak up his strength, letting it fortify me.

"Finish your food, Darlin'," he mumbles in my hair.

Without a word of protest, I let him go and sit down again, shoveling another spoonful of what I'm sure is delicious chili into my mouth.

"Can you access it?" Luna asks when Jasper plugs the key into his laptop.

"No, but I have data recovery software. Let me see

what I can do."

Paco steals a piece of bread from the plate in the middle of the table and I realize he hasn't eaten anything either. I managed to eat half the bowl and shove the rest at him.

"You sure?"

"Yeah, I've had enough."

Brick comes in again, this time with a large thermos of coffee and a collection of mugs he sets on the table.

"You can tip me after," he returns dryly when I try to thank him.

"Sure thing."

I try for a light tone, except there's no amount of money that would make up for what these people are doing for me.

"Got it," Jasper announces.

There's a scrape of chairs being pushed back as we all get up and crowd around the back of Jasper's chair.

He has a folder open on his screen showing a single file. Looks like a video. Jasper clicks on it and a window pops up, which he immediately enlarges to fill the screen.

"What is that?" Luna asks, leaning in farther.

A dim space appears and it takes me a minute to make out a wall filled with tools and mechanical stuff. The camera abruptly pans to what looks like a van. Its back doors are open.

All you can hear is the rapid breathing of the person filming and the light crunch of footsteps as he moves closer.

"It's a Ford Transit," Jasper mumbles.

"Same kind of van," Paco adds.

When the camera aims at the inside of the van, it's clear someone removed the seats. The entire interior is empty.

A hand appears in front of the camera and lifts the floor in one corner. The camera wobbles as he props it up. Then you see him brushing something, like dark sand, off a tidy row of white packages underneath.

"Coffee grounds," Luna says. "It's used to try and cover the scent of drugs. It can throw off the dogs."

In the background, you can hear a door slam followed by muffled voices. The camera jerks and for a few seconds it's impossible to tell what we're looking at, the picture blurred and constantly moving.

When it comes back into focus, you can tell we're underneath the van, the edge of a wheel obscuring part of the view.

A wet thud can be heard, and a body slams face-first on the concrete only a few feet from the van. It's a young man, his eyes open as he seems to stare right at the camera. His face is a bloody pulp. Then two pairs of legs come into view and a hand grabs the young man by the hair.

"You're making a fucking mess of my floor."

I hiss sharply. I'll never forget Mesina's menacing voice.

"Mesina," Luna confirms. "He's wearing some kind of work boots. The other guy has dress shoes, probably a suit."

"We know Mesina is a size ten, so the other guy wears

thirteens if I could venture a guess," Jasper adds.

They seem to be calmly analyzing the horrific scene playing out before us.

"A bigger guy, taller than Mesina and well-dressed," Luna says. "He might be our guy."

The camera shakes slightly. If this was Forbes filming, he must've been scared out of his wits. Only two voices are audible; Mesina's and the young man he is milking for information.

From what I can gather, the man is being accused of siphoning drugs from a shipment that came in. Mesina wants to know who he's told about the shipment, but the young guy keeps denying despite the beating he's receiving.

Suddenly one of the dress shoes hauls out and you can hear it connect with a sickening thud. This time it's the back of the man's head visible on camera. The shoe comes down on his neck and a hand holding a gun appears, pressing the barrel against his head. You can clearly see the sparkle of a cuff link in the white shirt sleeve peeking from a jacket.

"Last chance."

That's not Mesina. That's a different voice. One that raises the hair on my neck.

I'm not sure if it's the cuff link or the affected tone of his voice, but I suddenly know who it is. It makes sense he used voice distortion in his calls to me. That may have masked the depth and the timbre, but it doesn't hide his proper pronunciation.

"It's—"

Paco

Mel's phone starts ringing just as she's about to say something.

Her hands shake as she grabs for her cell.

"Wait," Luna says before Mel can answer. "What were you going to say?"

She looks at the screen of her phone.

"It's him. It's Mesina's lawyer, Howell Redfern."

"Are you sure?" Luna pushes.

Mel raises her eyes and her jaw sets firmly. "Positive."

Immediately, Jasper activates the tracer. Then he pulls up a search screen and types in Redfern's name.

"Okay," Luna tells her. "We need to stall. He's early. Answer it in the bedroom so these guys can work."

She grabs Mel and propels her in that direction.

Fuck, I want to go after her, but it looks like time has run out for Lindsey.

"What've you got?" I ask Jasper.

"A cell number listed in his name. A home address."

He pulls up a map, locating the luxury condo on the south side of town.

"No way we could've heard the train whistle from there. Besides, he wouldn't have been able to get her inside without someone seeing. Security cameras all over the place and neighbors would've heard her screaming. He called around dinnertime."

"What about the cell phone?" I suggest.

"I'll get on it."

I scribble down the address Jasper has up on the

screen and head for the door.

"I'll be downstairs."

I'm not even sure he heard me, already furiously typing on his laptop. Through the bedroom door I hear Mel's muffled voice rising in volume, but I can't let that distract me.

Not sure what I can find, but I'm not bound by law like Jasper is. I plan to hack into his financials. Maybe he has another property, somewhere he's holding her.

MEL

"You said twenty-four hours. I have thirty-five minutes left."

"Semantics, Ms. Morgan. You either have the boy or you don't."

My heart is hammering out of my chest as I throw Luna a panicked look. She gestures for me to go on.

"He's on his way to Durango now," I bluff.

"Need I remind you you're playing with your daughter's life?"

"No. Believe me, I wouldn't risk my daughter's life. She's all I have," I plead, letting emotion filter into my voice.

He doesn't need to know he's listening to pure fury. I swear I could tear that Bosch-wearing, manicured, stuck-up son of a bitch apart with my bare hands, the way I'm feeling right now. But rage makes my voice tremble and that's enough to have him chuckle arrogantly.

I have no trouble at all now recognizing his voice

under the electronic distortion.

"You have half an hour," he finally says. "Then I'll send you instructions via email."

"I'll need to talk to my daughter first," I blurt out when Luna motions for me to keep him on the line longer.

"You're stalling."

"I need to know she's alive."

"You'll have to take my word for it."

"But for all I know you've killed her already."

I don't have to fake the sob escaping when I wrap my mouth around those words.

The truth is, he could've. We may already be too late to save her.

"I assure you she's still breathing. For now."

"I need to know," I insist tearfully. "You're asking me to hand over an innocent child."

"Twenty-nine minutes. You'll have proof."

The line goes dead and I drop the phone on the bed, covering my face with my hands.

"You did good," Luna says, giving me a brief hug. "Let's see if it was long enough."

"And?" she asks Jasper when we walk out of the bedroom.

"Got him. It's pinging off a tower on Baldy Mountain. Northeast of town."

Luna grabs a map and spreads it on the table.

"That's closest to Evans's group. He's got a uniform, Honon, and Wapi with him."

She pulls out her phone and dials a number.

"We've got a signal from the cell tower on Baldy Mountain. Talk to Jasper," I hear her say before she places the phone on speaker.

"Evans. Concentrate north of the coordinates I'm texting him now," Jasper says. "Anything south of there would ping off the downtown tower."

"Can you be more specific?"

"Working on it," is the agent's response.

"Fair enough."

Luna contacts the other teams, redirecting them, while I stare at the clock, willing the hands to move slower. Already too much time has passed since his call.

"Bingo!"

Paco comes storming in, slapping a piece of paper on the table in front of Luna.

"It's an Airbnb listing of a hobby farm," he explains. "Pump the address in Google satellite."

Luna hands the sheet to Jasper, who does as he asks, and we all crowd behind him.

"There," Paco says, indicating a small structure at the back of the property bordering the Animas River.

Luna is already on the phone, barking out instructions.

There are nine minutes left.

Paco puts his arm around me and turns me into his body. I'm no longer aware of what goes on in the room. The only thing I hear is the sound of Paco's heart keeping me grounded and with every beat I silently call out to Lindsey to hang on.

He never lets go and I lose all sense of time, blocking out everything else except my internal mantra.

Suddenly I feel Paco's body jerk and he sets me back a few inches, leaning down in my face.

"Melanie, they found her. They've got Lindsey."

27

Paco

To MY SURPRISE it's Honon who is waiting for us at
the emergency entrance.

I was expecting Wapi.

I didn't wait to hear the details but whisked Mel out of
the clubhouse the moment we heard she was on her way
to Mercy Hospital. We left without talking to Mason, but
I trust Lisa will take care of him.

"Where is my daughter?" Mel immediately demands
to know.

The fierce woman I know is back. She was curt and to
the point when she contacted her sister on our drive over
here and told them to stay put until she knew more about
Lindsey's condition. Despite Mel's instructions, I fully
expect the family to show up in full force any minute.

"We got in five minutes ago, they're looking at her now."

"How is she?"

"A bit roughed up, but she'll be okay."

Mel blows out a big breath and starts heading toward the nurses' station in front of the emergency department.

"You sticking around?" I ask Honon, eager to stay close to Mel but also curious to hear what happened.

"Yeah. I'll wait."

The 'bit roughed up' Honon referred to turns out to be a laceration across her cheekbone and swelling and bruising to her face, but the most significant injuries are the spiral fractures of both bones in her left forearm, which is going to require surgery.

The young ER doctor gets up from the chair across from Mel in the waiting room.

"While we're waiting for the orthopedic surgeon, I'm just going to put a few stitches in the cut on her face, but if you'd like you can come back and sit with her until she goes up to the OR."

Mel is on her feet in a flash. I stand a little slower as she's already following the doctor out of the room.

"Paco?" She looks back over her shoulder.

"You go. I'm going to quickly touch base with Honon and then wait for your family to show."

I can tell from her reaction she'd forgotten about them.

"I'll call Beth from the room," she says before shooting me a little smile that only emphasizes the strain on her face. Then she's off after the doctor.

I find Honon outside the cafeteria, holding a carryout coffee cup and a cigarette.

"I could use one of those."

"The coffee or the smoke?" he asks.

"Both."

He hands me the cigarette and the coffee.

"Here, have this one, I haven't touched it yet. I'll go grab another one. Want anything to eat?"

"No thanks, I had a quick bite at the clubhouse before the shit hit the fan. You should probably grab something yourself."

Those guys were out all day searching, I doubt they took the time to eat.

I'm already done with the cigarette when Honon returns with a questionable premade sandwich and another coffee. We sit down at one of the two tables out here and he tosses his smokes on the table toward me.

Haven't smoked regularly since I started building my house, but every now and then I'll bum one off one of the remaining smokers among my brothers. Shit, five years ago almost every one of us smoked but by now there are only a few guys left. Usually when a woman got involved, a brother would lose that particular bad habit quickly.

While Honon consumes his sandwich in four bites, I light another one.

"Where's Wapi?" is the first thing I want to know.

It strikes me as odd he hasn't shown his face. He's been Lindsey's shadow for the past week or so and now suddenly he's not here.

"I don't know, man," Honon says, shaking his head. "He's fucked up. Wouldn't talk last night, he just sat at the bar for hours tossing them back and didn't say much today either." He takes a deep drag of his smoke. "That van was parked on the side of that building. More of a barn. The back doors were open and this guy was leaning in, taping down painter's plastic on the floor and up the walls of the van. Evans had taken the lead—told us to stick to the tree line—but when we realized what he was doing, Wapi lost it. Took off fucking running right for the guy. Guess having some crazy fucker running at him full speed startled him because he never had a chance to pull his gun before Wapi was on him. Took Evans and the uniform to pull him off or he'd have killed the guy."

"*Jesus*. He blames himself."

Honon snorts. "Yeah, that was obvious. Anyway, I went in after the girl. Bastard must've used a whole fuckin' roll of duct tape tying her to the frame of an old tractor. I cut her free and carried her out. Wapi took one look at her, turned on his heel, and took off."

Definitely feeling the guilt.

"How badly did he damage Redfern?"

"Is that the guy's name?"

"Yeah."

"Well, he didn't get any prettier, but I reckon he'll be fine once they patch him up."

He indicates the hospital.

"He's here?"

Honon's hand grabs my wrist and I realize I'm already halfway out of my chair.

"Sit your ass down. Our young brother already worked him over. He'll probably walk away, no harm no foul, but if you put your hands on a man in a hospital bed you won't be so lucky. Besides, it'll be crawling with cops and feds."

He makes a good point, but Redfern better get what's coming to him another way.

"I should get back up there. I promised Mel I'd catch her family when they arrive."

"I'm coming," Honon says, getting to his feet.

"Brother, you don't need to."

He gives me a sharp look. "Like fucking hell I don't need to. Family is family."

With that he heads for the door.

The small waiting room is empty. Guess they're still waiting for the surgeon to get here. No sooner have Honon and I sat down when Scott Beacham walks in, followed by his wife and who I assume to be Mel's parents.

I get to my feet and shake Scott's offered hand.

"Any word?"

"Mel's not back yet so I assume they're still waiting for the surgeon. She called you, right?"

"Yes." He turns to Honon and nods. Then he introduces his in-laws.

"Janet, Thomas, this is Paco."

I shake the reluctant hands but it doesn't take a genius to see they're less than enthused making my acquaintance or that of my brother who is introduced next.

I can see where the sisters get their looks, their mother looks like an older version. I'm guessing they must be in their seventies, at least, but both look well preserved and I suspect that's not just because nature was kind.

The father eyes me with clear distaste and suspicion. I figured if they're dumb enough to consider Mel a disappointment, they'd see me as the scum of the earth. Fine, I don't care, but they better not make a scene in front of Mel or Lindsey. I won't stand for it.

Instead of talking to me he turns to Scott.

"Who are these people?"

"Paco is Mel's...partner," Scott answers.

I can handle partner. I'm getting a little too old to be called someone's boyfriend anyway.

"Honon is my brother," I take over. "He's the one who carried your granddaughter to safety."

"Partner?"

The shocked echo comes from Janet, who is still staring at her son-in-law.

"Figures," her husband huffs under his breath.

Not quite sure what he means by that, but something tells me it's aimed at Mel.

Despite the parents' obvious unease, Beth steps forward and puts a hand on my arm.

"I can't thank you enough for being here for my sister and niece," she says before turning to Honon and offering her hand. "And you too."

The door to the waiting room opens and Ouray and Trunk walk in. This time I make the introductions.

"We just stopped in to see how Lindsey is doing," Ouray explains.

"Waiting for the surgeon, she has spiral fractures of

her forearm. The fucker must've twisted her arm."

"I hear Wapi put a hurtin' on him," Ouray states, looking around the waiting room. "Where is he anyway?"

"Took off," Honon answers. "He was in a state. I figured he'd be heading back to the clubhouse."

Ouray shakes his head. "He ain't there."

On the other side of the room the Morgans and Beth have taken a seat. Mr. Morgan is leaning across his wife talking to his daughter in a stage-whisper. I just catch the end of it.

"...now she's associating with a bunch of criminals? A motorcycle gang?"

I clench my jaw, itching to set the old fart straight, but it turns out I don't need to.

MEL

"ACTUALLY," I SNAP from the doorway after catching my father's comments. "It's a club, not a gang, and not a single one of these men is a criminal. In fact..." I move farther into the room. "If not for them, your granddaughter would've been dead. So instead of looking down your arrogant nose at them, why not be a decent human being for a change and show some fucking gratitude."

Mom clasps a hand to her chest, clutching her pearls. Literally.

I roll my eyes.

"Your language certainly hasn't improved," my father observes.

"That's enough," Scott suddenly barks, turning to his

in-laws. "You're in a hospital waiting room while your granddaughter is about to have surgery, and all you can do is belittle her mother and the men who rescued her? I just spent the entire day with them searching for her. What have you done, other than badger and complain? You're either here to support or you're not here at all. I'll personally put you back on that plane."

I don't think I've ever heard Scott blow up at my parents before. And judging by the startled look on Beth's face, she hasn't either. My brother-in-law and I have had a love-hate relationship but right now I could kiss him.

I leave him to handle my parents and make my way over to Paco, slipping an arm around his waist. He bends his head to brush my lips.

"She okay?" he asks softly.

"Yeah. The surgeon says she'll be a couple of hours."

I turn to Paco's brothers and make sure to hug and thank each of them. Yes, in part to stick it to my dad, I don't think that defiant streak in me will ever die.

Then I step over to Beth, who is now standing by her husband. I give her a side hug and smile at Scott.

"Thank you," I tell them.

"Sorry for—" Beth starts, but I cut her off.

"Don't take on what you don't own. Mom and Dad will never change, no matter how hard you try," I tell my sister, giving her waist a squeeze. "Stop putting yourself in the middle."

"I just want everyone to get along."

"Which is a lovely sentiment, but at what cost?"

"Your sister's right," Scott agrees.

That's twice he's jumped to my defense, I may be suffering hallucinations.

I feel a tap on my shoulder. It's Ouray.

"We're gonna head out and see if we can find Wapi. I'll check in later and see how she's doing."

"Sure."

Honon and Trunk follow him out of the room and I join Paco on the narrow love seat against the wall. He instantly tucks me under his shoulder.

"What's this about Wapi?"

I can feel my parents' eyes from across the room, but choose to ignore them.

"I suspect guilt is eating him. Apparently, they had to pull him off Redfern, but not before he gave the man a severe beating."

"Good," I comment. I have not even an ounce of sympathy for the sick bastard.

"Honon says Wapi took one look at Lindsey and took off. No one knows where the hell he is so they're gonna try and track him down. Wapi isn't a violent man. Far from it, but this year has been tough on him."

"Are you worried he might do something stupid?"

I reach up and rub the pad of my thumb over the worry lines between his eyebrows. He takes my hand, pressing his lips in my palm.

"Yeah."

Poor Wapi. Guilt can eat a person from the inside out, leaving nothing but a gaping hole. I hope they find him.

Talk about guilt, I ran out of the clubhouse earlier

barely even sparing Mason a look, I need to talk to him.

"Who are you calling?" Paco asks when I pull my phone from my pocket.

"I should talk to Mason."

"Darlin', he may already be in bed."

I check the time and see it's already after nine. I dial the clubhouse anyway.

"At least I can talk to Lisa."

It's Brick who answers, telling me Lisa went back to the cottage with the kids. Apparently, Mason had been quiet and stuck close to Kiara so Lisa put the two of them in Kiara's bed.

"He'll be fine. We can talk to him in the morning," Paco says when I share the information with him.

I know he's right, but I still wish I could be two places at once.

"BACK TO THE clubhouse?"

I look over at Paco, the deep grooves in his face making him look tired. I'd almost forgotten he got up before dawn this morning to start looking.

We just left the hospital after briefly seeing Lindsey. She was mostly out of it, still coming out of anesthesia. She has some hardware in her arm that will have to be taken out again at some point, but we've been assured she will heal.

My parents went in to see her as well before Scott and Beth took them home. It had been a tense few hours in that relatively small waiting room, and I don't envy my sister and brother-in-law having them in their home.

I'd planned on staying the night in the hospital but between the nurse, Paco, and my drugged-up daughter, I caved. They have my cell phone at the nurses' station in case they need me.

"Yeah."

The clubhouse makes more sense since Mason is there, that way we can see him first thing in the morning. I don't want him to feel we've forgotten about him.

"I would've thought Luna or one of the detectives would've been by to ask questions," I point out, as Paco navigates through town.

"My guess is they'll wait until morning. They would've checked in with the hospital and known she was in surgery."

Right.

The clubhouse is quiet when we arrive. It's a little after one in the morning and the only person up is Honon.

"Any luck?" Paco asks about Wapi after updating him on Lindsey.

"Nope. In the wind. Ouray put a call out to Red in case he surfaces there."

I stifle a yawn which Paco notices.

"We're heading to bed," he tells Honon, who nods.

"I'll lock up."

I give my teeth a perfunctory brush before rolling into bed, while Paco has a quick shower. I could probably use one but am too tired. I don't even notice when Paco comes to bed.

"Mel…"

There's a moment of disorientation when I open my eyes and find Lisa beside the bed with a bedraggled Mason by her side. I shoot up in bed immediately.

"What's wrong?"

"Nightmare. The boy needs ya."

I immediately reach down and lift Mason onto the bed. He wraps his spindly limbs around me as Lisa is already moving to the door.

"Thank you."

She wiggles her fingers over her shoulder and shuts the door behind her.

"Hey, kiddo. You okay?"

There's no answer, but his hold on me tightens a fraction. I lie back with the boy still attached to me.

"Hey, bud," I hear Paco mutter in a sleepy voice. "Bad dreams?"

I feel his nod against my shoulder.

"Wanna talk about it?"

"No," Mason mumbles.

I go to rub his back but encounter Paco's large hand already soothing the boy.

"You know…when you talk about dreams, they're not so scary anymore," I suggest.

Paco plucks the boy off me and rolls him between us.

"I couldn't find you and then you were floating in the river."

Oh dear Lord. The kid's breaking my heart.

"We're right here, kiddo. Not goin' anywhere." Paco beats me to it.

I catch his eye when he looks up. Something unspoken passes between us. An understanding that doesn't seem to require any words.

Paco reaches out, brushing the backs of his fingers down my cheek.

"Soon's your girl's back on her feet, we talk," he mumbles.

Yes, we will.

28

Paco

"How did you zero in on that Airbnb anyway?"

Luna tilts her head, her eyes locked on me.

"You're better off calling it an anonymous tip," I caution her.

Ramirez chuckles and Luna shakes her head.

"Fine. Keep your secrets."

We're in Ouray's office at the clubhouse. Luna was here with Ramirez to get statements from Honon and Wapi, but there's been no sign of him yet and the asshole isn't answering our calls. I'd just come back from the hospital when they called me in, wanting a word with me too.

I left Mel with Lindsey when her sister and parents showed up. I didn't want to go, but Mel urged me to go spend some time with Mason. Especially after last night.

"Is Redfern talking?" I want to know.

"A little tough with his jaw wired shut," Ramirez comments dryly.

Good. Glad to hear Wapi did some damage.

"Barnes and Greene are transporting him to our office and they'll be working on him," Luna volunteers. "Either way, we have him dead to rights."

"Would be nice to know how Forbes fit in. Who actually killed Kelly," I suggest.

"At this point we can only speculate, but I think it's safe to say Forbes's release from prison was a catalyst of sorts," Luna shares. "It's pretty clear Forbes did some side jobs for Mesina and either helped with or found out about the drug shipments hidden on imported vehicles. Maybe he wanted to record it for insurance purposes or his plan was blackmail."

"Did you find out who the victim was?" I interject.

"Yes," she confirms. "Lance Darr. Another employee at Capital Auto. We showed the tape to Peña this morning. He was able to identify him. Peña is under investigation as well, by the way. I suspect he is up to his eyeballs into the drug smuggling. So far he's cooperating with us."

"Whether or not Forbes used that video to blackmail anyone, I don't know, but catching a cold-blooded murder on tape may have caused him to think twice," Ramirez contributes. "He tucks it in what he deems a safe place, not realizing his ass would end up in jail not that long after."

"But why approach Mesina when he got out?" I want

to know.

"Who's to say it wasn't the other way around?" Luna counters. "Maybe Mesina kept tabs on him instead. He may have known about the video and forced Forbes to help him retrieve it."

"Either way," Ramirez picks up. "Yelinek was able to confirm with Kelly's landlord it was Redfern who stopped by the house with Forbes. Because of the state of the bodies when they were found, the best the coroner could do for either Kelly or Forbes was a range for time of death. Those overlap so we can't know if Forbes was there when Kelly was killed or if he was already dead at that point."

"Problem is that evidence against Redfern for Kelly's or Forbes's murders is circumstantial," Luna indicates. "Unless…"

I know where her mind is going and I don't like it.

"No. Mason is six years old. We're not going to put him through that again. Already he's plagued by nightmares. You're gonna have to find another way."

"Fair enough," she says easily, making me think she wasn't happy with the idea herself. "Let's hope we can put some pressure on Mesina who is probably the only person, other than Redfern, to know the full story."

"You mean pit them against each other?"

She shrugs. "Why not? With charges against both of them, the federal prosecutor will look for a maximum sentence, which is capital punishment. Maybe we can get Mesina to testify against Redfern in return for taking a death sentence off the table. I'll have to see what leverage the prosecutor will allow us."

"Whatever you need to do to leave Mason out of it."

I suddenly notice both Ramirez and Luna are grinning at me.

"What?"

"Never thought I'd see the day," Luna says getting out of her chair. "First, you fall for the woman and now a six-year-old boy. Instant family man. And to think when I first met you, I thought you were the biggest manwho—"

"All right, don't be spreading stories about me," I interrupt her. "Anything Mel needs to know; she'll get from me."

"I'm sure she can guess, Paco. The woman's no fool. A fifty-year old biker, looking like you, who's never been snatched up has surely seen his share of action."

I'm sure there's a compliment in there somewhere but I'm having trouble identifying it right now.

"I'm just saying, I've got this."

She walks around the table and gives me a quick hug.

"I know you do, brother. Happy for ya."

She pats my arm and heads out the door.

Ramirez punches my shoulder in passing.

"Welcome to the club."

Tonight, when Mason's in bed, I plan on discussing that club membership with Mel. It's not complicated. I love her, am pretty sure she loves me back, her girl is da bomb, and both of us are gone for the kid. I don't give a flying fuck what it takes to make that into a family, but I will.

I find Mason in the kitchen making cookies with Lisa.

He's covered in flour.

"Kid, you're a mess. I thought you were gonna come pick Mel up and say hi to Lindsey?"

"I am. Me and Lisa are making cookies to bring," he says in an earnest voice.

"Go on," Lisa says. "Go with Paco and get yourself cleaned up. I'll pack some of these up for you to take."

When Lindsey is released from the hospital—hopefully in a day or two—I plan to bring everyone back home. For now the clubhouse is easier with Mason.

As promised, Lisa has a container of cookies packed when we pop into the kitchen on our way out. She also hands Mason a baggie with a few.

"Those are for you two to share on the way."

Lisa gets one of the rare Mason smiles before he accepts the bag in one hand and automatically puts the other one in mine.

He's already chomping on a cookie by the time I have him buckled into the back of the cab.

"Hey. Didn't Lisa say share?"

He immediately holds out the baggie with his free hand and I dig in, shoving an entire cookie in my mouth.

"These are good. Great job, buddy."

There's that smile on his face again. Doesn't take much.

He clings to my hand when we walk through the hospital, looking around with big eyes as he clutches the container of cookies to his chest. It's a busy place today and I guess it might be a little intimidating for him, but like a little trooper he manages to keep up with me. But outside Lindsey's room, he stops in his tracks, his eyes on Mel's family in the room.

Scott isn't here, but Beth and her parents are. Beth looks up and smiles, her eyes taking in Mason half hidden behind me. Mel must've stepped out.

"Hey, Mason," Lindsey says, sitting up in bed. "Come sit here."

Her arm is strapped to her chest to immobilize it, but she pats the mattress beside her with the other hand.

Mason throws a suspicious glance at the other three in the room but I ignore them, aiming for the bed. I lean over and kiss Lindsey's cheek.

"Looking a lot better."

She grins, wincing slightly. "You mean aside from the messed-up face?"

Mason finds his courage and steps up to the edge of the bed, holding out the container.

"What's that?" she asks him.

"Cookies. I made them." He glances up at me before adding, "Lisa helped."

I wink at the kid; I'm thinking it was probably the other way around but let him take the glory.

"You did? That's amazing. Can I try one?"

Lindsey's chatter puts him at ease and when she pats the bed again, he wants to be lifted up.

"That's Aunt Beth," she tells him. "And that's my grandpa and grandma."

Beth waves, but the Morgans just nod.

"Hey, kiddo."

Mel's voice sounds behind me and I feel her hand

stroke my back as she passes to get to the bed. Mason launches himself at her.

I keep an eye on her parents—who have yet to say a word—and note their surprise at the familiar way Mason clings to Mel like a monkey. I'm not even sure they understand that kind of easy love.

MEL

THE TENSION IN the room has been thick today, until now.

I have to credit Beth for doing her best to keep things light. My parents can't seem to help themselves but to be critical and Lindsey wasn't putting up with it, so Beth would quickly change the subject.

I had to get some air.

Finding Paco and Mason already here is a relief.

"Guess what? Lindsey may be released tomorrow morning," I tell Paco.

"I still say it's too early," my mother pipes up.

"Grandma…" Lindsey warns.

"I'm just saying, you could've been killed."

Mason startles in my arms.

"Last I heard 'could've been killed' is not a recognized medical diagnosis," Lindsey fires back. "Besides, I didn't realize you had a medical degree."

"That doctor was barely out of diapers," Mom sputters but Lindsey isn't done yet.

"And thank God for that, I wouldn't want a geriatric wanna-be with one foot in the grave to decide my fate," she retorts dramatically.

I elbow Paco, who chuckles under his breath.

"Your grandmother is just concerned," Beth tries to mitigate.

"Apple doesn't fall far from the tree," Dad grumbles, glaring at my daughter.

I've had enough.

"This ends now," I say sharply. "First of all, I have a child here who has been through a tough time and does not need to be subjected to this."

"Your *child* is in a hospital bed, maybe you should worry about her," Mom says.

I can hear Paco's sharp inhale beside me and I can sense he's about to blow.

"My daughter is an adult with more common sense in her pinky finger than the rest of us combined," I fire back, trying to keep my voice calm. "She can look after herself just fine, unlike this boy who needs a place where he can be made to feel safe, and if you make that impossible, I'm going to have to ask you to leave."

"But we're your family," my father objects.

"Then maybe it's time you start behaving like it."

That finally seems to shut them up.

I feel Paco's hand land on my hip, giving it a squeeze.

"Brava, Mom," Lindsey mumbles before directing her attention to Mason. "Now, about those cookies. Wanna split one with me?"

Mason's head bops against my chin and I set him back down on the bed beside her.

Not long after that Beth convinces my parents to leave, citing the need to pick up some groceries. I watch as they say goodbye to Lindsey, who kisses them as if no sharp words were ever exchanged.

My daughter is a bigger person than I am, I don't manage more than an impersonal, "See you later." They don't even acknowledge Paco.

I'm about to comment on that when Paco bends down and whispers, "Not worth it."

He's right. They're not. I know it'll be a waste of energy.

Instead I focus on Beth, who steps in for a warm hug. My sister and I may never have been friends and there may be too much history to overlook, but she's a good woman and today I'm grateful for her.

"So, tomorrow?" Paco says when it's just us.

"Yes," Linds answers with a grin.

"Okay, then we need to talk about a few things."

I raise an eyebrow at him.

"Take a seat," he says, pointing at one of the chairs my parents were occupying.

"I think you should stay at my place." When I open my mouth to interrupt, he holds up his hand. "Hear me out. Your house still needs work. We haven't had a chance to replace the windows, let alone rebuild your garage. That's one." He holds up a finger and then adds another. "Two, you have a practice to run by yourself while Lindsey recuperates, you are going to have your hands full. I make my own time and don't have an office to worry about so I can look after her while you're working."

"My legs and one arm still work fine," my daughter

interjects.

Paco shoots her a pointed look and she quickly pretends to zip her lips. Then he turns his eyes back on me.

"It'll be a quick fix to put a bed in the home office. I can do the cooking since Linds won't be able to and you'll be too busy handling all the work by yourself. Admit it, it makes sense. For now," he quickly adds, but I have the distinct impression he only did that for my benefit.

"I'm game," Lindsey says, shooting a challenging grin in my direction.

I admit, it would suck to have to go back to sleeping alone. Who'd have thought? He's right, it all does make sense. Especially if you factor in Mason. I don't think either of us want to give him up and that would be complicated to navigate with two households.

So the question really is, what do I truly want, and the answer comes easy.

"Okay."

Paco's laugh lines deepen around his eyes.

"Yeah?"

I shrug.

"You're not gonna fight me on it?" he pokes with a grin.

"Well, I might if you keep pushing," I grumble.

He bursts out laughing, Lindsey joining in, and I can't hold back a smile of my own.

Damn. Something tells me I've just given in to something a lot more permanent than an emergency solution.

But the next moment reality hits when I hear Mason's soft voice.

"Where am I going to live?"

29

Mel

"Mom?"

I drag my eyes from the rustic picture Mason and Paco make as they pull the last of the carrots, Cookie chasing the clumps of soil flying around.

Lindsey is behind me, standing in the doorway.

"What's up?"

"Do you know where Wapi is? I've been trying to get hold of him, but he's not answering his phone."

I cross the deck to join her at the back door.

"I'm not sure, but from what I gather, he left shortly after you were rescued. Paco says he has some personal issues to deal with. Why?"

My daughter does a good job hiding the disappointment but I'm her mother, I can tell when she's hurting.

"Just wondering. He was up my ass the entire time and then suddenly disappeared off the face of the earth. I thought maybe something had happened to him." She shrugs. "Oh, well. I'm gonna give Dad a call back."

She turns and heads back to her temporary room, but I don't miss her mumbled comment.

"I don't even know why I care, Wapi's an asshole."

Stubborn like her mother.

I feel bad she's obviously upset, and it's clear there was something sizzling between those two, but I'm pretty sure neither of them was emotionally ready for the other. It would've been combustive, maybe even destructive, much like her father and my relationship.

I turn my attention back to the marinade I'm throwing together for the flank steaks we're having tonight. True to his word, Paco took care of dinner the last two nights, but it's Saturday and I only went into the office for a few hours, so I told him I'd be cooking tonight.

Part of the reason is also that my parents are coming for dinner.

They're leaving tomorrow—thank fucking God—and wanted to take us out to a restaurant. I wasn't going to subject us to sitting through a meal, trying to stay polite in public, while they would sit and find fault in everything and everyone. I wouldn't have been able to hold back anymore and there's a good chance Paco would blow as well. So I suggested it would be easier if they were to come here for dinner.

Anyway, I'm used to criticism and I didn't want to give them an excuse to pick on Paco. Besides, if things get out of hand here, one of us can whisk Mason to his room so he can be spared.

Poor kid. He about broke my heart when he asked where he'd be living. Whatever differences there may still be to work out for Paco and me, the one thing we didn't even need words to agree on was Mason and his place in each of our lives. We probably should've talked to him about it first.

As it turns out, when we told him that, of course, he'd be with us, he was so happy he cried. Which made me cry, then Lindsey started sobbing, and Paco had to leave the room. He really doesn't handle tears well. Good thing I don't cry. Much.

There's a knock at the front door and I quickly wipe my hands. If that's my parents, they're about two hours early. I groan at the thought of having to spend even more time with them.

But when I check the narrow window, I recognize Luna.

"Sorry to barge in," she starts when I open the door.

"Nonsense." I wave her in. "I'm just putzing in the kitchen. You can keep me company. Have a glass of wine with me."

"Three is a bit early for cocktail hour, but sure, what the hell."

"My parents are coming for dinner. Believe me, I need the wine."

She snickers as she sits down on the stool I direct her to. Then I pull out a couple of wineglasses and the bottle of chilled Pinot Grigio.

"This is actually perfect," Luna says, taking a sip of her wine. "I came with good news so there's cause for celebration."

"Oh? Pray tell."

I pour the marinade in the large Ziploc bag holding the steaks while Luna explains.

"Mesina took the deal. He turned on Redfern."

"Well, alleluia." I grab my glass and clink it to Luna's. "I'll drink to that."

"He was able to clear up a few details we weren't entirely clear on. Forbes was the one to approach Mesina, looking to finally cash in on that video he took. This was after your office was broken into. Guess he wanted to make sure he'd be able to find her."

"So that was definitely Forbes?"

"Sounds like it. Mesina notified Redfern and they told Forbes Redfern would accompany him to get the USB key from Kelly, in exchange for a set amount of money Mesina had provided. Mesina claims he had nothing to do with Forbes's murder, that when Redfern came back from Moab he told him it was all taken care of. He says he believed his lawyer and had no knowledge or part of whatever happened after."

"So he's denying any involvement in Lindsey's abduction?"

"Correct. He swears he didn't even know of Mason's existence."

"Bullshit," I spit out, taking an agitated swig of my wine.

"Clearly. He's trying to minimize his own involvement,

but he did hand us Redfern." She takes a healthy drink as well when she raises her hand. "Oh, and of course his claim is that he was just going to rough up Lance Darr a little to get information from him. Denying any responsibility in that murder."

"Lance Darr?"

"The victim from the video that started all this."

"Gotcha."

"Supposedly, Mesina hoped they could convince him to return the drugs he believed the guy stole from them, but Redfern lost patience and shot him. Carlos said that was not the plan."

"Of course," I mutter, not believing a word of it.

"Give us time," Luna tries to reassure me. "We're not done grilling him. He may give up some more details."

"I just hate the idea Kelly's murder may not get resolved."

"We don't know that. It's still early. With this new information, the FBI lab in Denver will be going over any evidence collected. We've also had both Forbes's and Kelly's bodies transported there from the Moab coroner's office. The lab will hopefully be able to get a better timeline on when exactly they died. It takes time."

Okay, that—and the bottom half of my glass of wine—make me feel a little better.

Good thing too, because there's another knock at the door. I think my parents have arrived.

PACO

OH, GREAT. THEY'RE here.

I watch Mel's parents peeking out the back door.

I know it's mostly for Lindsey's sake Mel proposed for them to have dinner here, but this is my house; one wrong word from either of them and I have no compunction tossing them out on their collective asses.

"Come on, Mason. Let's go wash up. Lindsey's grandparents are here."

I bite the inside of my cheek not to laugh at the expression on the boy's face. He's not a fan either.

Guess this is the reality of sharing a house and a life with someone. It comes with all the good and the bad.

Which reminds me, I still haven't really had a chance to talk with Mel alone. I'd like to rectify that tonight, after her folks are gone.

"You get the faucet, bud," I tell him and watch as he runs to the hose at the back of the house.

I follow a little slower carrying the bucket with the carrots and potatoes we pulled earlier. I'm in no hurry to get inside.

Who'd have thought just a few years ago, I'd have a house full of people. Heck, who'd have thought I'd even have a house, grow vegetables, let alone own a dog. I thought the clubhouse was all the home I needed. I guess you can't wish for what you don't know.

Now I know, and the only thing better is I get to share the things that give me pleasure with people I care about.

Like this little guy.

I ruffle Mason's hair.

"Ready to go in, buddy?"

Mel's dad is standing by the door when I slide it open. "You have a garden."

It's not really a question, more a puzzled conclusion, but it's the first time he's addressed me directly.

"I do. The soil's good and I've got the space for it."

Handing the bucket to Mason, I steer him into the kitchen.

"Go give those to Mel."

The bucket is pretty heavy but the kid seems to manage.

Thomas is still staring out at the view.

"Can I get you a drink?" I ask, mainly for something to say.

"I don't drink beer."

What the fuck?

"Your loss, Grandpa," Lindsey says, hooking her good arm in me. "Paco has some really nice micro brews. There's also wine, I think I saw some scotch, and I know for a fact there's tequila."

I grin when her face scrunches up at the mention of tequila. I'm sure she doesn't have very good memories of that particular bottle.

With Lindsey looking after her grandfather, I turn to the kitchen to see if Mel needs some help.

"Janet." I nod at her mom sitting at the island with a glass of wine in front of her. "Need a hand?" I ask Mel, putting an arm around her waist and pressing a kiss to the side of her head. She smells of the spices she's sprinkling over the apples for the pie and I inhale deeply.

Ignoring the sharp scrutiny I can feel from her mother,

I focus on the tight smile Mel throws me.

"Sure, if you don't mind tackling the carrots and potatoes so we can get them in the oven?"

"You've got it."

I go in search of another cutting board and knife when I hear Janet behind me.

"He cooks?"

Fuck. She's a piece of work, sitting in my kitchen, drinking my goddamn wine, and still unable to bring herself to address me directly.

I swing around and answer before Mel can.

"Yes, I cook. I also know how to do laundry, and will even occasionally run the vacuum."

At least she has the good grace to lower her eyes and pink up a little. I turn my back and start on the vegetables, listening with half an ear to Lindsey do her best to engage her grandparents in normal conversation.

After I slide the baking tray in the oven, I go in search of Mason who I find in his bedroom, playing with the new stuff Mel got him. Cookie, as always, is not far away, curled up beside him on the floor.

"How are you doing, bud?"

"Good."

The last couple of nights he's slept in our room, but this morning he announced he was ready to sleep in his own bed again. I could've cheered. Love the kid, but he's put a serious dent in Mel's and my love life.

Glad to see he finally seems to be settling down again. Poor tike has had more than his share of upheaval in his short life.

"I'm gonna fire up the grill outside. You want to come?"

He shakes his head. "I wanna play here."

Guess that's a good sign.

I look at Cookie, whose head perked up hearing the word 'come.'

"You coming?"

The dog tucks her head back down in response. I'll take that as a no.

My phone rings as I head toward the back door. I'm surprised when I see Wapi's name come up. Having a few choice words for my brother, I catch Mel's eye, point outside, and step onto the deck, closing the door behind me.

"Where the fuck have you been?" I snap, answering the call.

"How is she?" he asks, ignoring my question.

"She's got pins and plates holding her arm together, not that you'd care. You took off, brother. Not cool."

It's quiet on the other end.

"I care," he finally says. "Too fucking much. That's why I left."

"You're not making a lick of sense. She's been asking about you."

"Then it's even better I'm not there." The dejected tone in his voice has me worried. "I ain't the guy for her, Paco. I ain't got nothing to offer her. Fuck, man, I couldn't even protect her. I own every mark that son of a bitch put on her."

"Brother, you know that's not true."

"Do I? Doesn't matter either way, I have a thing for falling for women who are out of my league."

I know he's referring to Sophia, Tse's wife. Tse wasn't the only one with a serious thing for her when she first came into the picture. For a while there it pitted brother against brother, but Tse, being older and slightly wiser—by only a narrow margin—turned out the lucky one.

"I call bullshit. The right woman will be lucky to have you. Fuck, man, I've got a good twenty years on you, and I've just found mine."

"Happy for you, brother," he mumbles.

"You'll get yours."

"Yeah," he drawls, sounding like he doesn't believe it.

"Still haven't answered my question; where the hell are you?"

"Need a little time," he says. "Gettin' my head clear. Taking in the sights. I'll be in touch."

I get it. Man, do I get it. Like me, Wapi spent most of his life with the club. In Durango. Other than the occasional runs, of course, but you're always with your brothers, rarely alone. Maybe this'll be good for the kid, doing a little exploring, tasting a bit of life outside of the compound, and at the same time getting his head sorted.

But I still worry.

"Better not leave us hanging too long, Wapi," I warn him. "What do you want me to tell Ouray? The brothers? Heck, what the fuck should I say to Lindsey?"

"Tell them…" There's a thick pause. "Tell them I'll be back…eventually."

I look out at the view, my heart hurting for him, but if this is what he needs I won't stand in his way.

"I will. Ride safe, brother. And Godspeed."

30

MEL

I WATCHED PACO from the kitchen window.

Not sure who he was on the phone with but the call clearly weighed heavy on him. He's been quiet all throughout dinner.

"That was good," Dad says, patting his mouth with a napkin. He ate every last crumb of the apple pie I made for dessert.

The compliment settles warmly under my skin. Not often have I heard praise from either of my parents in my life, but I've collected each treasured memory carefully. This one will join the scant others I recall.

It's not that I need their approval to add value to my existence—I know my own worth—but those rare glimpses validate the love I still have for my shitty parents.

"It could've used a bit more sugar," Mom immediately neutralizes Dad's praise. "I found the apples a little tart."

I guess it's like muscle memory, they almost can't help themselves.

Glancing up, I catch Lindsey's rolling eyes and wink at her. We've both learned to hold on to the good and let the bad slide off our backs.

That's all you can do.

Mason is fidgeting on his seat beside Linds.

"You can get up if you want, kiddo," I tell him.

He's off his chair in a flash but before he gets very far, Dad pipes up.

"It's polite to say 'thank you for dinner.'"

Paco's head shoots up, glaring at my father, but Mason looks back at me.

"Thank you for dinner, Mo—Mel," he corrects himself at the last second before darting down the hall to his room.

"I'd appreciate it if you left the parenting to us," Paco says through clenched teeth.

"I didn't realize you had experience parenting?"

There are times I could do my parents physical harm; this would be one of them.

"Dad..." I warn him, but he's obviously not done.

"I thought you were just looking after the boy until his family is found. I admit I'm not quite sure what the plan is."

"Mason's staying," Paco bites off.

"Where? Here? With you?"

"With us," I state firmly, putting a hand on Paco's knee.

"Aren't you a bit too old for that?" Mom puts in her two cents' worth. "He's only six and you're almost fifty."

"Grandma, you really have to get with the times," Lindsey says, her mouth full of pie. "Mom's only forty-eight and I know plenty of women these days that don't even start a family until they're in their late thirties, even early forties. Besides," she adds, shoving her now empty plate away. "Mom and Paco are the kind of people who'll never be too old for anything. Also…" She grins at me. "I've always wanted a little brother."

In my peripheral vision I see the corner of Paco's mouth twitch with amusement. God, I love my girl.

"Just to be clear," I find myself sharing. "We hope to officially adopt Mason eventually."

"Cool," Lindsey chirps. "You'll finally have that grandson you always wanted, Grandpa."

Jesus. My daughter…

"Poor guy," I mumble.

I tuck up my legs and snuggle farther into Paco's side. He has his socked feet on the coffee table, his arm draped around me.

The parents are gone, heading back home in the morning, and miraculously no blood was shed.

Mason has been asleep in his own bed for an hour or so, and Lindsey went to bed as well, right after Paco finished telling us about Wapi's phone call.

"He'll figure it out," he says, but I can't tell whether it's to convince me or himself. "You think Linds is gonna be okay?"

My daughter played the news Wapi left indefinitely off as inconsequential, but I'm pretty sure her stiff upper lip got a workout. She likes him more than she's willing to admit, even to herself, but the fact he'd been able to get under her skin so easily gives her away. Any other time a guy she's been even remotely interested in disappointed her, she'd get pissed, drunk, or both, but was over it within a day or so. Most recently with Dale—the guy I suspect Wapi chased off—which lasted about as long as it took for her hangover to wear off.

Yet she's been moping around for days now, and instead of getting angry or grabbing for a drink after hearing the news, she retreats.

"Hope so. She's resilient."

"Yeah," he rumbles, chuckling. "Feisty too. Love how she handles your parents."

"She's a pro at killing with kindness. I don't seem to have that ability; telling my parents off in a way they don't know whether to be offended or pleased."

We sit in silence for a few minutes, staring at the blank TV screen over the fireplace.

"I think it's time we—"

"We should probably—"

I snort and finish for both of us. "Talk. You go first," I add.

Separating from him, I twist my body so I sit with my

back to the corner, my legs in a modified lotus position. This way I can look him in the eye.

He shifts slightly too, putting his arm along the back of the couch, his fingers just reaching my shoulder. Maintaining contact. I like it.

"Not sure where to start now," he admits, grinning a little sheepishly. "So much has already happened. Hard to believe there is anything about me you don't know yet."

Didn't think it was possible to appreciate the man more than I already did.

"I know the important things."

His fingertips softly stroke my skin.

"Probably, but I want you to know it all. There's stuff in my past I'm not exactly proud of, but it's what brought me to this point."

"Then tell me," I prompt him.

"I'm not sure how much you know about the history of the club."

"Enough to know you weren't choirboys. I did my homework."

I know they were rumored to have been involved in the weapons trade, maybe even drugs. I also know when Ouray was voted in as president of the club, he was the wind of change.

"Right. We partied, and we did it hard. There wasn't a mood-altering substance I didn't try at some point, a drink I said no to, or a woman I refused. We were hound dogs, but some of us took a little longer to grow out of it."

Nothing really shocks me, and this doesn't either. I haven't exactly been an angel either, I've tried my share of stuff. Heck, in the days I was following Lindsey's father around the various racetracks, there was a lot more questionable stuff going on behind the NASCAR scenes than was common knowledge.

"We used to have quite a few hangers-on at the club. Other clubs call them sweetbutts. Women who—"

I place a hand on his arm.

"I know what they are."

"I fell for one. Britney. Thought I had something there, but she turned out to be a conniving bitch. Almost got Luna killed."

That last bit catches my interest. "Luna?"

"Yeah, but that's a long story for a time I'm not trying to get to the good stuff."

I widen my eyes. "There's good stuff?"

I laugh when he growls in response.

Then, with a serious expression on his face, he proceeds to render me speechless.

"Darlin', as long as I've got you under this roof, it's all good stuff."

He takes my hand, entwining his fingers with mine.

"In fact, if not for you I wouldn't've built this house. That kitchen? For you. The soaker tub in the bathroom? Also for you. And the giant-ass walk-in closet I could never hope to fill? All yours."

He brings my hand to his mouth and kisses my knuckles.

"This was a house before. All it needed was you to

make it a home."

Paco

Mel's mouth is hungry on mine, her hands clawing at my shirt.

"Easy, Darlin'," I mumble against her lips.

"Screw easy. You can't say stuff like that and expect me to have any restraint."

I barely manage to guide her to the bedroom before she has my shirt off and starts on my fly. I'm so hard I'm afraid the fucking zipper's gonna leave a permanent imprint on my cock.

When she releases me, I can't hold back a groan. Then she slowly sinks down to her knees, tugging my jeans down to my ankles. Her hair brushes against the sensitive tip of my dick as she bends her head, working my jeans and socks off my feet. She runs her hands up my legs as she tilts her face up, looking at me with a little smirk playing on her lips.

With her gaze locked on mine she leans in, takes a firm grip of my cock at the root, and slides me between her lips. I lock my knees and sink my hands into her wild hair.

I'm already in heaven and haven't even managed to take a stitch of clothing off her.

Unfortunately, if I don't stop her right here, I won't get to feel her clamp down on me later.

"Fuck, Darlin'. That mouth of yours is lethal," I mumble as I reach down, put my hands under her arms, and lift her to her feet.

With that smirk back on her face, she slowly steps back from me and holds up a finger, indicating for me to wait. Then she proceeds to strip…agonizingly slowly.

I narrow my eyes and follow every move carefully. When she finally stands naked before me, looking at me with a challenge in her eyes, I clear the distance between us in a flash. My control only goes so far.

We land on the bed in a tangle of limbs and a clashing of mouths.

I wish I'd met her twenty years ago when my recovery time was a lot shorter, but I probably would've done something to fuck us up. Maybe I won't have as much time ahead as I left behind, but I'll die a happy man if I get to spend the rest of my years with this woman.

Suddenly I need to know. I want to hear everything about her. I want to know who she was before she became this woman. I need to hear what she meant when she told her parents Mason would be staying with us and that we were hoping to adopt him. Was that for their benefit?

Is she ready to give up the life she had and move forward with me?

Fuck.

"Melanie…"

"No, don't stop," she complains, wrapping her legs around my hips.

"Just slowing us down a touch, Darlin'."

"Why?" she snips.

"Because we never really finished our talk."

Her eyes pop open and she looks at me like I'm out of

my mind. And maybe I am.

"You wanna talk more? Now?"

"I do."

I lift up on my arms and stare down in her incredulous face. When she catches on I'm not budging, she rolls her eyes and removes her legs from around me.

"Fine. Talk."

"Not me, you. I wanna know all of you."

Her hands come up and she presses the heels of her hands in her eyes.

"I can't believe this," she mutters.

I shift off her, pull her hands away from her face, and brush the hair off her forehead. How am I going to explain this?

"I wanna make love to you, Mel."

She huffs. "Well, isn't that what we were doing before you decided you wanted to talk?"

She shakes her head and starts yanking on the sheets, pulling them up to cover her.

"We were rushing, I don't wanna rush. I don't want to feel like there's a time limit. That *we* have a time limit. I—"

"Paco." She stops me with a hand on my chest. "Where is this coming from?"

I roll on my back and cover my eyes with my arm.

"I don't know. Circumstances brought you here. Guess I wonder what'll happen when the dust settles. Whether you'll choose to be here. With me."

It's her turn to prop herself up on an elbow.

"Have you heard anything I said tonight at dinner?"

I lift my arm and look up at her.

"Every word. Just like I've heard every word you've said to me since we first met. Been waiting, Mel. Bidin' my time. Wondering if I'd ever get my shot, but at the same time scared shitless I'd blow it if I did."

I roll toward her, lifting a hand to her face and tracing her mouth with a finger.

"Guess part of me still can't quite believe you're here, in my house, in my bed."

She grabs my wrist.

"I'm as real as the dirt in your garden," she says, her eyes dancing. "In your house and in your bed is exactly where I want to be, however…" The corner of her mouth twitches. "I'd prefer to make it *our* house, and *our* bed, so I want to buy in."

I shake my head. "I don't think—"

"Do I look like a woman who needs to be taken care of?" she snaps, cutting me off.

"Mel, I may not look it, but I'm not exactly hurting. I'm handy with investments," I explain.

"Good for you. That doesn't change the fact I'll be talking to the bank on Monday." She tugs at the short hairs of my beard. "And in case you're still not getting the message. Me buying in means I'm in, Paco. All the way in."

With a hand to her shoulder, I roll her on her back and cover her with my body. She immediately welcomes me by opening her legs and I settle my hips between them.

"I'm also buying a new vehicle because eventually Linds will want hers back."

"I'll come," I tell her.

"No, I don't think so."

"Why not? I've got a few contacts. Bet I can get you a good deal on a nice Chevy Traverse, or a Ford Expedition. Solid American SUVs."

"Make that a hell no then. I'm getting myself a nice Japanese Subaru Forrester, just like the one that was sitting in my garage."

I can tell from the stubborn set of her chin I'm not going to talk her out of it.

Fine, if she wants to go out and get herself a Japanese dinky toy, so be it. As long as it's parked outside my house—*our* house—every day.

I give up my argument and focus on the woman underneath me.

Getting rid of the sheets covering her, I take Mel's hands, pin them to the mattress, and drop my head to kiss her deeply.

Even with only a kiss and the friction of our skin, it doesn't take long before she squirms underneath me. I roll my hips between her legs, slicking my cock through the wetness collecting there, before poising the tip at her core.

Then I lift my mouth from hers and stare down into eyes that shine with life.

"Love you, Melanie," I confess. "Have for a while now."

"Getting that picture, Paco."

My eyebrows crawl into my hairline. "And?"

She smiles. "Thought I loved a man once. Turns out

I had no idea."

"The words, you wench," I growl.

"Oh, all right," she sputters, but her grin grows. Then she gives me what I want. "Love you right back, Paco."

I close my eyes, savoring her words.

With a buck of my hips, I plant myself deep in her heat, *"Fuck yeah,"* and let myself fall off the edge, into a new reality.

ARROW'S EDGE MC

EPILOGUE

Paco

One month later…

IT'S FUCKING FREEZING.

"Can we light the fires now?"

I look down at Mason, whose face shows every ounce of anticipation.

We're on the back deck, Mason with a hot chocolate Luna made him and I have my hands wrapped around a mug of coffee to stay warm.

"Soon, buddy. Soon."

It had been Mel's idea, doing it in our backyard. Never mind that it's been below average for days now with early snow expected this afternoon. Even now, in the middle of the day, the temperature is hovering around the freezing mark.

Some of the brothers helped set out a total of six fire barrels that are supposed to keep us all from freezing to death. Heck, I hope I can get the words out through my chattering teeth.

But this is what she wanted, so this is what she'll have.

Unconventional as fuck, of course, but that's Mel too. According to her this was the only way to ensure people wouldn't come dressed up, because that would mean she'd have to. When I asked her what she wanted me to wear, I was told whatever I'd put on any other day. Mason is proudly wearing the new jeans, winter coat, and boots Mel bought him last week.

I turn my head to see if I can catch a glimpse of her, but I just see Luna and Janet, Mel's mother, in the kitchen. Lisa is in there somewhere as well, along with the other club wives, which means there'll be a shitload of food. Lindsey and Beth arrived earlier and carted Mel off to our bedroom, where they've been holed up ever since. I was relegated outside.

The door opens and Thomas Morgan steps onto the deck. I brace myself.

"Heads-up," he says, stepping up to the railing beside me, his eyes on the view. "David Zimmerman just arrived."

Lindsey's father. I knew he was coming, but I guess no one told Thomas. I met David a few days ago when he first arrived in town. He'd apparently been in Europe last month and just got back, wanting to check on his daughter. Nice enough guy, who stepped right up when

Lindsey announced she was ready to move back to Mel's old house. Two days ago he showed up to help Lindsey pack her stuff and told Mel he intends to hang around for a while, until Linds has the use of both arms again.

"Yeah, Mel invited him," I tell Thomas, letting him know it's not a surprise.

He looks at me, shocked.

"That doesn't bother you?"

"No, why should it? He's Lindsey's father, he and Mel have forged a friendship in more recent years. He's no threat to me."

Mel made sure I understood whatever she'd had with him almost thirty years ago was nothing compared to what we have. As far as I'm concerned, David came out the loser on that end. Besides, whether I like it or not is irrelevant, he's part of the family and we decided family would be part of today.

I hear Thomas mumble something unintelligible but I choose to ignore it. I'm not going to let him spoil this day.

"Shouldn't we light those barrels?" he asks a minute later.

At that moment I hear the rumble of motorcycles. Sounds like my brothers have arrived. All but one.

Wapi sent a text earlier, telling me he was happy for me. I guess he's been in touch with someone at the club because I hadn't heard from him since that one phone call.

"I guess we can, my family just arrived," I tell Mel's father.

"How about it, son?" he directs at Mason, holding out his hand for him. "Wanna help Grandpa light them up?"

Mason looks up at me for approval and I nod at him.

Guess Lindsey was right, the old man's not averse to adding a grandson. And I can put up with my soon-to-be in-laws as long as they treat my boy right.

Twenty minutes later, I'm standing in front of Ouray—who is marrying us—with Tse beside me, as I watch Lindsey make her way through the small crowd toward me, a big smile on her face.

Getting married was kind of a foregone conclusion the moment we decided we wanted Mason in our lives. Doing it as soon as possible was also a given, since applying for adoption is still easier as a legalized couple. We found out, two weeks ago, the only living relative the boy has is a grandmother—suffering from Alzheimer's—in a long-term care facility in Salt Lake City and our plans went into overdrive.

When Linds reaches me she goes up on her toes and kisses my cheek. Then she quietly whispers, "Word of warning. Mom's pissed 'cause we're making her walk down the aisle."

I look over her shoulder and see Mel approaching, her eyes drilling holes in her daughter's back. I can't keep the grin off my face because even ticked off, she's easily the most beautiful woman I've laid eyes on.

Her hair is in loose curls piled up on her head with random fall leaves poking out of the silver, and a few random tendrils framing her face. She's wearing some kind of cream-colored throw draped over her shoulders and around her neck, and holds a bouquet made of autumn branches in her hands.

But underneath I can see she's wearing her bib overalls—my favorite—with white Chucks on her feet.

Completely unconventional, but totally Mel.

"I look ridiculous," she mutters, as I hold out my hand for her.

"You take my breath away," I counter.

MEL

Six months later…

I DUMP MY bags on the counter and shrug out of the zippered hoodie I put on this morning. It had been chilly when I left, but it's warmed up nicely.

I love these in-between seasons. Fall and spring. The only thing I'm not a fan of is the bugs, which there are plenty of this time of year. Especially up here in the mountains.

Glancing out the window, I spot the red of the do-rag my husband likes to wear tied around his head when working outside. Bugs don't appear to bother Paco, who is outside with the dog every chance he gets, tending the garden he just finished planting last week. Although right now he looks to be finishing his project for tomorrow.

Missing is Mason's matching head covering. He's at the clubhouse hanging with Lisa and Kiara until tomorrow when they're bringing him home to a surprise.

Tomorrow he turns seven years old and in a few short

months he'll be going to regular school, along with the other kids. Hard to believe more than half a year has gone by since he came into our lives. He's a great kid and we love him to bits.

About three months ago, he asked if we were his mom and dad now and if he should call us that. I almost blurted out yes, until I noticed he seemed a little conflicted at the prospect. It had been Lindsey's idea to baptize us Mimi and Papa, and that's what he's been calling us ever since.

I know some—namely my parents and sister—worried having a young boy in the house might be too much for people our age to handle, but if anything, Mason is keeping us young.

Although he's not the only thing keeping me young; a healthy and frequent love life might have something to do with that as well. We've been married six months, and together just fractionally longer, but it feels like we've known each other all our lives. Neither of us were big talkers before, but these days we do a lot of sharing.

However, I've kept one thing from him and it's been burning a hole in my knapsack all week, waiting for the right moment.

I left Lindsey to mind the office for the remainder of the day and zipped over to the City Market before coming home. I have a cake to bake, a house to decorate, and a husband to turn into an even happier man than he already is.

When Paco eventually wanders in from outside, the kitchen is a disaster but the cake sitting on the island is perfect.

"That is some cake for a little boy," he comments.

"He's gonna have to share with the rest of us tomorrow."

My parents announced they're driving up and staying with Beth and Scott for a few nights. They're all going to be here, as well as the club kids and their parents. Mason has no idea.

Paco walks up to me and tilts his head down for a kiss.

"Mmm, sweet," he mumbles, licking his lips.

I may have tested the frosting once or ten times.

"Quality control," I tell him with a straight face.

"I'm sure." He grins.

"How is it going out there?"

"All done. I'm just hoping it won't rain between now and tomorrow."

I love this man. He came up with the idea to create a treasure hunt for the kids. It's like a nature walk, where they have to follow clues for directions and pick up random things like a pine cone, or specific leaf, maybe a rock, at each station to get their next clue. The final stop will be at the new tree house. He's got the brothers involved, setting them up at each stop through the woods.

Paco's never had children, but I'm so glad he's getting a chance to shine as a father. It would've been a tragedy if he never had that opportunity.

"That was a great idea. I bet the kids are gonna love it." I take in the pleased smile on his face. "You're a wonderful father, you know that? Mason is a lucky boy."

He nods and I can tell what I said touches him.

Then I walk to the fridge and grab the envelope I

placed on top.

"What's this?" he asks when I hand it to him.

I simply smile, waiting for him to find out for himself.

He slips the papers out and I watch his eyes scan the document. Then they shoot up and lock on mine.

"Is this for real?"

I nod, tears welling in my eyes to match his.

THE LOOK ON Mason's face when he walked in the door and took in the full house, the decorations Paco and I put up last night, and especially the cake, was priceless.

Having a houseful of people sing "Happy Birthday" turned out to be a tad overwhelming and he pressed his face in my chest during that.

But the gifts are a massive success. Yes, the kid is being spoiled senseless, but we figured for his first birthday in this family we wouldn't put on any restrictions. We need to make up for the ones we missed and going forward we'll keep it more moderate. Maybe.

"Can we go out now?" Mason asks, his eyes on the balloons Paco tied up outside.

"Actually, we have one more thing for you."

I wave Lindsey over, who comes to stand with Paco and me behind the stool Mason is perched on. Then Paco hands him the gift.

It takes Mason two seconds to rip off the paper and he almost looks disappointed to find a picture frame with a photo Lindsey took of Mason working in the garden with

Paco last week.

"Read what it says on the frame," Lindsey prompts.

"Mm…Mason…P…P…"

"Philips," Linds whispers in his ear. "Say it again."

"Mason…Philips? But that's your name," he says twisting his head to look at Paco.

"Yup. That's our last name, but it's your last name now too."

"It's official, kiddo," I explain. "See that date?" I point at the date engraved on the frame next to his name. "That was four days ago, when the adoption became official."

He's only six—well, seven now—but we wanted to make sure he was okay with us adopting him, even if the full understanding of the concept is still a little over his head.

"Are you for real my mom and dad now?"

"We absolutely are, buddy," Paco says, visibly moved.

"Can I still call you Mimi and Papa?"

I respond with a lump in my throat.

"Honey, you can call us whatever you like."

THE END

ABOUT THE AUTHOR

USA Today bestselling author Freya Barker loves writing about ordinary people with extraordinary stories.

With forty-plus books already published, she continues to create characters who are perhaps less than perfect, each struggling to find their own slice of happy.

Recipient of the ReadFREE.ly 2019 Best Book We've Read All Year Award for "Covering Ollie, the 2015 RomCon "Reader's Choice" Award for Best First Book, "Slim To None", Finalist for the 2017 Kindle Book Award with "From Dust", and Finalist for the 2020 Kindle Book Award with "When Hope Ends", Freya spins story after story with an endless supply of bruised and dented characters, vying for attention!

www.freyabarker.com

ARROW'S EDGE MC

CPSIA information can be obtained
at www.ICGtesting.com
Printed in the USA
LVHW012158141021
700457LV00013B/598

9 781988 733692